THE GHOST

AND THE POLTERGEIST

HAUNTING DANIELLE

HAUNTING DANIELLE - BOOK 34

THE GHOST
AND THE POLTERGEIST

USA TODAY BESTSELLING AUTHOR
BOBBI HOLMES

The Ghost and the Poltergeist
(Haunting Danielle, Book 34)
A Novel
By Bobbi Holmes
USA TODAY BESTSELLING AUTHOR
Cover Design: Elizabeth Mackey

ROBETH
PUBLISHING, LLC

ISBN: 978-1-949977-78-3
A

Dedicated to my best friend, Don.
In less than two months we celebrate our
48th Wedding Anniversary. No regrets. I love you.

ONE

Spring arrived in Frederickport several weeks before the birth of Walt and Danielle's twins. The impatient pair was supposed to arrive in mid-May yet showed up on the last Saturday in April. Two weeks after their birth, Danielle sat with her best friend, Lily, in the living room of Marlow House, while Walt worked upstairs in his attic office, and the newborns napped in their bedroom on the second floor. Nearby, the baby monitor emitted a soft hum, keeping tabs on the sleeping babies.

Lily sprawled out on the living room sofa with her shoes abandoned on the floor. She lounged against a throw pillow propped against the upholstered arm, while her stockinged feet rested on the opposite end of the sofa, and her hands absently stroked her protruding baby belly.

Danielle sat on a recliner facing Lily, her feet up on its footrest. Lily had brought her golden retriever, Sadie, over with her, but the dog stayed in the backyard with Danielle's cat, Max. It was too lovely a day for them to stay inside. Lily's young son, Connor, was at story time at the library, with his grandmother and aunt.

Lily, her red hair fastened into a high ponytail, glanced briefly at her watch and then looked at Danielle. "June and Kelly should be dropping Connor off any time now. I texted them earlier that I'd be over here."

"It was nice of them to take Connor today. Give you some quiet time."

"Yeah. And I must admit, June's been pretty good lately. I think it's that talk Ian had with her a while back." Lily paused a moment and looked over at Danielle. "Oh, I was wondering, did you hear about Pearl Cove's new Monday brunch?"

"What's that?"

"Pearl Cove expanded its Sunday brunch to Monday brunch. Same menu, just two days a week instead of one."

"I can understand adding another day. Their Sunday brunch has gotten crowded."

Lily let out a sigh and slumped back against a throw pillow. "Although, I don't know when I'll be going out for Sunday brunch again. Not with Connor and a newborn."

"You could go now. We can watch Connor," Danielle suggested.

"To be honest, I'm not sure I feel like getting all dressed up and going to a fancy restaurant right now. I'm so ready to have this baby. But I have another two months." Lily groaned. "I'll also be so freaking happy to have this addition done. I'm sick of dealing with all the mess, chaos, and noise. And it's just going to get worse. Last night Ian explained what they need to do before they finish. I really hate living in the middle of a construction zone."

"There's no reason for you to deal with all that. Come stay here. We have plenty of room for all of you. We told you, you're more than welcome."

Before Lily could respond, the doorbell rang. Both glanced at the living room window. So engrossed with their conversation, neither one had noticed anyone walking by the window to the front door.

"It's probably June and Kelly, dropping off Connor." Lily started to stand.

"I'll get it." Danielle stood up. "You stay there. I need the exercise. You rest."

A few minutes later, Danielle returned to the living room with Lily's mother-in-law, June; her sister-in-law, Kelly; and Connor, who immediately ran to a basket of toys by the fireplace. He promptly dumped the toys onto the floor before sitting down to play.

June laughed at her grandson. "He certainly makes himself at home."

"How was he at story time?" Lily asked without standing up.

"I think we now know what his imaginary friend, Marie, looks like," Kelly said with a snort.

Danielle arched her brows and exchanged a quick glance with Lily.

"What do you mean?" Lily asked.

"He was sitting like a little angel during story time," June began. "They were reading a book while showing the children the pictures. But then—"

"She turned to a page with a little old lady with gray hair, wearing a straw hat and a flowered dress, and Connor immediately pointed to the picture, stood up, jumped up and down and started saying Gamma Marie. Over and over again," Kelly said after interrupting her mother's explanation.

Lily smiled weakly. "Really?"

June nodded. "Really."

"I remember when Laura told me about your imaginary friend, Rupert. I just assumed imaginary friends were imaginary kids. Or something from a storybook, like a dragon or hobbit. But a little old lady?" Kelly chuckled. "What was Rupert?"

"As best I remember, a little boy," Lily lied. Fact was, Rupert wasn't an imaginary friend; he had actually been a ghost, but he had been the ghost of a little boy.

"My guess," Danielle improvised. "The book they read at the library is one Heather has read to Connor, and she probably pointed to the picture of the little old lady and said she reminded her of our friend Marie."

Lily resisted her temptation to roll her eyes at Danielle's suggestion.

June shrugged. "He seemed to recognize the book." She looked at Danielle and asked, "Are the twins napping?"

"Yes. Although they'll probably be waking up pretty soon." Danielle motioned to the recliners for them to sit down, while Lily moved over, giving Danielle room to sit on the sofa with her.

"Kelly told me about the quilt Lily bought you," June said right after she sat down.

"Yes, I love it."

Lily had purchased the quilt the previous Sunday while thrifting with her sister-in-law, Kelly. Lily had affectionally dubbed it the Twins Quilt because the large, square, handmade, colorful quilt appeared to have been made for twins, considering its unique appliques. It was the type of blanket one might spread on the floor or at the beach for the babies to play on. While it looked old, it did not look used. It currently hung over the back of one rocker in the nursery.

"I'd love to see it," June said. "When I was at the library this morning, I enrolled in a quilt class. The flyer suggested we bring pictures of our favorite quilts to the first class. I really have nothing to bring. But how Kelly described the quilt, I'd love to share a photo of it."

"It would be awesome if your teacher recognized it or suggested someone who might," Danielle said. "I'd love to learn its history. Of course, it's possible it just ended up in Frederickport, and no one locally made it."

Sound interrupted their conversation when the hum of the baby monitor competed with the faint cries of an infant. Danielle immediately stood and looked at June. "You can come upstairs with me if you want. I'll show you the quilt. You can take a picture of it now."

A few minutes later, June and Kelly walked upstairs with Danielle while Lily remained in the living room with Connor.

———

BY THE TIME Danielle reached the nursery and opened its door, both infants were awake, squirming, and making faint sounds.

Danielle walked into the room, hesitantly followed by June and then Kelly.

"I thought they'd be crying up a storm by the time we got up here," June whispered.

Danielle thought the same thing, yet instead of commenting, hurried to the closest crib and picked up Addison. She stepped to her son's crib and placed Addison next to her brother and then proceeded to change their diapers.

Now standing at the edge of a crib beside Danielle, June and Kelly watched the squirming babies while Danielle adeptly changed both their diapers. Had they watched her do this a week ago, it would have looked comical instead of efficient.

"They are so little," Kelly cooed.

"Which is a good thing for Danielle, since she had to deliver them. And she wasn't even at the hospital!" June turned to Danielle and asked, "Now, what is the boy's full name again?"

"Jack Brian Marlow."

While Kelly and June knew the Brian was for Brian Henderson, who had helped deliver the twins, they didn't know Jack was for Walt's best friend, from Walt's previous life.

Danielle picked up Jack and turned to Kelly. "Could you hold him for a second while I get Addison and sit in the rocker so I can feed them?"

"Are you going to feed them both at once?" Kelly asked.

Danielle nodded, handed Jack to Kelly, and then said, "Yes."

Kelly gently cradled Jack while June watched. Jack eagerly rooted for a nipple. Kelly chuckled and whispered, "Sorry, little guy, but mama will help you in a minute."

The rocker Danielle and Walt had selected for the nursery had upholstered and padded arms, making it more comfortable for nursing two babies. Lily and Ian had given them a second, matching chair as a shower gift.

Danielle took her place in one rocker, adjusted Addison on one side, and before opening her blouse, she looked up and said, "If the sight of a couple of boobs bothers either of you, I suggest you look away. Frankly, having two to nurse, I don't have the energy for modesty in the nursery."

"It doesn't bother me," June said, "but if it makes you uncomfortable, I can leave."

"Hey, after having Brian help deliver my babies, I think my modesty died when these two arrived," Danielle said with a laugh. A moment later, Kelly gently placed Jack on Danielle's lap, and soon both babies eagerly nursed.

"The quilt you're asking about is on the other rocker," Danielle told June.

June moved to the empty rocker and picked up the quilt. "This is beautiful." She looked at her daughter. "Kelly, come hold it up. I want to take a picture."

A few minutes later, Kelly stood facing the window, holding up the quilt while her mother snapped several pictures. Meanwhile, Danielle focused her attention on the babies in her arms.

When she finished taking pictures, June looked at what she had just taken and frowned. "Something's wrong with the camera on my phone."

Kelly set the quilt back on the empty rocker and walked to her mother. Standing beside June, she looked down at the pictures as June scrolled through each one.

"It's like they have spots of water on them," June muttered, her eyes still on her phone's screen.

"They look like orbs. Did you see them when you took the pictures?" Kelly asked.

"I wasn't looking behind you when I took the pictures. I was looking at the quilt. What do you mean, orbs?" After asking, June looked up and froze. She stared at the rocker next to Danielle. It silently rocked in tandem with the one Danielle sat in, while Danielle, engrossed by the babies in her arms, failed to hear the conversation going on between June and Kelly, or notice the empty chair rocking next to her.

Kelly, seeing her mother stare blankly ahead, turned to the rockers. With a frown, she walked toward the empty rocker. Yet once she reached it, it stopped rocking. The next moment, a small stuffed elephant, sitting on a shelf behind the rocking chairs, flew from its place toward June. It hovered a moment just inches in front of June's nose and then fell to the floor when June let out a scream before she collapsed to the floor in a faint.

Startled by June's abrupt scream, Danielle looked up, inadvertently pulling her nipples from the infants' mouths. The babies cried.

TWO

After his death in 1925, Walt Marlow had spent the next ninety-one years confined to Marlow House. While he hadn't spent his entire time in the attic, it had been his preferred area of the house, perhaps because that was where his spirit had left his body. Yet much had changed in the past three years, which included no longer being dead. During these brief years into his new life, he and his wife, Danielle, had remodeled the attic, first to serve as his bedroom, and later, when they awaited the birth of their twins, as his office.

Walt had discovered his new calling early into his newest life, as an author. He took the cliche writing advice: *write what you know.* And so Walt wrote stories which took place in the 1920s during prohibition. His first book had become a *New York Times* bestseller and was supposedly making it to the big screen. Of course, he had been told that before. His second book showed promise.

After spending the morning writing, Walt walked down the stairs from his attic office to the second floor. His first stop was to peek in on the twins and check if they were still napping. The moment he stepped on the second-floor landing, a woman screamed, followed by a loud thumping and then crying.

Walt raced to the nursery, and the moment he swung open the door, he found June Bartley sprawled out on the floor, with her daughter, Kelly, kneeling by her side. Behind them in a rocker sat Danielle, struggling with the squirming infants while looking confused at the scene on the floor. The babies were no longer crying and were again nursing.

Walt was about to ask what happened when June's eyes fluttered open and looked up into Kelly's face.

"Mom? Are you okay?"

"What happened?" June asked.

"Umm, well…" Kelly struggled to explain to her mother what they had witnessed but paused a moment and looked up at Walt.

Dazed, June, who hadn't tried to sit up, turned her head to one side and came eye to eye with the stuffed elephant now sitting inches from her nose on the floor. June let out another scream and, like the one before, startled Danielle, making her jerk, causing the twins to unlatch from her nipples again. The babies cried. But she quickly got the situation in hand.

Walt focused his attention on the two women on the floor. Kelly had wrapped her arms around her sobbing mother and attempted to soothe her.

"What happened?" Walt asked gently as he knelt before the women.

Still wrapping her arms around her mother's shoulders, Kelly gave Walt a shrug while saying, "Umm, the rocking chair started rocking on its own, and then the stuffed animal…" Kelly paused and nodded down to the stuffed elephant. "It sorta, well, flew across the room." Kelly turned to look over at Danielle. "You saw it. Right?"

Danielle shook her head. "No. I was fussing with the babies, not really paying attention to what was going on while you were taking pictures."

"You didn't see the stuffed animal fly across the room?" Kelly asked.

Danielle shook her head again.

"I noticed Mom staring at something, and I turned to see the chair next to you rocking. And then the stuffed animal flew across the room toward Mom."

June, who had stopped crying, gave a sniffle and pulled herself from Kelly's hold. She looked up at Walt. "I never believed in ghosts before, but I think your house is haunted. This isn't a safe place for those babies."

With Kelly's help, June stumbled to her feet.

Once standing, June looked at Walt and said, "We need to get out of here, and I think you should, too."

As the women hurried from the room, Walt called out, "I'm sure there is a logical explanation!"

"Yes, Marie," Danielle grumbled after June and Kelly were out of earshot.

Walt turned and frowned at Danielle. "Did Marie do something? What happened?"

The twins, no longer wanting to nurse, squirmed again, and without being asked, Walt took one from Danielle. It wasn't until they stood by the cribs, each holding a baby, did Walt ask again, "What happened? I could hear June screaming from down the hall."

Resting Addison against a cloth diaper draped over her right shoulder, Danielle gently burped the baby while Walt did the same with Jack. "You heard what Kelly said. Apparently, the other rocker was moving, and the stuffed animal flew across the room. I didn't see any of it because I was looking at Addison and Jack. I knew they were taking pictures of the quilt, but I wasn't watching them."

With the burping done, they wiped excess milk from the corners of tiny mouths and began checking the status of diapers when Walt asked, "But why did you say Marie?"

"I just figure, if the rocker was really moving on its own, and the stuffed animal flew, then it had to be Marie. Unless you snuck in here and messed with them."

"I didn't see Marie. Was she here?"

"I haven't seen Marie all day. But if those things really happened, who else did it? Eva can't move things." Danielle let out a sigh and picked up Addison now freshly diapered and swaddled in a receiving blanket. "It's entirely possible Marie was in here, and I didn't notice her."

Walt and Danielle went to the living room a few minutes later, each holding a swaddled baby. Lily was still lounging on the sofa while Connor played with the toys from the basket. The moment the new parents walked into the room, Lily called out, "Okay, Walt, what did you do to June and Kelly?"

"I didn't do anything."

Walt and Danielle walked to the recliners and sat down, each holding a baby. Connor looked up from his toys and called out, "Babies!" before standing up and running over to have a closer look.

"Just look; don't touch," Lily warned her son, who now hovered curiously by Walt and Danielle's side. Lily looked at Walt and asked, "Are you sure you did nothing to them?"

"Nothing," Walt insisted. After allowing Connor to inspect the babies, Walt distracted the toddler so he wouldn't wake the twins; he sent a toy airplane flying. Seeing the miniature aircraft, Connor lost interest in the babies and followed the airplane, which landed amidst his pile of toys.

"What did they tell you?" Danielle asked Lily.

"The minute they got downstairs, June demanded we all leave. Not just her and Kelly, but me and Connor. She said something about the place being haunted."

Danielle shifted the sleeping baby in her arms and looked over to Lily. "But you stayed here?"

Lily grinned. "I told her I wasn't afraid of ghosts. Reminded her I had lived in Marlow House and always got along with the resident ghosts."

Walt chuckled.

"What did she say to that?" Danielle asked.

"She got a little flustered and dragged Kelly out before they could explain what exactly happened. What happened?"

Danielle told Lily, as best she could, what had occurred in the nursery.

Lily frowned. "You think Marie was messing with them?"

"Who am I messing with?" a new voice asked. Everyone in the living room could hear it except Lily.

Connor looked up from the toys and cried out, "Gamma Marie!"

"Hello, love," Marie greeted Connor after giving him a quick kiss on the forehead. Like the illustration in the storybook that morning, Marie wore a floral housedress and a straw hat over her short gray hair.

"Marie's here?" Lily asked.

"Yes." After answering Lily, Danielle turned to Marie and asked, "What were you thinking earlier, messing with June and Kelly?"

Marie, who had just bent down to pick up a toy, glanced over at Danielle. "So it's June and Kelly I supposedly messed with? When did I do this? And what did I do?" Marie handed the toy to Connor and then walked toward the adults.

"You know very well what you did, not twenty minutes ago," Danielle scolded.

"Dear, I was with Eva in Astoria twenty minutes ago. I just stopped here to see how you and the babies are doing. I didn't expect to get blamed for something I didn't do." Marie sounded amused, not offended.

Now standing at Walt's side, Marie looked down at Jack and smiled and then looked over at Addison. Both babies slept.

Danielle studied Marie for a moment. "You're serious? You just got here?"

"Yes, dear. I'm serious. Now tell me, what happened?"

A few minutes later, Marie sat in an imaginary chair between the recliners and sofa. When Danielle finished explaining what had occurred in the nursery, Marie let out a sigh and asked, "Do you think Kelly threw the stuffed elephant?"

Danielle repeated Marie's question for Lily.

"Is Marie saying she wasn't responsible for June freaking out?" Lily asked.

Danielle nodded. "She is."

Lily considered Marie's question for a moment before saying, "Well, you did say, according to Kelly, June was staring at the chair that seemed to rock by itself when the stuffed animal flew across the room. I could see Kelly trying to be funny."

"Funny, how?" Walt asked.

"Danielle said Kelly removed the quilt from the chair. It's possible she accidentally sent the chair rocking. If she noticed her mom staring at the chair a few moments later, maybe she realized her mom thought it was rocking on its own, and she impulsively picked up the stuffed animal and threw it in June's direction, sort of like saying *boo!* But when June freaked out, Kelly regretted the stunt and didn't fess up to what she'd done."

"That's entirely possible," Danielle said. "I wasn't paying any attention when this was all going on."

The sound of barking from the hallway interrupted the conversation. A moment later, Lily's husband, Ian, walked into the living room with Sadie by his side.

"I found this dog in your backyard," Ian teased. The golden retriever moved quickly around the room, greeting everyone with a wet nose and sniff, even Addison's and Jack's blanket-wrapped feet, before joining Connor and the toys.

"Did you see Max?" Danielle asked.

"Yes. He's still outside, sleeping on one of the patio chairs."

"Did your mom stop by the house?" Lily asked.

"That's why I'm here. Mom and Kelly came by, and Mom insisted I come over here and bring Connor home because Marlow House is haunted."

"She didn't tell you to bring me home? She was fine leaving me in this dangerous haunted house?" Lily teased.

"When she told me what happened, I assumed it was Marie or Walt trying to be funny."

"It wasn't me," Walt said. "And Marie insists it wasn't her. By the way, Marie's sitting right there." Walt pointed to the spot Marie occupied.

Ian glanced to where he imagined Marie sat and said, "Hello, Marie," before pulling his cellphone from the back pocket of his jeans. "Maybe it wasn't Marie, and after seeing the pictures my mother took, I didn't think it was Walt."

Danielle frowned at Ian. "What are you talking about?"

Ian stepped toward Walt and Danielle. "Kelly told me Mom took pictures of the quilt. But when she looked at the pictures, she noticed something strange. Kelly airdropped these to me from Mom's phone."

Danielle took the phone Ian offered while saying, "Your mom said something was wrong with her phone's camera. Said something about how the pictures looked like they had water drops." She looked down at the phone's screen.

"Not water drops. Orbs. The kind of orbs paranormal investigators talk about," Ian explained.

THREE

Frederickport's city manager, Fred Lyons, hadn't planned to spend his free Saturday afternoon entertaining his rambunctious nine-year-old nephews. Nor had he ever imagined he would be expected to step up and become a surrogate father for the boys and assume responsibility not just for them, but for their mother, Debbie Bowman. Fred's wife, Robyn, had insisted her little sister and nephews remain in the garage apartment now that Debbie's husband, Clay, had skipped bond and took off with not just Fred's valuable coin collection, but any hopes of being reimbursed for the bond Fred had paid, and left people questioning Fred's judgment.

Fred sorely regretted ever recommending Clay for the position as acting police chief during Chief MacDonald's medical leave, and his resentment towards his wife grew daily. Things might have gone differently had Robyn simply told him about Clay's affair with Camilla Henderson. From what he had recently learned, both Robyn and Debbie had been aware of Clay's affair with the then-married woman before the twins were even born.

It wasn't that Fred could have predicted Clay might murder Camilla to keep her quiet. After all, Debbie already knew about her husband's infidelity, so technically, there was no reason to shut

Camila up to keep her from telling Debbie about the affair. But to bring Clay in to act as a supervisor over a man whose wife Clay had slept with was wrong on so many levels. Had Robyn shared that bit of information with him, he would never have recommended Clay for the job, and he wouldn't be spending his Saturday afternoon taking his nephews to the museum.

Fred remembered his brief jealousy of Clay after the twins' birth. He had always wanted a son, and Clay had ended up with two. While Debbie had visited over the years since leaving Frederickport and having the twins, they had been brief visits, and Fred had never spent much time with his nephews.

Over the last month, Fred had gotten to know the boys better, and he now suspected Clay's real motive for jumping bail had nothing to do with avoiding a murder conviction. He simply wanted to get away from his obnoxious and unruly sons.

Whenever Fred complained to his wife about the boys' behavior, Robyn reminded him that poor Eric and Zack were going through a rough time, losing their father and hearing such nasty rumors about him around town.

Fred wasn't sure how Eric and Zack had heard anything around town about their father since Debbie homeschooled the boys. Plus, Fred no longer felt they were rumors. He believed Clay had murdered Camilla, yet Debbie continued to believe in her husband's innocence, and insisted the only reason he ran was from fear, which she sympathized with. Apparently, she wasn't angry that he had deserted her and their sons, or that he had helped himself to Fred's valuable coin collection. When discussing this with Robyn, his wife refused to say if she believed Clay was innocent or guilty, claiming she just wanted to support her sister.

Seeing the museum up ahead jolted Fred from his mental musings. He slowed down and turned his car into the museum parking lot.

"Do we have to go to the museum, Uncle Fred?" Zack called out from the back seat.

"Yeah, let's just go to a movie," Eric suggested.

Fred glanced in the rearview mirror as he parked his car. "Your mom asked me to take you to the museum today. She said it's for your school."

"It's dumb," Eric grumbled. "I want summer vacation like everyone else."

"The local schools aren't out yet," Fred said as he turned off the ignition and then unhooked his seatbelt. "So they aren't on summer vacation, either."

MILLIE SAMSON STOOD in the museum gift store, chatting with another docent, when she heard someone coming into the museum's front entrance. A few moments later, Millie stepped into the entry hall from the gift shop, and she immediately recognized the city manager. While she wasn't familiar with the two boys in his charge, she immediately knew who they were. The entire town knew.

"Afternoon, Fred," Millie greeted.

Fred flashed Millie a smile and silently grabbed the back of Eric's hoody sweatshirt with his right hand while using his left hand to grab hold of Zack's. He pulled his nephews back towards him, holding them in place before they could run into the exhibit area without him. "Boys, this is Mrs. Samson. She volunteers at the museum. Millie, these are my nephews, Zack and Eric."

Millie smiled down at the pair. "Hello, boys, welcome to the museum."

"Do you have dinosaurs?" Eric asked.

Millie chuckled. "No. I'm afraid we don't have dinosaurs."

Eric turned to Fred and asked, "Can't we go to the movies instead?"

Fred took a deep breath and exhaled. "No, we can't." Fred looked back at Millie and said, "Robyn took her sister to Portland today to do some shopping."

"Aww, you're babysitting?" Millie said.

"We're not babies," Zack snapped.

Fred flashed Zack a frown. "Quiet." He looked back at Millie

17

and said, "They're homeschooled, and their mother asked me if I could bring them to the museum today. As you probably noticed, they're not exactly thrilled about the idea."

"Really?" Millie smiled down at the boys. "Not even interested in learning about a secret tunnel?"

"Secret tunnel?" Zack looked up at Millie.

"What secret tunnel?" Eric asked.

"Over a hundred years ago, the founder of Frederickport built a secret tunnel under part of the town. No one knew it was there until it was discovered a little over a year ago," Millie explained.

"What's down there?" Eric asked.

"I wanna see." Zack turned to his uncle and asked, "Can we go in the tunnel?"

"I'm afraid no one can actually go into it now," Millie said. "The town locked it up, but before they did, they took lots of pictures. And someone even made a model of the tunnel, so you can see what it looks like inside. I could show you."

"I thought that exhibit was opening in July?" Fred asked Millie.

Millie looked up at Fred and nodded. "Yes. Over July Fourth weekend. Although the Fourth falls on a Thursday, that's when the exhibit officially opens." She glanced down at the boys and smiled before saying, "But if your nephews let you show them around the museum to look at the other exhibits, and if they prove they can be on their best behavior, then I'll be happy to take them into the back storeroom to give them a special pre-viewing of the tunnel exhibit."

"I'd like to see that myself," Fred said.

"Me too!" Eric chimed before offering Fred his right hand to hold. Zack then offered a hand to his uncle. A few moments later, as Fred led two submissive nine-year-olds into the exhibit room, he flashed Millie a smile and mouthed, *Thanks*.

MILLIE WALKED with Fred and the boys through the museum, with Fred explaining the exhibits while Millie added additional commentary. Of all the displays, the boys seemed most interested in the taxidermy exhibit showcasing local wildlife. Eric wanted to put his hand in the mountain lion's mouth to feel the fangs, but Fred reminded him they could not touch the exhibits.

Neither boy was interested in visiting the art room featuring the paintings of Eva Thorndike and the Marlows. Instead, they begged to go to the storeroom to see the tunnel exhibit. Fred, understanding how the portraits probably wouldn't appeal to the boys, asked Millie if they could go see the tunnel exhibit now, and she agreed. Another reason Fred made the request, he wanted to go home, where he planned to sit the boys in front of the television set to watch a movie while he returned to a book he had started.

They saw the scale model first, which included miniatures of the houses that had existed back when the tunnel had been built. Both the boys recognized the miniature of Marlow House. A plate of glass covered a portion of Beach Drive on the model, giving the boys a peek inside the tunnel, allowing them to see how it ran from Marlow House to another house across the street.

"That is so cool," Eric said.

"Those were the only houses on Beach Drive when they built the tunnel. But this one." Millie pointed to the house on the opposite end of the tunnel from Marlow House. "That's how it looks now. The original house burned down. And that corner brick section was all that remained. When they removed the debris after the fire, they left the brick section," Millie explained. "The owner at the time wanted to preserve something of the original house when rebuilding, never realizing it was actually the entrance to an underground tunnel."

"Wow!" the boys exclaimed.

"There are pictures over on that board." Millie pointed to a nearby display partition covered with photographs.

Both Eric and Zack rushed to the photo display. After a few minutes, Eric asked, "How come nobody can go in the tunnels now?"

"For one thing," Millie began, "there is no real public access into the tunnels." She pointed to Marlow House on the model. "One way to get into the tunnel is from the basement of Marlow House."

She then pointed to the house on the other end of the tunnel. "Or from this house. And both houses are private residences. I don't think they want people using their homes to get into the tunnel."

"I wonder if the people who live in those houses go back and forth to visit each other through the tunnel. That's what I'd do if I lived in one of those houses," Zack said.

"No, they can't do that." Millie pointed to the end of the tunnel leading into Marlow House. "See that door?"

Both boys moved back to the display and looked through the glass covering the top of the tunnel.

"There are two doors separating Marlow House from the tunnel, and unless you have both keys, no one can get into Marlow House from the tunnel," Millie explained. She then picked up a small box from a shelf behind her. She opened the box and showed it to the boys. It held two ornate brass skeleton keys.

"Are those the keys that open the doors?" Eric asked.

"Not the originals. These are replicas," Millie explained.

"Do they work?" Zack asked.

"Yes. Of course, they wouldn't really do anyone any good because they would still need to get into one of the houses," Millie explained. "But if you were in the tunnel, they would open the door. Of course, it is dark in the tunnel, so someone would need to bring along a good flashlight."

"What are you going to do with the keys? They're really cool looking," Eric asked.

Millie closed the box holding the keys and set it back on the shelf. She looked at the boys and said, "We're having a special display built for them. One that locks."

WHEN THEY RETURNED to the front of the museum, Eric and Zack asked to look around the gift shop before going home. As they browsed the store, Fred told Millie, "Thanks for making this trip to the museum fun for the boys. I think they enjoyed it."

"That's my job." Millie smiled.

A few minutes later, Eric called out from across the gift shop, "Uncle Fred, I need to go to the bathroom."

"Go on. You know where it is," Fred told him. Eric dashed off to the restroom at the back of the museum, down the hall from the office and next to the storage room.

———————

TWENTY MINUTES LATER, Eric and Zack climbed into the back seat of their uncle's car and closed the door. As they put on their seatbelts, Fred, now sitting in the front seat and adjusting the rearview mirror, said, "You guys did pretty good at the museum today. I'll tell your mom."

"It was cool," Zack said.

When Fred steered his vehicle out into the street several minutes later, Eric nudged his brother and placed a finger over his lips, signaling to his twin not to say anything. He then pulled his hand out of his pocket and moved it closer to his brother. Zack looked down at Eric's fist, waiting for him to show him what he had pulled from his pocket. The next moment, Eric opened his palm, revealing two ornate brass skeleton keys. Zack's eyes widened as he looked up into his brother's face.

Eric grinned at Zack and then closed his palm, returning the keys to his pocket.

FOUR

On Saturday evening, Danielle left Walt reading in the living room with the twins sleeping in a playpen while she visited in the kitchen with her neighbor and fellow medium Heather Donovan.

Heather, who had spent her day off cleaning her house, doing laundry, and baking four loaves of sourdough bread, wore a dark green blouse and black denims she had slipped on after returning from her morning run and taking a shower. Dusty white handprints, from Heather carelessly wiping flour from her hands, stained her denim-clad hips. She wore her black hair pulled up in a ponytail, mostly to keep hair out of the food she prepared, and she told herself that when she returned home, she would need to take a second shower, considering all she had done that day. But the day wasn't over yet. First, she intended to make Walt and Danielle dinner.

"You don't have to do this," Danielle said as she sat at the kitchen table and watched Heather pull a freshly baked loaf of sour-dough bread from a brown paper bag. Heather set it on the counter. Next, she removed glass jars from the bag and set them on the counter with the bread.

Heather turned to Danielle and smiled. "I know. But it's only been two weeks, and I can't imagine how exhausted you must be taking care of two newborns! Let me make you dinner."

"I love the offer and the sentiment. But I feel a little guilty."

Heather frowned. "Guilty, how?"

Danielle let out a sigh. "To be honest, it's been kind of easy so far."

Heather arched her brows. "Easy?"

"For one thing, they've been sleeping most of the time."

"It's probably because they came early," Heather suggested.

Danielle shrugged. "Probably. Plus, Walt's always there to help. Things like bath times we do together, and I have to say, his telekinetic ability is a big help. And while Joanne is gone this week, before she left, she cleaned the house from top to bottom and made sure we had enough groceries for until she gets back."

"Dang, girl, you are spoiled." Heather laughed. "But I'll still make you dinner. I've been wanting to try this recipe, anyway. And Brian's working tonight. So you and Walt can be my guinea pigs."

"I appreciate it. And pizza sounds good. Plus, I suspect it being easy is the universe messing with me."

"Why do you say that?"

"I doubt this easy stage will last forever."

"You're probably right." Heather pulled a large cast-iron skillet from a cabinet and placed it in the oven. After turning the oven on and closing its door, Heather turned to Danielle. "I'm making the pizza dough with sourdough discard. Just discard, nothing else except for some olive oil and fresh herbs. It's supposed to be a super easy recipe, and I love finding new ways to use my discard. I refuse to throw it away."

While Heather waited for the oven and cast-iron skillet to heat up, she arranged the items for the pizza on the counter while Danielle told her about June and Kelly's visit that afternoon.

"So you think Kelly threw the stuffed animal at her mom?" Heather asked.

"She must have. I never saw any ghosts aside from Marie, who insists she wasn't even here when it happened. And Walt saw nothing. Although, the pictures June took had those orbs, but it was probably dust on the lens or something."

A few minutes later, Danielle watched as Heather, wearing large oven mitts, pulled the cast-iron skillet from the oven and set it on the stove. After removing the oven mitts, Heather grabbed a bottle of olive oil from the counter, removed its lid, and liberally added oil to the hot skillet. She then used a spatula to disperse the oil in the pan.

When Heather finished with the olive oil, she opened a large jar holding her sourdough discard and began pouring it into the skillet.

"You said you're just using discard for the crust?" Danielle asked.

"Yep. But I fed it this morning. So technically, I suppose it's sourdough starter."

"Interesting," Danielle muttered as she watched Heather spread the discard around in the skillet.

"There's something magical about mixing water and flour to capture wild yeast, and then feeding it with more water and flour to keep it alive. Sourdough starter is a living thing."

Danielle chuckled.

Heather looked at Danielle. "What?"

"Look at you. You've really gotten into baking."

After adding a splash of olive oil to the top of the starter she had just spread in the pan, along with some freshly chopped herbs, Heather slipped on the oven mitts, set the cast-iron skillet in the hot oven, shut its door, and turned back to Danielle. "I'm not really interested in making bread with manufactured store-bought yeast. Sourdough bread is more aligned with nature. Not to mention, it's been around for centuries. I feel like it connects me to my ancestors." Heather paused and then added, "Umm, not the one who was a serial killer."

ABOUT TEN MINUTES LATER, Heather removed the cast-iron skillet from the oven and added sauce and toppings to the pizza, before returning it to the oven. When it finished cooking, Heather slid the pizza onto a cutting board, careful not to burn herself. With a long knife, she cut the pizza into slices and then moved them onto a clean baking sheet. Heather took the pizza along with napkins and small plates to the living room with Danielle. Before Danielle could try her pizza, the twins woke up and wanted to be fed.

A few minutes later, the new mother sat on a recliner, holding both babies, and with a bit of adjusting and fussing, she got them both nursing.

Walt sat on the recliner next to Danielle, while Heather stood near the sofa, the baking sheet with the pizza, napkins and plates sitting on the coffee table. Heather set two pieces on a plate and handed them to Walt. She looked at Danielle and asked, "Are you sure you don't want me to bring you a piece?"

"My hands are kind of busy," Danielle said. "After I feed them, I'll have some. It looks delicious."

"Maybe I can help," Walt offered. The next moment, one slice of pizza from his plate floated over to Danielle and hovered in front of her mouth.

"I appreciate the offer." Danielle giggled. "But I don't want to drop crumbs on the babies. And I imagine it's still warm."

Walt cringed. "Good point." The slice floated back to his plate.

"Did you hear about Chris's neighbor moving?" Heather asked a few minutes later after she sat on the sofa and took a slice of pizza for herself.

"Which neighbor?" Danielle asked.

"The Crawfords. They're getting a divorce," Heather said.

"Really? I haven't seen them around much lately," Danielle said.

"Mia talked to Chris yesterday morning. Told him Austin moved out last week. From what Chris was saying, I got the feeling Mia was letting Chris know she was available if he was interested."

"I thought you said they were moving?" Walt asked. "Or did you mean just Austin?"

"I assume they're both moving because Mia asked Chris to recommend a real estate agent. Of course, he recommended Adam."

"Why do you think she was hitting on him?" Danielle asked.

"She just kept telling Chris how lonely she was. How Austin hadn't been…umm…taking care of her. And crap like that. And then she asked to see what kind of view Chris had from his house. Wanted him to take her inside and, umm…give her a tour." Heather let out a snort.

"Did he?" Walt asked.

"That's when I arrived to pick Chris up for work. It was my turn to drive. Mia didn't look happy to see me. She was kinda rude. And when we were driving to work, I asked Chris what Mia's problem was. That's when he told me what she'd said."

"I guess I need to call Adam in the morning and see if he's listing the property," Walt said.

"Why?" Heather asked.

"We've been putting off dealing with the tunnel and its access to Crawford's house. Right now, the doors on our end are locked, so there really isn't an issue with anyone gaining access to Marlow House. But we need to do something about the Crawford entrance, and it should probably be done before they list the property," Walt explained.

WHEN THE BABIES FINISHED NURSING, Heather offered to hold Jack while Walt held Addison so Danielle could enjoy some pizza.

After Heather eventually went home, Walt and Danielle took the babies upstairs and gave them a bath. Afterwards, Walt took a shower while Danielle laid the babies on her bed with her. In a soft voice, she began talking to them. Her cat, Max, jumped up on the mattress and curiously sniffed the infants' tiny toes and fingers.

After his shower, Walt traded places with Danielle. He stretched out on the bed with the twins and Max. He silently conversed with Max, answering questions the feline had about the new family members.

"I'm exhausted. But not sure what I did today," Danielle said after wandering back into the bedroom after her shower.

"We've both walked up and down those stairs more than we normally do in a day. On top of that, your body is busy producing enough milk for not just one, but two babies."

Wearing a nursing nightgown, Danielle glanced down at her breasts. "I used to be jealous of Lily."

Walt chuckled. "Why?"

"You know why. One thing nursing has taught me, it's a pain being this big. None of my regular blouses fit me."

IT WAS after ten before Walt and Danielle got the twins down in the nursery and they returned to their bedroom. As Danielle drifted off to sleep, she thought about how lucky she was to be married to a man who didn't expect her to do all the work taking care of the babies. While she had told Heather it had been easy, she knew it wouldn't be so without Walt by her side, even with Joanne's help.

PERSISTENT KNOCKING WOKE DANIELLE. Jolted awake, she sat up in bed, glanced over to the alarm clock, and saw they had been asleep for hours. She heard the knocking again. This time it woke Walt. Drowsy, he sat up in bed.

"Walt? What is that?" Danielle asked.

The knocking started again. It sounded like it came from the wall separating their bedroom from the twins'. Without another word, both Danielle and Walt jumped from the bed and raced out of the bedroom, heading to the nursery.

The knocking stopped the moment they stepped into the hallway. When they reached the nursery, they found both babies fussing and rooting, yet neither one was crying.

"What was that knocking?" Danielle asked as she stood between the cribs.

"I don't know. It sounded like it was coming from in there." Walt pointed to the closet.

Danielle stood protectively in front of the cribs and silently watched as Walt approached the closet. She held her breath as he reached for the closet door, comforted by the knowledge of Walt's telekinetic powers. A moment later, Walt opened the closet and took a closer look.

He turned, faced Danielle, and shrugged.

"Is it windy outside? Was that a tree hitting the house?" Danielle suggested.

Before Walt could respond, a meow interrupted their conversation. Walt and Danielle glanced at the open doorway and watched Max stroll into the room. Walt used his telekinetic power to shut the bedroom door while silently communicating with the cat.

"According to Max, it's not windy outside. He also hasn't seen anything unusual in the house."

"I know I heard knocking," Danielle insisted.

"I did too."

The babies' fussing intensified. They wanted to eat. A few minutes later, Danielle sat in one of the rocking chairs, nursing the twins.

"I think I should check out the rest of the house. I'll lock the bedroom door," Walt told Danielle.

Danielle gave Walt a reluctant nod. He turned from her, walked toward the door, and as he reached for the doorknob, Danielle cried out, "Walt!"

Walt turned to Danielle and found her staring at the empty rocking chair next to her. Of the two rocking chairs in the nursery, there was only one rocking. And it wasn't the one Danielle sat in.

FIVE

"Whoever you are, show yourself," Danielle demanded. The rocking chair stopped rocking. "We know you're here. Who are you?" Danielle held her arms protectively around the nursing babies. She looked at Walt. "Does Max see whoever it is?"

Walt glanced down at the black cat, who stood by the empty rocking chair, staring at it while his tail swished. Walt called out Max's name. The cat turned to him, and the two stared in silence at each other. After a moment, Walt shook his head. "He doesn't see anything."

The bedroom door abruptly opened. Walt stepped to the open doorway, looked out into the hall, and saw nothing. After a moment, he turned back into the room and looked at Danielle, who still held the twins. They had each fallen asleep.

"Did it leave?" Danielle asked.

Walt shrugged. "I guess." Confused, Walt walked to Danielle and took Addison. He gently patted her back while Danielle stood up with Jack. They walked toward the cribs.

"This is bizarre." Danielle laid Jack in his crib. "I've been seeing ghosts most of my life. The key word: *seeing*."

"I'll confess, I'm comforted by the fact Eva insists a ghost won't harm an innocent."

Danielle reached out and ran her fingertips across Jack's pink cheek and watched as he slept. "I guess." She glanced over to the adjacent crib, where Walt had placed their sleeping daughter. Danielle frowned and then looked back into Jack's crib.

Noticing Danielle's change of expression, Walt asked, "What's wrong?"

"Did you put the stuffed animals in the cribs when we put the babies down earlier?"

Walt looked back at the cribs. A stuffed teddy bear sat in the corner of Jack's crib, while a stuffed lamb sat in the corner of Addison's crib. He shook his head. "No. I didn't."

Danielle removed the stuffed animals from the cribs, tossed them on the floor, and walked over to the rocker she had been sitting on earlier and sat down. She pulled the quilt off the other rocker and used it to cover her lap.

"What are you doing?" Walt asked.

"Until we figure out what is going on, I'm not leaving my babies alone."

"You can't sleep on a chair all night. I'll go down to the living room and get the playpens. We can set them up in our bedroom. They can sleep in there with us."

"Don't leave," Danielle pleaded, not wanting him to leave her alone in the nursery with the babies.

Walt smiled and then took a seat on the empty chair. "Ghosts rarely scare you."

"I kind of understand how poor June felt today."

"What do you mean?"

Danielle snuggled up in the vintage quilt; her bare feet pushed against the floor, making her chair rock. "It's sort of different when you can't see them. I've always been able to see when there is a ghost. But witnessing paranormal activity and not seeing where it's coming from, that's different."

"The only difference now, they've made their presence known."

"What do you mean the only difference? The difference is I can't see them."

Walt reached over from his chair and patted Danielle's left hand while he, too, rocked. "No. You couldn't always see when there was a ghost in the room with you. There were many times—before—when you didn't know I was in the room with you."

Danielle frowned at Walt. "Really? Like when?"

"At night, sometimes. I liked to watch you sleep. But I didn't want you to wake up and find me standing there. I didn't want to scare you."

"Gee, Walt. That sounds sorta creepy."

Walt chuckled. "I suppose it does."

"Were you stalking me?"

"I was a ghost, Danielle. Ghosts haunt. Haunting is a form of stalking."

Danielle wrinkled her nose. "And it's creepy."

Walt chuckled again. "I suppose it is. But the difference between a living person stalking someone and a ghost, a ghost won't harm an innocent. You can't say the same thing about living people."

Danielle glanced toward the cribs. "Are our babies safe?"

"I was thinking about that." Walt leaned back in the rocker and stretched out his legs while his hands rested on the chair's arms. "Why does someone typically set a stuffed animal in a crib with a baby?"

"I suppose they're trying to comfort the child. But I don't like the idea of a stuffed animal left with an unsupervised baby. I read a tragic story about a baby who smothered to death under a stuffed animal in his crib."

Closing his eyes, Walt leaned farther back in the chair, making it rock. "You're talking like an overprotective mother. Which is not a bad thing. But considering our elusive spirit set each stuffed animal in a far corner of each crib, the chances of Addison or Jack reaching the stuffed animal at this age is not a significant risk. And I have to wonder if the ghost placed the stuffed animals in the cribs for our benefit, not for the babies'."

"Why would they do that?" Danielle asked.

"Because I've also been thinking about that knocking. Had the knocking happened when the babies slept, I'd expect the sound to jolt them awake, and then they would start crying. Had our visiting ghost noticed the babies waking up, rooting, and felt they were hungry, and knocked on our wall to wake us up. Maybe that's why they put the stuffed animals in the cribs. They were trying to find some way to comfort the babies until you came and could feed them, and signal to us they mean no harm."

Danielle rocked in silence while considering Walt's words. Finally, she said, "While I like your theory of a shy ghost that's a kind and helpful spirit, it did hurl the stuffed animal at June. Scared the crap out of her."

Walt opened his eyes, stopped rocking, and looked at Danielle. He smiled. "Come on, Danielle, haven't there been times when you wanted to throw something at June?"

CHRIS JOHNSON, aka Chris Glandon, had talked to Heather Saturday night after she returned home from Marlow House. She had told Chris how she'd made dinner for Walt and Danielle that night, trying out a new recipe. Somewhere during the conversation on food and baking, Heather mentioned she wished she would have thought to pick up some cinnamon rolls for Walt and Danielle, as Danielle had mentioned during dinner she hadn't had cinnamon rolls since before the babies were born.

Chris offered to stop by Old Salts the next morning and pick up some fresh cinnamon rolls for Walt and Danielle. Heather liked the idea and suggested she and Brian join them in the morning. With the chief being out for medical leave and his replacement being arrested for murder, Brian had been working long hours, but he had Sunday off.

On Sunday morning, Chris arrived at Marlow House with his pit bull Hunny and a large sack of cinnamon rolls. Chris used his key and let himself in the back door and left Hunny outside to sniff around. Chris entered the kitchen and dropped the bag of cinnamon rolls on the kitchen table and walked to the coffeepot. No one had made coffee yet, so Chris filled the pot with water.

Hunny entered the house through the doggy door just as the coffee started to brew. Snatching up the bag of cinnamon rolls, Chris left the kitchen and headed down the hallway, Hunny trailing behind him. Chris wondered if Walt and Danielle were still sleeping. But when he walked into the living room, he saw them sitting together, huddled on the sofa, reminding him of a pair of exhausted homeless vagrants. Nearby sat two portable cribs, each holding a sleeping baby.

Walt and Danielle looked up at him yet said nothing. Chris walked to the sofa and stopped. In a soft voice, he said, "Damn, you guys look like crap. Rough night?"

"What are you doing here?" Danielle asked in a less than friendly tone.

Chris held up the bag with the Old Salts logo.

Danielle's eyes widened. "Tell me those are cinnamon rolls."

"I brought you cinnamon rolls." Chris grinned and tossed Danielle the sack. She quickly opened it, pulled out a fresh sticky roll, and handed the sack to Walt.

Chris glanced over at the playpens and looked back at Walt and Danielle. "You guys want some coffee?"

"Please," they chorused. Now holding a cinnamon roll, Walt set the sack with the rest of the rolls on the coffee table.

Chris left the room while Hunny greeted Walt and Danielle with a wet nose. Several minutes later, Chris returned with three cups of coffee. He set them all on the table and then picked up one and handed it to Danielle and then handed another to Walt. After taking a cinnamon roll for himself, Chris took it and a cup of coffee with him as he took a seat in a recliner across from Walt and Danielle.

"Brian and Heather are coming over. We figured you'd be up by now. This baby thing rough?"

"It's not the babies." Danielle took a sip of coffee, set the cup on the table, and used her free hand to try straightening her morning hair while her other hand held what remained of her cinnamon roll. "It's the ghost."

"Ghost? What ghost?" Chris asked.

Walt told Chris about last night's haunting, beginning with what June and Kelly had witnessed.

"Heather told me about what happened with June and Kelly, but she said Kelly threw the stuffed animal."

"That's what we thought before last night. We eventually brought the babies down here," Danielle said. "Walt was going to bring the playpens upstairs to our room. But I fell asleep in the rocker."

"And then it came back," Walt said.

"What happened?" Chris asked.

"Like Danielle said, she had fallen asleep on the rocker. I didn't want to wake her, so I tried to doze but couldn't get comfortable. I got up and noticed the quilt Danielle had put over her had fallen to the floor. When I went to pick it up, well, our ghost did it for me."

"What did it do with the quilt?" Chris asked.

"It covered Danielle up again."

Chris arched his brows. "Well, that's kind of nice."

"It woke me up. And we realized the ghost had obviously returned. I tried talking to it again. But nothing. I just didn't want to stay upstairs, so we came downstairs and put the babies in the playpens. We curled up here to sleep."

"Did the ghost follow you back down here?" Chris asked.

Danielle shrugged. "I don't think so. Nothing's happened down here."

"How about when you were asleep?" Chris asked.

Danielle glared at Chris.

Chris frowned. "What?"

Walt let out a sigh. "That's why we look so terrific. We couldn't get to sleep. We haven't slept all night. Danielle was afraid something might happen to the babies if we dozed off."

"I thought you said Danielle dozed in the rocker?" Chris asked.

"That was only for about fifteen minutes," Walt explained.

Chris looked at Danielle, who continued to glare in his direction. He flashed her one of his charming smiles and said, "Well, not only does a lack of sleep do nothing for your appearance, it doesn't help your disposition, either."

Walt wrapped his arm around Danielle and pulled her close. She looked as if she might cry. "If you make her cry, I'm going to hurt you."

"Fair enough. But when Brian and Heather get here, I want you two to go upstairs and try to get some sleep. We'll watch the babies. Just let us know when you think they'll need to nurse again. I don't want to wake you up unless we have to."

"Are you going to change diapers?" Walt asked.

"No. But Heather will."

"She will?" Walt asked.

"Sure. I'll pay her twenty bucks a diaper." Chris grinned.

SIX

Before going over to Marlow House on Sunday morning, Heather took her daily jog along the beach. By the time she returned home, her boyfriend, Brian Henderson, was at her house waiting for her. He had already stopped at his house after leaving work that morning and had changed clothes before heading to Heather's. Eager for a cup of coffee and a cinnamon roll, Heather didn't bother changing out of her jogging clothes or removing her long black hair from its messy bun before walking with Brian over to Marlow House.

"JUST YESTERDAY, Danielle was telling me how easy it has been," Heather told Brian and Chris. Minutes earlier, Walt and Danielle had reluctantly gone upstairs to get some sleep while their friends stayed in the living room, looking after the babies. The twins were still sleeping, and Danielle had told Heather they shouldn't need to eat for another three or four hours. But if they got really fussy in two hours to call her, and she'd come downstairs and feed them.

Heather and Brian sat together on the sofa, drinking coffee and splitting a cinnamon roll, while Chris sat across from them on the recliner. He had already finished one cinnamon roll and was on his second cup of coffee.

"Easy until the mystery ghost showed up," Chris said.

"That's what I don't understand. Why can't Walt and Danielle see this ghost?" Brian asked.

Chris shrugged. "It happens sometimes. Somehow they can, well, hide. Annoying, that's for sure."

"I'm curious what Eva will have to say about this," Heather said.

Brian noticed Hunny rested her sleeping head on Chris's shoe. "Hey, Chris, how's Hunny doing?"

Chris glanced down at his dozing pit bull and then looked back at Brian. "I took her to the vet on Friday. He said she's doing great. Right after it happened, when they first brought her in, he was afraid they might lose her. But she pulled through like a trooper. It helped that Walt could explain things to her. Like to not try jumping up on the bed and leaving her stitches alone."

Heather smiled at Hunny. "She's my hero."

While framing Heather for the murder of Brian's ex-wife, Clay Bowman had attempted to stage Heather's suicide, but Hunny had intervened and saved Heather's life. It had also gotten Hunny shot.

Chris looked at Brian. "Heather tells me you've been putting in a lot of hours."

Brian nodded. "It'll be a while before the chief can come back. He comes in a few hours each week, and we talk to him every day. But Joe and I have been filling in for him."

"Any word on Bowman?" Chris asked. Bowman, who had been the chief's temporary replacement, had jumped bail after his arrest.

Brian shook his head. "No. He's basically disappeared into thin air. Some of those coins he took off with should have popped up by now, but nothing. If he's pawned them, whoever he sold them to are lying low. There is also speculation that he made it over the border to Canada."

"Heather was telling me Bowman's wife and sons are still staying with the Lyonses," Chris said.

"Yeah. And from what I've heard through the grapevine, Lyons isn't thrilled about it. I guess those nephews of his are a handful."

"I talked to Evan about Bowman's kids," Heather said, "and he was telling me what brats they were at the Easter egg hunt."

The twins started making noises. Heather got up and walked to the playpens. A few minutes later, she finished diapering them both. "Okay, that will be forty bucks."

Chris laughed. "Did Danielle tell you?"

"No. But before going upstairs, Walt told me to make sure to change their diapers frequently because you were paying twenty bucks a diaper change."

Chris laughed again.

"And if that's the case, I need to run upstairs and get more diapers. I used the last ones down here."

Heather re-swaddled Jack, handed him to Brian, and then re-swaddled Addison before handing her to Chris. Both men gingerly held the infants while looking down into the tiny faces. "You two are in charge. Don't let them cry."

"Which one is this?" Chris asked as he gently bounced the baby.

"Addison. I figure you're better with girls," Heather said before leaving the room.

BEFORE GOING INTO THE NURSERY, Heather stopped by Walt and Danielle's bedroom door on the second floor. She eased the door open a few inches and peeked inside. The new parents appeared to be sound asleep on the bed. Heather smiled as she gently shut the door.

The first thing she noticed when she walked into the nursery was the quilt folded neatly over the back of one rocker. She had seen the quilt before, but she wanted to take another look. Heather walked to the rocker, picked up the quilt, and took it to one crib, where she draped it over the crib's rail, spreading it out to inspect it. Heather marveled at the intricate hand stitching, telling herself whoever had made it hadn't used a sewing machine. She couldn't help but wonder about the quilt's story.

Just as she was about to pick up one corner of the quilt to have a closer look, the quilt flew from the crib rail, sliding between her and the crib as if someone had grabbed it. Startled, Heather turned to the quilt and watched as it folded itself in midair and then returned to its place on the back of the rocker before the chair started rocking, a steady back and forth.

After a moment of stunned silence, Heather took a deep breath, stared at the rocking chair, and said, "So you're the ghost who is too chicken to show itself."

The next moment, the stuffed animals flew off the shelves behind the rocker and hurled in Heather's direction. One by one, Heather intercepted each stuffed animal before it hit her face by blocking each one with an elbow until all the stuffed animals fell to the floor by her feet. She looked down briefly and then turned her attention back to the still rocking chair.

"I guess I should be glad it was just stuffed animals you threw at—"

Before Heather could finish her sentence, a bronze bookend hurled in her direction from a bookshelf on the other side of the room. By the time she saw it in her peripheral vision, it was already inches from her temple. Yet it froze in the air, hovering a moment before it dropped to the floor with a loud thud.

Her heart now racing, Heather leaned down and picked up the heavy bookend before turning back to the rocking chair. Testing the weight of the object in her hand, Heather glared at the chair. "Why do I suspect the Universe stopped this? You didn't want to just scare me. If that had been the case, why choose something I didn't see coming? No, you wanted to do something more sinister. But listen, you soulless specter, every time you do crap like that, the Universe is keeping a tab, and when you cross over, my guess, you'll find yourself someplace with intolerable heat. It's not just the bad things we do that get us in trouble with the Universe, it's also our intentions. Trust me, if I planned a murdering spree and was shot and killed before I could implement the evil plan, it would not earn me brownie points when I face my creator. No. The powers that be will know what was in my heart, and that's what I'll be judged on. So save the theatrics and move on. You already disrupted Little Mama's sleep, and she needs all the rest she can get if she is to feed her babies the milk they need to get a healthy start on life. I'm pretty sure there is a special hell waiting for those who do things to hurt babies."

The chair stopped rocking.

"WHAT TOOK YOU SO LONG?" Brian asked when Heather finally returned to the living room. The babies, whom Brian and Chris had been holding when Heather first left to fetch more diapers, were now sleeping in their portable cribs.

"Telling off a ghost and picking up the nursery." Heather dumped the diapers she had been carrying on the coffee table, snatched a cinnamon roll from the bag on said table, and then plopped down on the sofa next to Brian.

"What ghost was that?" Chris asked. Heather then told them what had happened.

"You really think it was trying to hurt you?" Brian asked.

"Unfortunately, I do. I suppose there is an upside to that." Heather shrugged.

"What upside?" Brian asked.

Chris started laughing.

Brian looked at Chris and frowned. "What's so funny?"

"I know what Heather meant. She's saying it proves she really is an innocent, because the ghost couldn't hurt her."

Heather shrugged again. "Yes and no. Sure, it sorta validates that the Universe considers me an innocent. Yet it also confirms what Eva always says, that a ghost can't hurt an innocent."

"How do you know it's a ghost?" Chris asked.

Heather frowned at Chris. "What else could it be?"

"A poltergeist?" Chris suggested.

Heather scoffed. "Poltergeist just means noisy ghost."

"Some people say a poltergeist isn't a ghost at all, but a sponta-neous recurring psychokinesis. While Danielle refers to Walt's abili-ties as telekinesis, some people use the terms interchangeably, while others insist they might be similar, but not the same thing," Chris explained.

"Are you suggesting Walt is responsible for this?" Brian asked.

"No way," Heather answered for Chris. "For one thing, those who think a poltergeist's behavior stems from a living person also say that person is typically a teenager or female."

Chris glanced at the sleeping babies. "Or the babies who inher-ited a special gift from their father?"

"That's ridiculous," Heather grumbled. "Are you suggesting those innocent babes tried to kill me upstairs?"

"Certainly not. Poltergeist behavior has nothing to do with the intent of the person whose energy is causing the havoc. Their birth could have been more stressful than we realize and one—or both of them—are inadvertently moving things."

Heather shook her head. "No. For one thing, I said teenagers or preteens, not babies. Anyway, they were down here, and I was upstairs when all that happened. If it was coming from the babies, then things would fly down here, not upstairs."

They continued to debate the subject.

IT HAD BEEN ABOUT three and a half hours since Walt and Danielle had gone upstairs when the babies fussed. Chris followed Heather over to the portable cribs and watched as she checked their diapers.

"They're soaked. And I imagine hungry," Heather announced.

Chris handed Heather a diaper and picked up one for himself. "I'll change Jack; you change Addison."

"Are you trying to save twenty bucks?" Heather teased.

"Maybe."

"Ever changed a diaper before?" Heather asked.

"No. But I'm sure I can figure it out."

"I'll give you a tip. When changing Jack, his squirt gun might be loaded. Keep your mouth shut."

When they finished changing the diapers, Heather picked up Addison, while Chris picked up Jack. Heather was about to ask Brian to call Danielle or Walt on the phone to wake them up, so Danielle could come downstairs and feed the babies, when Danielle and Walt stepped into the living room.

"We were about to call you," Heather said as she shifted the squirming baby into her arms. "You woke up at the perfect time. These guys are hungry."

"We didn't wake up by ourselves," Danielle said as she walked into the room. "The persistent knocking on our wall woke us up."

SEVEN

Adam Nichols's friend Danielle Marlow once told him a woman should never be with a man who expects her to be less so he can feel like more. It was a private conversation they'd exchanged not long after Melony, his now wife, moved back to Frederickport. While they weren't discussing Melony, Adam often wondered if Danielle was trying to plant a seed so he wouldn't sabotage his future with Mel. Although, back then, he didn't think he had a shot, much less a future with the woman, although they had dated in high school.

Back in those days, Adam thought Mel was the prettiest girl he had ever seen. It was still true. She had the looks to be a fashion model, but she had chosen law, like her father. Yet unlike her father, whose law firm had closed in disgrace and scandal, Mel had become one of the top and respected criminal attorneys in the state.

Adam had always known she was wicked smart—much smarter than him. It was possible their relationship might have hit the rocks from his personal insecurities, but ironically, it was Mel who reminded him of his own worth. Before she had moved back to town, he had built a successful real estate and vacation rental company in Frederickport despite his parents' lack of support and constant berating. Of course, there had always been his grand-mother, Marie Nichols, who not only had faith in him, but helped him grow his business and, when she died, had left him the majority of her estate, which in itself he saw as a testament of her faith in him.

Those were Adam's thoughts while he sat alone in a booth at Pier Café on Sunday afternoon, waiting for Melony to join him. Carla had offered him some coffee when he first sat down, but he'd opted for iced tea. He was just taking a sip of the tea when Melony walked into the diner. He saw her immediately and gave a little wave when she glanced around, looking for him.

"Did you get the listing?" Mel asked when she joined Adam in the booth a few moments later. Prior to meeting up at the café, Adam had met Mia Crawford at his office to talk about listing her house on Beach Drive.

"I sent it off to her husband. But it's entirely possible he'll tell me he wants to get another Realtor. From how Mia talked, it doesn't sound like an amicable divorce."

"Isn't amicable divorce an oxymoron?" Mel teased.

Adam grinned. "You have a point."

"Didn't you tell me Chris referred you?"

"Yes. Why?"

"They're neighbors. From what I remember, they always got along. If Chris is the one who recommended you, then I don't see why he wouldn't use you. It's not like the recommendation is coming from Mia."

"That might be true if Chris didn't look like he does." Adam took another drink of his tea.

Melony laughed. "What is that supposed to mean?"

"Think about it. The wife you're divorcing comes to you with a name of a Realtor she got from her hot neighbor."

Melony laughed again. "I see what you mean."

"Anyway, I won't be disappointed if Crawford tells me he's going with someone else."

"That doesn't sound like you."

"I'm not sure if I want to deal with the tunnel. To be honest, if the referral hadn't come from Chris, I'd probably be finding an excuse to turn it down. The idea of filling out that property disclosure gives me a headache."

After taking their orders, Carla returned a few minutes later with Melony's drink order. She set the glass of iced tea in front of Melony and asked, "Have you seen the Marlow twins yet? I mean, aside from when they were born. I still can't believe Danielle had the babies at your house. That must have been terrifying."

"It was a surprise, that's for sure," Melony said. "But all the drama was over before we knew anything was going on."

"I'd always heard having a baby involved a lot of screaming and took hours," Adam said. "But Danielle just excused herself to go to the bathroom and came back with two kids. She's kind of a showoff."

Melony laughed.

"I'm glad it all worked out and there wasn't a problem having a surprise home delivery," Carla said.

"Adam and I have stopped by Marlow House several times since they were born. Danielle and Walt seem to have everything under control. I'm very impressed with how Walt's handling fatherhood. He's right there with Danielle, changing diapers and giving baths, and I never noticed Danielle having to tell him to do something. He just does it. The feminist me says I shouldn't be impressed because that's what a new father should do. After all, no one praises a new mom for doing basics like changing diapers. But the fact is, a lot of new fathers don't do half of what Walt does," Melony said.

"So Walt impresses you because other fathers are slackers?" Adam teased.

Melony flashed Adam a smile. "Well, not all of them."

"Back when Walt first walked into the diner, when he was engaged to that other woman, if someone had asked me what type of father I thought he'd someday be, I would've gone with the slacker," Carla snarked.

"I couldn't stand Clint," Adam said. "We should give all jerks amnesia to improve their personality. I actually like Walt now."

"I still don't understand how amnesia changed his personality so much," Carla said.

"Some sort of reset? But maybe we shouldn't be gossiping about my cousin's husband." Melony grinned.

"Cousin?" Carla frowned. "Oh, that's right. You guys are related somehow through that aunt who left Danielle Marlow House."

Melony nodded. "That's right."

"Tell your cousin she really needs to bring the babies into the diner. I'd love to see them."

"I doubt Danielle plans to bring them out in public for a while," Melony said. "Too many germs, and they were premature."

Carla let out a sigh. "I guess I understand. Hey, did you see the quilt Lily got Danielle from the estate sale?"

"The twin quilt?" Melony asked.

"Yes. She and Kelly stopped in for lunch after they went thrifting. Lily showed it to me. While sewing is not my thing, my grandma was a quilter. Can't imagine getting rid of the quilts she made me. I have to assume whoever made it made it for someone who had twins. I just don't know why they would get rid of it."

"Danielle showed Mel and me the quilt when we stopped over there," Adam said. "It came from the Beckett estate. And what I know about the Becketts, there weren't any twins in the family. At least not anyone who lived in the house for the last hundred years."

"How would you know about all the people who lived there over the last hundred years?" Carla asked.

"My guess, Marie told him," Melony said.

Adam flashed his wife a smile. "Yep. Grandma knew the son of the man who built the house. They were about the same age. He was an only child. No twins. He inherited the house when his parents died, raised his family there. He had a big family, twelve kids. But none of them were twins. Dad was friends with one son."

"Twelve is a lot of kids. Are you sure there weren't some twins in there?" Carla asked.

Adam shook his head. "No. Once, when Dad was talking about them and telling me how many kids they had, he made a point of saying that didn't include any twins. Only two of them stayed in Frederickport. A son and the youngest daughter. The daughter inherited the house because she took care of her parents until they died. She never married, and when she passed away a few months ago, she left her house to her nieces and nephews. Her trustee is one of her nephews, the only one who lives in Frederickport. He's the son of her brother who stayed in town. He's already talked to me about listing the property, and he's been cleaning out the house before we list it. That's how they got the quilt."

Someone called out, "Carla."

Carla turned toward the voice and cringed. "Excuse me," she told Adam and Mel before dashing off.

Melony and Adam assumed they were alone again when Carla left to take care of another customer. They didn't realize the ghost of Adam's grandmother, Marie Nichols, had just taken a seat in the booth next to Melony. A few minutes later, a familiar couple walked by the booth and stopped. It was Joe and Kelly Morelli.

"Hi, guys," Kelly greeted Adam and Mel.

"Hey. Haven't seen you two since the infamous baby shower," Mel greeted.

They all laughed.

"Want to join us?" Adam offered.

Marie grumbled the next minute when she had to move after Mel slid over to make room for Adam, who was giving his side of the booth to Joe and Kelly.

"The craziest thing happened over at Marlow House yesterday," Kelly said the moment she sat down.

"Come on, Kelly, there has to be a logical explanation for what happened," Joe said.

Kelly turned to Joe. "Yes. Marlow House is haunted."

Marie, who considered leaving after losing her place, quickly changed her mind and hovered nearby, listening.

"Haunted?" Adam snickered. "I've always thought Marlow House was haunted."

"No, I'm serious," Kelly said.

Adam shrugged. "So am I."

Melony shushed her husband and asked Kelly, "What happened?"

Kelly recounted what had happened during her visit to Marlow House with her mother, while Joe gave an occasional eye roll. After she finished telling her story, Kelly looked at Joe and flashed him a scowl. "Stop doing that."

Joe feigned innocence. "What did I do?"

"The eye rolls, Joe. It's insulting. You weren't there. Ask my mother what happened."

"I believe you," Mel said.

Joe frowned at Mel. "You do?"

"Sure. I've encountered some strange things before. Things that don't have a logical explanation," Mel said.

"Everything has a logical explanation," Joe insisted.

Mel considered Joe's words a moment before saying, "I suppose they do, as long as you find ghosts logical."

"Come on, Mel, certainly you aren't saying you believe in ghosts," Joe said.

"There are countless things in this world we don't understand. That we aren't meant to understand," Mel insisted. "And it's a little presumptuous to assume there aren't ghosts—just as it might be presumptuous to assume there is no such thing as God just because you haven't seen him...or her."

"Thank you, Mel," Kelly said. She turned back to Joe. "See, not everyone thinks I'm crazy."

"I never said you were crazy," Joe insisted.

"Oh my," Marie muttered. "If Kelly didn't throw the stuffed animal at her mother, is there a ghost hanging around at Marlow House that I don't know about? One that's haunting the nursery?" The next minute, Marie left the diner to go find Eva before heading to Marlow House.

EIGHT

When Carla brought the food to Melony and Adam's booth, she found two more guests had joined them. After taking Kelly's and Joe's orders, Carla quickly left their table without visiting.

Kelly watched as Carla hurried away. "You know, I actually like Carla's hair that way."

"You like purple hair?" Joe snarked.

"I wouldn't want purple hair. But you have to admit, it kinda compliments her complexion. I didn't like it when she had it green. Although, green would be a good hair color if you wanted to dress up as a Martian for Halloween."

Adam chuckled. "I think Carla gets bored, and changing her hair color every month gives her something to do."

Kelly shrugged. "I guess."

Melony picked up her burger and looked over at Joe and Kelly. "So, what are you guys doing for the rest of the day?"

"Joe has to go back to work," Kelly grumbled.

"On a Sunday?" Mel took a bite of her burger.

"Joe works a lot of Sundays," Kelly said.

"Yeah, Adam works some Sundays too. In fact, he worked this

morning." Mel set her burger on her plate and used a napkin to wipe off her hands. "I just figured since you guys were here for lunch, Joe had the day off."

"I go in a little later today. Brian and I have been putting in a lot of extra hours, helping the chief until he can come back full time," Joe explained.

"I dropped by Eddy's the other day. He's doing pretty good." Melony was the only one in their group to call Police Chief Edward MacDonald Eddy. She had been the chief's late wife's best friend, and despite the fact Melony had grown up in Frederickport, she had met Eddy during her college years, before Edward took the job as police chief and moved to Frederickport with his wife.

Several minutes later, Carla returned to their booth with Joe's and Kelly's drinks. She deposited the sodas in front of the pair without saying a word, and then turned and rushed back toward the kitchen.

"Hey, isn't that Clay Bowman's wife and kids?" Adam asked.

Mel, Kelly, and Joe turned toward the front of the diner, where Adam stared. Two women stood by the entrance with two young boys. The women looked around before one pointed to an empty booth near the entrance.

Joe turned back to Adam. "Yes. The one in the red sweater is Clay's wife. The other one is her sister, Robyn Lyons."

"If I were Clay Bowman's wife, I sure wouldn't stay here. I can't imagine how embarrassing it is for her having everyone in town know what her husband did. I would want to start somewhere fresh, especially since she has kids," Kelly said.

"I doubt Debbie Bowman has anywhere else to go," Melony said. "From what I understand, she's always been a stay-at-home mom, no job experience. She homeschools her sons. Her only family is her sister. Even if she and her husband have assets, those could be lost if Camila's family sues Clay's estate. And if Clay is found, he'll have more legal fees unless he makes a plea deal."

"I WANT to go treasure hunting for shells," Zack told his mother after they sat down in the diner booth.

"Me too. I'm not even hungry," Eric said.

"Me either." Zack slumped back in the booth with his arms crossed over his chest.

Debbie looked up at her sons from over her menu while her sister quietly listened. "That's because you guys helped yourself to the leftover fried chicken in the refrigerator an hour ago. That was supposed to be our dinner."

"Then why do we have to have another lunch? That was a lot of chicken," Eric said.

With a sigh, Debbie closed her menu and set it on the table. "Because I haven't eaten. And I was looking forward to going out to lunch with your aunt."

"You guys went out yesterday," Eric reminded them.

"And if I wanted to stay home, what am I supposed to eat? You two ate all the chicken."

Robyn chuckled and reached over to her sister, giving her hand a pat. "Deb, let the boys go play on the beach. They'll be okay. They're old enough to understand they need to stay out of the water."

Eric scowled. "I don't want to go in the water. It's too cold."

"See," Robyn told Debbie. "You and I can have a nice lunch, and they can play on the beach. It's perfectly safe. I have friends who drop their kids off at the beach during the summer, and they aren't much older than Eric and Zack." Robyn smiled at her nephews. "They could use a little fresh air. And running up and down the beach would do them some good, too."

"Can we, Mom? Please, please," Eric begged.

"Please, Mom," Zack added.

Debbie let out a sigh. "Okay, but I want you both to check your watches. I expect you back in twenty minutes."

"Come on, Deb, they're going to be okay. Twenty minutes isn't enough time. They haven't even taken our order yet. Let the boys have some fun."

Debbie looked from her sister to her sons' faces, back to her sister. Finally, she looked back at the boys and said, "Okay. But I want you back here in forty minutes. Show me on your watches where forty minutes is." For their last birthday, Debbie had bought both of her sons a watch and had refused to buy them digital ones, wanting them to understand how to read time on a clock with hands.

Eric and then Zack showed her when forty minutes would be. She nodded her approval and then reminded them both to behave themselves and stay on the beach.

After they ran off, Robyn laughed.

Debbie looked at her sister. "What?"

"I can't believe you gave them forty minutes."

Debbie smiled. "I rather like the idea of enjoying a quiet lunch with my sister. And maybe, if they wear themselves out running around on the beach, they'll go to bed earlier tonight."

HE FIGURED people would notice a man wearing a wig and find that odd. The last thing he wanted to do was draw attention to himself. But if he wore a baseball cap, they would assume the short hair was his. He had chosen gray because he knew when he grew out his beard, it would likely come out gray. And he had been right. The beard wasn't as long as he'd wanted, but with the wig and sunglasses, he doubted even his wife would recognize him.

For shoes, he chose ones with lifts to give him extra height. Denims and flannel shirts worked for clothes, with a bulky puffer vest and jacket, making him look heavier than his actual body. He didn't carry a backpack or anything to signal he might be homeless. The last thing he needed was someone from the local police department approaching him. Instead, he was going with the tourist vibe.

While he didn't have a working cellphone, he had found an older iPhone in a house he had broken into. Its owner had obviously upgraded, and instead of turning in the old phone, they kept it. He had found it when looking through their closet. He doubted they realized it was missing. The reason for carrying a nonworking phone, it gave him something to talk into, so people would assume he was on the phone and wouldn't approach him. And he could use it to pretend to take pictures, to help him appear like a visitor to the area.

He had come down to the pier to use the public restrooms and was just leaving the men's room when he saw the two boys leaving Pier Café and heading to the beach. They walked right by him without giving him a second look. Resisting the temptation to follow them down to the beach, he instead walked along the pier and looked over the rail to the beach below. The two boys ran north, kicking up sand. He glanced back at the diner and wondered who had brought them down to the pier, and why they had left the two young boys alone and unsupervised.

ERIC AND ZACK ran down the beach, looking for a house that resembled the one they had seen in the model at the museum. Zack saw it first. He stopped running and shouted, "That's it!"

Eric slid to a stop and looked at where his brother pointed. "Looks like the one in the model." He glanced around and didn't see anyone. "Come on."

Together, Eric and Zack approached the house. The ground they walked transformed from sand to dirt as they approached green shrubbery running along the house's west property line. When they reached the shrubbery, they heard a woman's loud, shrieking voice. Zack grabbed his brother by a wrist and gave it a tug, signaling for him to drop out of sight. The boys hid behind the bush.

Slightly out of breath from the running, the boys looked through the leaves and saw a woman standing by a car in the driveway on her cellphone. She paced back and forth while talking, several feet from the shrubbery.

"It's really none of your business where I'm going," she angrily ranted, her right hand clutching the cellphone to her ear. "What do you care? You're not here...Look at those real estate papers he emailed you so we can get this done...No, I'm not coming back...

Are you serious? No, I didn't clean out the freaking refrigerator. Just like you to take off and expect me to do everything…I don't care if you can't get back until July. Not my problem…then sign the damn listing, and I'm sure the Realtor can arrange for someone to clean out the refrigerator!"

The woman shoved her cellphone in her back pocket a moment later and then marched over to the parked car. After loading two suitcases into the car, she climbed into the driver's side of the vehicle, slammed the car door shut, turned on the engine, and drove out of the driveway and down the street.

"She's gone," Eric whispered.

"Think anyone else is there?"

"Let's see." Eric jumped up and raced to the house and to the side door.

"What are you doing?"

"Gonna see if anyone else is here." Eric knocked on the side door.

"What if someone answers?"

"Then we tell them we lost our dog. Ask them if they've seen it."

"What kinda dog?" Zack asked.

"It doesn't matter."

"Sure it does. We have to tell them what it looks like."

"Make up something." Eric knocked again.

"How about a poodle?"

"Poodles are lame."

"I don't think anyone is home." Zack cupped his face between his hands and pressed his nose up against the pane of glass in the door, trying to peek inside the house.

Eric pulled a credit card from his back pocket. "Move."

Zack moved back from the door and looked at his brother and the credit card in his hand. The credit card was cut on one side.

"Where did you get that?"

"Mom's purse."

"What you going to do with it?"

"Last night, when Mom was taking a shower, I got her phone

and started watching YouTube videos. I watched one showing how to break into a house using a credit card."

"Why is it cut?"

Eric shrugged. "The credit card in the video was cut. So I cut Mom's the same way."

"Mom's gonna kill you for cutting her credit card if she finds out."

"If she finds out, she's gonna kill me for watching YouTube, anyway. She can't kill me twice."

Moving closer to the door, Eric shoved his mother's credit card along the edge of the door, near the doorknob. Zack watched as his brother imitated what he had seen on the YouTube video. A moment later, he let out a whoop as the door opened.

"Dang, you actually did it!"

"Come on." Eric grabbed his brother and shoved him into the house before walking in himself. He closed the door behind him.

NINE

While Danielle nursed the babies, Heather told her and Walt about what had happened in the nursery while they slept. They concluded that whatever was going on seemed to be confined to the nursery—for now. They all agreed the best course of action was to talk to Eva and Marie, and hopefully the two spirits could unravel the paranormal mystery.

Eventually, the conversation drifted to the topic of the day's warmer than normal May weather, and Danielle urged her friends to go do something fun and enjoy the sunshine and absence of rain. Instead of taking Danielle's suggestion, Chris ordered food to be delivered, and they enjoyed a makeshift indoor picnic lunch in Marlow House's living room.

It proved to be a lazy Sunday afternoon at Marlow House. Chris, who had moved to a recliner and had the footrest up, had been holding Addison when she nodded off after being nursed and changed. She napped on a receiving blanket draped over Chris's denim-clad thighs.

Heather had been holding Jack when he fell back asleep, and now he napped on the sofa between Danielle and Heather while they discussed sourdough discard recipes Heather wanted to try.

Across the library, Walt sat with Brian at the small table with the chessboard while Walt reintroduced Brian to the game. After Danielle had suggested her friends go do something fun and enjoy the weather, someone suggested they stay in and play a game. When they couldn't agree on a game, someone mentioned chess, and Brian told them his father had taught him chess, but he hadn't played in years, which led to his playing with Walt.

Chris, who stretched out lazily on the recliner, looked down at the sleeping baby. Nearby, Danielle and Heather discussed discard pretzels and pizza, both of which sounded disgusting to him, because when he envisioned discard, the image of something spoiled and disgusting came to mind. To his right, he overheard bits of Walt and Brian's quiet conversation involving knights and pawns.

Taking a deep breath, still staring down at the infant, Chris said, "They don't do much at this age, do they?"

Heather and Danielle looked over at Chris and smiled.

"Just eat, sleep, and poop," Heather said.

"But she is damn cute," Chris added, still staring at Addison. "Look at that tiny little rosebud mouth. That delicate nose."

Brian looked over at Chris from the chessboard. "Yearning to start a family?"

Before Chris could respond, Hunny jumped up and ran from the living room. A moment later, she returned with Sadie by her side, and trailing behind the dogs were Ian and Lily, with Ian holding Connor.

"Hi, guys," Lily greeted a little too loudly, but immediately cringed when she noticed the sleeping infants, one on the sofa and the other on Chris's lap. Yet neither baby woke up, not even when Sadie gave them each a quick sniff while her tail wagged.

"I doubt anything wakes these two besides an empty stomach," Heather said.

"Where have you been?" Danielle asked Lily. "I tried calling you this morning."

"Sorry. We had some errands, and my phone died. Forgot to charge it," Lily explained.

Walt and Brian stopped playing chess. After everyone exchanged greetings, the adults all sat down, Connor dumped the basket of toys out, and the sleeping infants returned to their portable cribs.

With Connor playing on the floor nearby, Lily looked at Danielle and said, "Ian and I were talking about your offer yesterday to move over here while they finish the remodel. We would like to take you up on your offer."

"You sure you want to live under the same roof as a poltergeist?" Heather asked Lily. "Dealing with objects flying off the shelf?"

Lily looked at Heather. "If you're talking about what happened when Kelly and June were over here, I'm sure it was Kelly playing ghost."

"Although the orbs in those photos were interesting," Ian muttered.

Lily glanced at Ian and rolled her eyes.

Danielle was about to tell Lily it hadn't been Kelly, but she paused when she saw two people walking by the living room window to the front door. One was the topic of their conversation, and the other one was Joe.

Before anyone could tell Lily and Ian about the possible poltergeist, Walt went to answer the front door and then brought Kelly and Joe into the living room.

Brian greeted the couple by asking Joe, "Aren't you working today?"

"I am." Joe glanced at his watch before looking back at Brian. "I don't start for another hour. We just had lunch at Pier Café, ran into Melony and Adam. Kelly told them about what happened to her and June here yesterday. I don't know if you've heard."

"Yes, June says Marlow House is haunted." Lily chuckled.

"Kelly said the rocking chair started rocking on its own, and a stuffed animal flew across the room. I told her there is a logical explanation, and it's not ghosts."

"You weren't here, Joe. I know what I saw," Kelly grumbled.

"I don't doubt you saw something. Never did I say I don't believe you. I just don't agree with your conclusion. There is a logical explanation for everything." Joe turned to Danielle. "I'm sorry we just barged in. But before I go to work, I was hoping we could put this thing to rest. Would you let me go up to the nursery with Kelly and help her figure out what really happened?"

Knowing they couldn't come up with a good reason Joe and Kelly shouldn't go up to the nursery—it wasn't like they could claim the babies were upstairs and they didn't want to wake them—Walt decided it best to take them upstairs himself so he could use his telekinetic gift to intervene if necessary.

Ian and Lily, who still assumed Kelly had thrown the stuffed animal, followed them upstairs. They were halfway up the stairs when Heather said, "I gotta see what's going to happen." She dashed from the living room and hurried up to the nursery. Tempted to join Heather, Chris figured that was too many people crammed into the nursery, so he stayed downstairs.

WALT WALKED into the nursery first and looked around. While nothing seemed unusual, he knew that could change in a moment. In the hallway, Kelly paused a moment at the open doorway, not wanting to go in, but Joe gave her a gentle nudge and said, "Come on. I'm going to prove there is no such thing as ghosts."

Looking unconvincingly at Joe, Kelly entered the nursery, finding it looking just as it had been when she and June had first come into the room the previous day, with the stuffed elephant on a shelf.

Ian and Lily, still believing Kelly had thrown the stuffed animal, followed Joe and Kelly into the nursery, with Heather trailing behind them.

"Now what?" Lily asked.

Joe looked at Kelly. "Tell me what you did before the rocker supposedly started rocking on its own."

Nervously chewing her lower lip, Kelly glanced around and then looked at the rocking chair Danielle had been using when nursing the babies. She pointed to the chair. "Danielle was there, nursing the twins. I walked over to the other rocker, picked up the quilt, held it up for my mom to take a picture, and the empty rocker just started rocking."

"Like this?" Joe walked to the rocker and jerked the quilt from the chair, sending the chair rocking.

"No, not like that. I didn't yank it like you did," Kelly grumbled.

"Maybe you didn't think you yanked it," Joe said, still holding the quilt. "But that has to be what happened." Joe reached out and put his hand on the chair, stopping it from rocking. Kelly was about to ask Joe how that explained the stuffed animal flying across the room, when the chair started rocking again.

Joe, who hadn't yet noticed, continued to hold the quilt, a smug smile on his face, while Lily and Ian exchanged quick glances and Heather resisted the temptation to giggle.

Kelly pointed to the rocking chair. "Explain that!" Her voice quivered.

Joe looked down at the chair and frowned. Tossing the quilt on the other chair, he placed his hand back on the moving rocker; once again, it stopped. He glanced around at the floor, looking for an answer. Lifting his hand from the chair, he stared at it a moment and smiled when it stayed still. But a moment later, it began rocking. Convinced there was a logical explanation for the rocking, Joe continued inspecting the chair when something hit the back of his head. Kelly let out a scream.

Heather stood by the corner near the door and watched as stuffed animals started flying off the shelves behind Joe, hitting him in the head. Both Lily and Ian glanced over to Walt, believing he was responsible for the attack, and both silently questioned his actions.

Joe, so preoccupied with batting away the stuffed animals, failed to see them flying off the shelves. But after a moment, the assault stopped, leaving stuffed toys scattered on the floor.

The chair stopped rocking. No one spoke. Finally, Joe walked to Kelly, took her hand, and said, "Okay, I believe you saw something. But it's not ghosts. Let's go."

THEY HAD HEARD Kelly's scream from the living room, so they assumed the mystery spirit was up to its old tricks. Unsure how they were going to handle this, or if they should even bother, since it wasn't like any of them knew what the heck was going on, they all remained where they had been sitting when Joe and Kelly first left to go upstairs.

Joe and Kelly entered the living room first, with Joe holding Kelly's hand. Ian, Lily, Heather, and Walt entered next. Lily and Ian looked annoyed. Kelly looked terrified. Walt looked like someone trying to figure out a problem, and Heather looked like someone watching a good movie and waiting for the surprise ending. Joe looked amused.

"Cute trick," Joe said after they were all back in the living room. "But I don't think you should have played it on June. Sounds like it terrified her."

"What are you talking about?" Danielle asked.

Joe smiled at Danielle. "Come on, Danielle. You guys obviously rigged the rocking chair to rock on its own."

Danielle frowned at Joe. "We did?"

"Joe, what about the stuffed animals?" Kelly asked.

Joe shrugged. "Obviously thrown from one of those ball-throwing devices."

"They flew off the shelves," Kelly insisted. Joe rolled his eyes at her comment.

"Did you find a device like that?" Walt asked.

Joe looked at Walt and smiled. "No, I didn't. But I didn't check around. Joanne's told us how you consider yourself an amateur magician. I didn't feel compelled to figure out how you do your tricks. If Houdini can make an elephant disappear, I'm sure you can make a rocking chair rock and toss around some stuffed animals. It's a good trick, but you did freak out my mother-in-law. She's convinced Marlow House is haunted."

Kelly frowned. "It was all a trick?"

Joe smiled at Kelly. "Certainly. Do you really believe the nursery is haunted?" He glanced around at the others and then looked back at Kelly. "And obviously everyone else knows it was a trick, too. You were the only one screaming up there when things started flying and rocking. It didn't seem to scare anyone else." Joe looked back at the others and said, "Next time, you should all act scared, too."

Kelly, unlike Joe, was not amused that it had supposably all been a magic trick. She glared at Walt and then everyone else in the room, who she now believed was in on the joke, like always, even her brother.

"I guess you guys just love making me look like a fool!" Kelly shouted before breaking into tears and running from the room. Joe, who looked a little shocked at Kelly's outburst, froze a moment before he ran out of the room after his wife.

After the door slammed, Ian turned angrily to Walt and said, "Why would you do that?"

"I don't know what happened upstairs," Danielle said, "but if things started flying, it wasn't Walt. That's why we have the babies napping downstairs and not in the nursery."

TEN

Ian sat on the living room fireplace hearth in Marlow House, hunched over with his right palm cupping his forehead. Danielle and Walt had just explained what had happened in the nursery the night before and earlier that day with Heather. Since Lily had failed to answer her phone when running errands, she and Ian didn't know about the unexplained paranormal activity taking place in Marlow House's nursery until now.

"I don't know how I'm going to fix this with my sister," Ian groaned. "I understand why she's upset. She already feels all of us have been keeping secrets from her. That she's not included in what's going on." Ian looked up at his friends, who all sat quietly watching him. "And she's not wrong."

"Perhaps it's time to tell her the truth," Danielle suggested.

"Are you serious?" Ian stood up and began pacing. "If I do that, she'll tell Joe, and the last thing I want to do is cause problems in her marriage."

"I understand where you're coming from," Heather said. "After all, you were kind of a jerk when Lily told you. You even dumped her."

Ian stopped pacing and turned to Heather. He cringed at the

memory. "Which is why I'm aware of the problems this truth can cause my sister."

"Ian," Walt began, "it's already causing her troubles."

"Walt's right," Chris agreed. "You've always been close with your sister. It's clear she idolizes you, so when she feels left out or excluded from your friend group, she'll naturally get jealous."

"But what do I do?" Ian asked.

"You have to tell her something," Lily said.

"Like what?" Ian asked.

Lily shrugged. "I had a similar problem with my sister after she witnessed certain things over at your parents' property. I didn't tell her everything, but enough to move past it."

"The difference, Laura isn't married to Joe," Ian reminded her. "I know my sister. She doesn't believe you should keep secrets in a marriage. She'll feel compelled to tell Joe, and he'll refuse to believe her, which will only cause more problems. He'll probably convince her we're all in on some elaborate practical joke."

"Ian has a point. Joe is one of my closest friends, but he will have a difficult time wrapping his head around this," Brian said.

Walt nodded in agreement. "Yes. He quickly found his logical explanation for what just happened in the nursery."

"Something like this was bound to happen," Heather said.

Ian looked at Heather. "Why do you say that?"

"You hang out with a bunch of mediums. Your son's favorite babysitter is a ghost, and you have to admit, Beach Drive seems to attract not only mediums, but an inordinate amount of paranormal activity," Heather said.

Flower petals fell from the ceiling. The mediums looked up.

"Eva, is Marie with you?" Danielle called out.

"Yes, dear. I'm right here." The next moment, Marie appeared in the middle of the living room, followed by Eva Thorndike, the spirit of a silent screen star with an uncanny resemblance to the Gibson Girl. Once Eva's vision appeared, the flower petals vanished.

"Gamma Marie!" Connor called out. He stood up and toddled over to Marie.

Marie reached down and picked up Connor. "I was at the diner, and I overheard Kelly talking about what happened in the nursery when she was here with June, and I no longer believe Kelly threw the stuffed animal. Not the way she was talking to Adam and Melony. Which is why I brought Eva with me to talk to you."

"Yes, Marie. We already know Kelly wasn't involved." Danielle then explained what had happened earlier.

Lily, who stood quietly next to her husband, watching her son float around the room, finally spoke up. "You guys, I think Ian and I should go home and let all of you discuss this. I want to talk alone with Ian, anyway."

Brian stood. "I'm going too. I worked late last night, and I haven't slept since I got off work. Going home to crash."

LILY AND IAN had taken Connor and Sadie and headed back across the street to their house. Brian had kissed Heather goodbye, telling her he'd call later after he woke up, and took off. The twins stirred after the non-mediums left, again hungry.

A few minutes later, Danielle sat on the sofa with Walt and the twins, while Chris and Heather sat in the recliners across from them, and the two spirits sat in imaginary chairs nearby. While Danielle nursed the infants, Walt recounted all the unusual paranormal activities that had been happening over the last twenty-four hours.

"And it's only been happening in the nursery?" Eva asked.

"There was the knocking on our bedroom wall. But technically speaking, that was coming from the closet in the nursery," Danielle said.

"And none of you saw anything?" Eva asked.

"Only flying stuffed animals and chairs that rock on their own," Walt said.

"Also, that flying bookend," Heather reminded him. "If that thing hit me, I'd probably be on Eva and Marie's side by now."

"You didn't see it coming?" Eva asked.

Heather shook her head. "No. I saw the stuffed animals flying at me, and just knocked them away with my arm. No big deal. But I only got a glimpse of the bookend from the corner of my eye, and I think that's just because it stopped. Hung there in midair for a moment a couple of inches away from my head. That's when I noticed it in my peripheral vision. And then it fell to the ground."

"Either the spirit just wanted to scare you, or—"

"The Universe intervened," Heather finished for Eva.

Eva nodded in agreement.

"Eva and I have discussed the situation, and we think it best if we spend some time in the nursery, see if we can figure out who is doing this and why," Marie said.

Danielle let out a sigh. "That would be wonderful." She looked down at her nursing babies.

"While I don't believe Addison and Jack are in any danger sleeping in the nursery, I can understand if you don't feel comfortable having them sleeping in there while we figure this thing out," Eva said.

"Walt and I already talked about moving the portable cribs in our bedroom until we resolve whatever it is," Danielle said.

"Marie and I will pop up to the nursery and have a look now." Eva disappeared, and Marie followed her.

"I hope we figure this thing out soon," Danielle grumbled.

Outside, a woman walked by the living room window.

"Someone's coming to the front door," Heather said.

While Walt left to answer the door, Heather helped Danielle with the babies, who had finished nursing. When Walt returned to the living room a few minutes later, carrying a large grocery bag, Danielle and Heather were busy changing the babies' diapers on the sofa. Walt wasn't alone. Millie Samson from the museum stood by his side, holding a small package wrapped in pink and blue gift-wrapping paper.

"Millie," Danielle greeted her while she picked up the freshly diapered baby.

"Millie has brought us some food," Walt told Danielle.

"It's just a little something you can have for dinner or toss in the freezer and save for another night. I figure the last thing you want to think about is what to cook for dinner, and you need to keep up your strength." Millie moved closer to the sofa to see the babies. "Oh my, they are so adorable." She then handed Danielle the small package. "I also brought you this."

Danielle took the package from Millie. "How sweet."

"I'll be right back. I'm going to put this in the kitchen," Walt said before leaving the room. Chris and Heather exchanged greetings with Millie while she took a seat on the now empty rocker, and Heather remained sitting on the sofa, holding Jack while Danielle held Addison.

They exchanged pleasantries. Millie asked questions about the babies, and a few minutes later, Walt returned from the kitchen, taking a seat on the sofa between Heather and Danielle. He took Addison from Danielle so she could unwrap the gift Millie had brought. Everyone watched as Danielle unwrapped Millie's gift. A few minutes later, she held up two crocheted infant baby bonnets, one in pink yarn, the other in blue.

"These are adorable. Did you make these?" Danielle asked Millie.

"Yes. I usually like to make a baby blanket, but since there are two babies, I thought the bonnets might be nice instead."

"I love them. Thank you so much. Yours is the first homemade gift we've received. I'm going to cherish them." Danielle neatly folded the bonnets and placed them back in the gift box.

"I've a quilting friend who's known for making baby quilts for baby showers. But when one of her nieces had twins, she gave her something else. The niece was hurt, but I imagine making two quilts is a lot of work," Millie said.

"Now that I think about it, I do have something homemade for the twins, a quilt. Although it wasn't actually made for them." Danielle then told Millie about the handcrafted quilt Lily had purchased at the estate sale.

"Oh, I'd love to see it."

Walt stood. "I'll get it." He quickly left the room before Millie asked to go see the nursery.

"ANYTHING HAPPEN?" Walt asked when he stepped into the nursery and found Marie sitting in one rocker, and Eva in the other one.

"No. It's been quiet," Marie said.

"We've been trying to start a conversation with whoever—or whatever it is—but I wonder if they have already moved on," Eva said.

"I just came up to grab the quilt Lily gave us. Millie Samson is downstairs," Walt explained.

MILLIE ONLY STAYED for about thirty minutes. After she left, Heather asked Walt if Eva and Marie had made any progress in the nursery. He told her what Eva had said.

Chris stood. "I'm going to take Hunny and head home. Want me to help you move the portable cribs upstairs to your room before I go?"

Walt flashed Chris a smile. "I can do it myself."

Chris chuckled. "That's right. Sometimes I forget."

Heather stood. "I need to get home to Bella."

"We really appreciate all your help. Also, thanks for the cinnamon rolls," Danielle said. "And for the lunch."

Heather kissed the babies on their foreheads before leaving with Chris and Hunny. A few minutes later, after they heard the front door shut, Walt and Danielle sat quietly on the sofa, each holding a baby.

Finally, Danielle looked at Walt and said, "Wow, it's quiet in here."

Walt grinned at Danielle. "Won't be if one of these starts crying."

Danielle glanced down at the baby in her arms and then looked over at the one in Walt's arms. Addison and Jack were almost asleep.

"You know, Heather is right. At this age, all they do is poop, eat, and sleep."

Walt chuckled and then looked over at the portable cribs. After showing the twin quilt to Millie, they had draped it over the side of one crib. "Should we put them down?"

"Sounds like a good idea."

Walt gently laid the sleeping baby on the sofa, intending to stand up before picking him up to place him in the portable crib, while Danielle remained sitting on the sofa, holding Addison.

Danielle looked up over at the cribs and froze. "Oh crap. Walt, look."

Instead of picking up Jack from the sofa, Walt glanced over at the portable cribs. The twins quilt was no longer hanging over the side of one crib. Instead, it floated above them.

ELEVEN

Not long after Lily and Ian left Marlow House, and while Chris and Heather were still there, Lily and Ian sat together on their living room sofa, with Lily leaning against Ian's shoulder, her stockinged feet propped up on the coffee table. Connor sat in a nearby highchair Ian had dragged into the living room from the dining room, where the toddler sat eating goldfish crackers and slices of banana. Sadie lay on the floor by the highchair, prepared to clean up any food Connor might drop off the tray.

"We never discussed staying at Marlow House when we were over there," Lily said.

Ian glanced down at his wife's face. "Not sure I want to now."

"No kidding. I hope they figure this thing out."

"What I need to figure out, what I'm going to say to Kelly." Ian absently fiddled with strands of Lily's hair.

Lily considered his question a moment, let out a deep sigh and said, "Maybe you should tell her the truth. Not all of it. But tell her you don't know what's going on over at Marlow House, just that Walt had nothing to do with it."

"Yes, but Joe has a point. We didn't really react. If we'd shown some surprise or fear, then I could convince her. The truth of the matter, I assumed Walt was responsible."

"Everyone reacts different to fear. You could tell her we were in shock. We didn't know what was going on." Lily patted one of Ian's knees.

"You just said everyone reacts different to fear. But you and I, Walt and Heather, we all reacted the same by not reacting."

"Ian, you know what's kind of funny about all this?"

"What?"

"All along, you've refused to tell your sister about—about any of it. Because you love her, and you've been trying to protect her. You didn't want to do anything to jeopardize her relationship with Joe because she seems happy with him. And Joe, being Joe, could never wrap his head around any of it."

"I'm not seeing the funny part yet," Ian grumbled.

"Kelly's relationship with you is also important. I'll admit, sometimes your sister drives me nuts, but I understand how close you two are, and I understand how much you love each other."

"Still waiting for the funny part."

"When I said funny, I meant ironic."

"Go on."

"While you've been keeping secrets from Kelly to protect her marriage, Joe comes along and basically blows up your relationship with her."

Ian's cellphone rang. Instead of responding to his wife's observation, Ian reached over to the side table and picked up his cellphone. He looked at it and said, "It's my mother." He accepted the call. Lily silently listened to Ian's side of the conversation, and soon it became obvious her mother-in-law was upset over something, considering Ian's one-word responses. He kept starting sentences, only to be cut off before he could finish. After a few minutes, the call ended.

"What was that about?" Lily asked as Ian tossed his cellphone back onto the side table.

"Kelly called my mother after she left Marlow House. Mom's

pretty upset and not thrilled with our friends for pulling such a trick on her."

Lily groaned.

"She feels Walt and Danielle owe them both an apology, and she says I need to make it right with my sister, or I'm going to destroy my relationship with her. She reminded me family comes first, and I've allowed my friends in Frederickport to come between me and Kelly."

"This is so unfair. It's hardly Walt and Danielle's fault."

"I realize that. I couldn't even get two words in to tell Mom the truth."

"You were going to?"

"I have to tell her something. But first, I need to see my sister. Joe's at work by now. Mom said Kelly's at home alone, crying."

KELLY SAW her brother's car pull up in the driveway from her kitchen window. No one was in the car with him. She suspected their mother had called him, and she wanted to close her blinds and not answer the door. But she didn't because she was curious to hear what he had to say.

She opened the front door before he rang the doorbell, and instead of giving him a greeting, she left the door wide open, turned, and walked to her living room and sat down on the sofa.

Ian walked into the house, closed the door behind him, and followed his sister into the living room. Instead of sitting on one chair in the living room, he took a seat on the sofa next to her.

"Mom called you. Didn't she? That's why you're here," Kelly asked dully while staring ahead, refusing to look at Ian.

"Yes, and no."

Arms folded across her chest, Kelly turned to Ian and frowned. "What do you mean?"

"Mom called, but that's not why I'm here."

"Then why are you here?"

"You stormed out of Marlow House this afternoon without giving me a chance to say anything."

"What was there to say? That it was just a joke? I should lighten up?"

Ian shook his head. "No. Because it wasn't a joke."

"What do you mean?"

When Ian had walked into Kelly's house several minutes earlier, he had been carrying his cellphone. When he sat on the sofa with her, he hadn't slipped it in his pocket or set it on a table. He held it in his hands, absently fidgeting with it, moving it from his right hand to his left and back to his right again, and so on.

"Kelly, I'd like to have a conversation and keep it between you and me for now. I'd rather you not say anything to Joe."

"Ian, I don't keep secrets from my husband. Do you keep secrets from Lily?"

Ian took a deep breath. "Remember when we worked together on the Eva Thorndike story? And I couldn't tell Lily about it?"

"Yeah, but you weren't married back then. You weren't even really dating yet."

"If we had been dating, if we had been married, would you have felt comfortable with me sharing information with Lily early on?"

"Are you saying you're working on a new story?"

"In a way. Sort of."

"What does that mean?"

"Kelly, what happened at Marlow House in the nursery, Walt didn't do it. He didn't make the rocker rock. He had nothing to do with stuffed animals flying across the room. He didn't do any of it."

Kelly frowned at her brother. "Then who did?"

"We don't know."

"Are you saying Marlow House is haunted?"

Ian stopped fidgeting with his phone and instead looked at it, opened his photo app, found an image, and offered it to Kelly. "Have you forgotten the orbs?"

Kelly grabbed the cellphone and looked at the image on its screen.

She then used a finger to flip through the other pictures her mother had taken yesterday, and she had airdropped to Ian's phone, each showing the orbs in a different location in the room behind her while she held up the quilt. After a moment, she shrugged, handed the phone back to Ian. "Joe says lots of things can cause orbs in photos, like dust or moisture."

"True, but it doesn't explain the chair rocking on its own or things flying in the room."

"Joe says—"

"Please, can we leave Joe out of this for the moment? I know he's your husband, and I don't want to cause problems with him, and that is one reason I didn't want to say anything to you about this, because I knew what he'd say. I have no desire to convince you something supernatural was happening at Marlow House, because I knew Joe would say someone was making this up. But unfortunately, I had no control over what happened in the nursery."

"The way you reacted. You all seemed unfazed."

"Lily's and my reaction can be attributed to shock. You see, until we went upstairs, we assumed you had thrown the stuffed animal at Mom the day before."

"Why would I do that?"

Ian shrugged. "We figured you were just messing around, and when Mom freaked out, you said nothing."

"What did everyone else think?"

"That you'd thrown the stuffed animal. But last night, some strange things started happening in the nursery, which is why Walt and Danielle were downstairs with the babies, letting them sleep in the portable cribs, instead of upstairs in their bedroom. Lily and I arrived at Marlow House today right before you did, and they didn't have time to tell us you hadn't thrown the stuffed animal. Walt and Heather hoped nothing would happen, yet knew it was possible. So their reaction only proves they weren't surprised, not that Walt made it happen."

Kelly stared at her brother. "Are you serious?"

BACK AT MARLOW HOUSE, the floating quilt had fallen after a few minutes, landing inside a crib. Danielle headed upstairs to get Eva and Marie, while Walt stayed with the babies. By the time Danielle returned to the living room with the two spirits, she had already told them about the floating quilt.

"Any activity upstairs?" Walt asked when they entered the living room.

"No. But it sounds like whatever it is, is down here now," Eva said.

"Whoever you are, please show yourself," Danielle called out.

Marie took a seat on the sofa with Walt and the babies while their mother paced the room in frustration. Absently, Danielle walked over to the cribs, retrieved the quilt, and folded it. She carried it to the fireplace and set it on the hearth. As she turned away to walk back to the others, a figurine sitting on the fireplace mantel fell from its place, landing on the quilt. Danielle swung around and faced the fireplace.

Eva stared at the quilt. "Are you trying to get our attention?"

The figurine floated up from the quilt and returned to its place on the mantel.

"I just did that," Walt told them.

The next minute, the figurine fell back off the mantel, onto the quilt.

"Did you do that, Walt?" Danielle asked.

"No."

"Marie?" Danielle asked.

Marie shook her head. "No, dear."

"If it wants our attention, why doesn't it just show itself?" Danielle asked.

Eva moved closer to the fireplace and stared down at the figurine and where it had landed. "Danielle, how long have you had this quilt?"

"Lily gave it to me Thursday. Why?"

"Where did Lily get it?" Eva asked.

"From an estate sale. She found it last weekend. Why?"

"Do you think the quilt has something to do with all this?" Marie asked.

Eva turned to the others. "Was this the quilt Ian's mother wanted pictures of?"

Danielle studied Eva, wondering what she was thinking. "Yes."

"From what you've told me, the first incident occurred when Kelly picked up the quilt so her mother could take pictures of it. You bring the quilt down here to show Millie, and another incident occurs. Initially, you assumed the haunting was isolated to the nursery. But perhaps it's connected to the quilt. It's not upstairs or downstairs, it's wherever the quilt is."

"Are you suggesting the ghost is haunting the quilt?" Danielle asked.

Pausing a moment, Eva absently tapped her forefinger against her chin as she considered Danielle's question. Finally, she said, "Perhaps it's not a ghost at all, but the residual energy of a past trauma attached to the quilt, which would explain why none of us has witnessed an apparition normally attached to a ghost. And if that's the case, it might be a good idea to learn more about the quilt's history and whatever incident triggered this paranormal activity."

"Wouldn't it be easier to just get rid of the quilt?" Danielle asked.

"No. Because it's entirely possible that energy might attach itself to another object before you get rid of the quilt. Our best plan of action is to find out as much as we can about the quilt's history."

TWELVE

S everal neighborhoods away, in Fred Lyons's garage apartment, two nine-year-old boys sat in front of the television while their mother was in the apartment's bedroom with her sister, talking.

During the commercial, Eric got up from the sofa and headed to the bathroom. When he got out of the bathroom, instead of returning to the sofa, he paused at the partially open bedroom door and eavesdropped on his mother and aunt.

"I haven't had a decent night's sleep since Clay left," his mother told his aunt.

"What about that sleep medication the doctor gave you? I thought you said you slept great that night."

"I did. But that stuff knocked me out within fifteen minutes, and I didn't wake until nine the next morning. I didn't even wake up to go to the bathroom."

"Then take it tonight," his aunt urged.

"I can't do that. I have the boys to worry about. They're both up by seven in the morning. I can't have them running around while I'm knocked out."

"What happened when you took it the last time?" his aunt asked.

"When I got up, they were watching TV and eating cereal. But I got lucky. What happens if they decide they want bacon and try cooking it and burn the place down?"

"Just tell them they're not to use the stove."

"My sons would see that as a challenge to prove they could do it while I slept," his mother scoffed.

"How about this? I get up at six, anyway. I can come over in the morning, let myself in, and hang out here until you get up."

"I can't let you do that."

"Debbie, please. Take the medicine. You need to sleep. You've got dark circles under your eyes, and you're not doing you or your boys any good how you are now."

His mother let out a sigh. "Okay, I'll do it. I need a good night's sleep."

"Alright, now that's settled, I should probably get home. Fred and I have a movie we want to watch tonight."

Eric hurried back to the sofa and sat down. A few minutes later, his aunt and mother came out of the bedroom. After his aunt left, their mother picked up the TV remote and paused the show they were watching.

"Hey, what did you do that for?" Zack whined.

"I'll turn it back on in a minute. I wanted to tell you I'm going to take a shower, and when that show is over, don't start watching something else. Because when I get out of the shower, I want you both to get ready for bed." The next moment she unpaused the television show and left the room.

Eric sat quietly next to his brother and turned around. He watched his mother go into the bathroom and shut the door. He turned back to his brother. "Hey, I have an idea."

Zack elbowed his brother to stop talking. "I'm watching this."

"You wanna go into the tunnel tonight?" Eric asked.

Zack turned to his brother and frowned. "What are you talking about?"

While they had found the entrance to the tunnel after breaking into the Crawford house, they hadn't brought a flashlight with them and had returned to the pier without entering the tunnel.

"I know where a flashlight is. We could ride our bikes over there and have all night to explore."

"Yeah, right. And what happens when Mom wakes up in the middle of the night and we're not out here? She'll freak."

"She's not going to wake up." Eric then recounted the conversation he had just overheard.

ZACK TOOK HIS BATH FIRST. After Eric finished his, he came out of the bathroom and found the sofa couch had already been pulled out and made into a bed, with Zack under the covers on his side of the mattress. Eric climbed into bed. Debbie tucked them both in and then turned off all the lights before going into the bedroom and shutting the door.

"I think she took the medicine when you were in the bathroom," Zack whispered to his brother.

The two boys lay quietly in bed, waiting for their mother to fall asleep. Thirty minutes passed, and Zack said, "Should we go now?"

"We need to make sure she's really asleep before we leave."

"How do we do that?"

Eric climbed out of bed. "You stay here."

"What are you going to do?"

"See if she's asleep. Or if I can wake her up easy."

Zack frowned at his brother. "What if she wakes up?"

Eric considered the question for a moment before saying, "I'll tell her I'm afraid and ask if I can sleep with her. She'll let me. That way, when she falls asleep, it'll be easier to tell."

A few minutes later, Eric stood by his mother's bedside. A nightlight broke up the darkness. By the gentle snores coming from Debbie, Eric knew she had fallen asleep, but he wondered how deeply she slept. He stared at her for a moment and then picked up her right wrist, raised it about two feet, and let it drop. Her hand fell back onto the sheet, and instead of waking up, she moaned softly, turned to one side, and continued to snore. Eric grinned and then ran from the room, gently closing the door behind him.

After Eric returned to his brother, they both changed out of their pajamas into the clothes their mother had laid out for the next day and put on their jackets. Before leaving the house, Eric retrieved the flashlight he had found earlier.

There were lights on next door, and Eric assumed his aunt and uncle were up watching television, considering what his aunt had told his mother. Eric figured they were on the other side of the house, where the windows didn't face the garage apartment, so he wasn't concerned about his aunt and uncle catching them leaving the house. Overhead, the quarter moon provided sufficient lighting so they wouldn't need to turn on the flashlight. The plan was to stay on the sidewalks and try to keep out of sight from oncoming cars, because the last thing they wanted was someone calling the police and reporting two boys riding bikes in the dark.

Most houses they passed had their blinds closed or interior lights turned off. When they turned down one street, a dog started barking at them, but fortunately the dog was in a fenced yard, so once they turned the corner, the sound of barking faded away.

It took them less than twenty minutes to reach their destination. Once they pulled into the driveway, they rode to the rear of the property, which faced the ocean, and dropped their bikes on the driveway.

FOLLOWING the boys from the pier today had to be one of the smartest things he had done since this all began. If he was to believe the phone call he'd overheard earlier, no one would show up at the house until July—except for a possible Realtor, but Realtors rarely showed up at night, so that didn't worry him. He could make himself scarce during the day, but at least now he had somewhere comfortable to sleep, and he was no longer hungry, thanks to all the food he found in the refrigerator and pantry.

He hadn't bothered locking the door because he didn't want to get in the habit of locking it when he left in the morning. It would make it easier to come and go if he wasn't always jimmying the door. When the Realtor showed up, he would assume the home-owner had forgotten to lock all the doors, and then lock it. When he returned at night and found the door locked, he would know it was time to be on high alert, as that would probably mean the Realtor had shown up. Of course, it wouldn't keep him out of the house during the evenings. If a little boy could get a locked door open, he was certain he could do the same.

Before getting in bed, he took a shower and helped himself to a clean pair of jogging pants and a sweatshirt, which he assumed belonged to the husband of the woman he'd seen in the driveway earlier that day. Fortunately, he wore the same-sized clothes as the man.

He started thinking about the box of graham crackers he had found in the pantry and the open carton of milk in the refrigerator. He had checked the expiration date on the milk and given it a sniff. It smelled good, and he told himself he should probably finish it before it spoiled, or before the Realtor showed up and got rid of all the food.

Not wanting the neighbors to notice his presence in the house, he hadn't turned on any lights. Fortunately, there was enough moon-light coming through the blinds, so he wasn't in total darkness.

He climbed out of bed and headed for the door, planning to go to the kitchen and help himself to a glass of milk and some graham crackers. But once he opened the door, he froze. Someone else was in the house.

"IT'S kind of creepy in here," Zack told Eric.

"Don't be a chicken."

"We probably should have locked the door when we left today."

"Why? Then we would be standing outside in the dark, trying to get the door unlocked with the credit card," Eric reminded him.

"Yeah, but maybe someone else got in since we were here."

"Don't be a baby. No one got in."

"Can't we turn a light on?" Zack asked.

"Don't be stupid. Someone will see. We got the flashlight."

The boys walked to the corner of the room, where they'd found the entrance to the tunnel earlier that day. Had the lady at the museum not been so helpful in telling them all about the tunnel entrance, and shown them pictures, they might not have been able to find it so easily and quickly.

"I wonder if we can get it open. You think they have it nailed shut?" Zack asked.

"Dang. I didn't even think about that. We should have brought some tools with us. But I bet we can find some here if we need them."

"Let's look at the tunnel door first."

When they had been there earlier that day, they had found the tunnel behind the bookcase, but because of all the books weighing down the cabinet, all they could do was use their body weight to help shove the bookcase out a few inches, just enough to see the tunnel entrance. It looked just like it had in the pictures at the museum. Before they had left to return to Pier Café, they had pushed the bookcase back against the wall.

Instead of trying to move the bookcase again, the boys began removing the books and stacking them nearby. Once all the books had been removed, they worked together to slide the now empty bookcase down the wall, revealing the tunnel's entrance.

Excited, Eric and Zack scrambled to the entrance and tried jiggling the metal plate that served as its door. To their surprise, it swung open, revealing what looked like a dark hole.

"We did it!" Eric squealed. Shoving his brother out of the way, he poked his head into the hole with the flashlight and looked down. "Wow, this is cool."

"Let me see," Zack asked.

"I'll climb in, and you follow me." Eric shoved the flashlight under his chin, holding it there to free his hands.

"I hope no one comes and shuts the door on us."

"No one's gonna come in and shut the stupid door. Anyway, I have the keys to open the other side of the tunnel. We can always get into the basement of Marlow House."

Eric entered the tunnel without dropping the flashlight. After they were both inside, they stood together while moving the flashlight beam along the walls of the tunnel.

"This is really creepy," Zack muttered.

"You aren't afraid, are you?" Eric asked.

"Aren't you?"

"No. The lady from the museum said no one can get down here. So there is nothing to be afraid of. Let's check it out."

Hesitantly, Zack followed his brother, careful to keep close by his side, since he held their only flashlight. After about five minutes, Zack grabbed hold of his brother's wrist and pulled him to a stop.

"Did you hear that?" Zack whispered.

"Why are you whispering? Nobody's in here but you and me."

"I heard footsteps."

"It's probably ours. It echoes in here."

"I guess," Zack muttered, but then he heard the footsteps again, and he and Eric were not walking.

The next moment, both Zack and Eric each felt a hand drop on the top of their heads, holding them in place. They screamed; it echoed ominously through the tunnel.

THIRTEEN

Danielle Marlow had a reputation for being an excellent cook and baker, which had helped build her bed-and-breakfast business. Heather had no desire to compete with Danielle's culinary acumen. Heather's baking expertise was limited to sourdough bread.

Early on she realized she proofed her bread too long, taking Lily's original instructions of proofing for ten to twelve hours as set in stone, as opposed to a ballpark, and now Heather looked for her dough to double and pass the touch test she'd learned from other sourdough bakers on social media.

Heather had also learned new ways to use her sourdough discard, because the idea of throwing away discard when feeding her starter seemed ridiculously wasteful, and having a room full of glass jars filled with the starter wasn't practical.

On Monday morning, Heather stood in her kitchen, wearing the clothes she had worn jogging, and measured two and a half cups of discard into a large bowl. She loved this waffle recipe, because it didn't call for additional flour, just discard. Heather then added two tablespoons of real maple syrup, six tablespoons of melted butter, two eggs, a teaspoon of vanilla, a half a teaspoon of salt, and one teaspoon of baking soda.

Before starting breakfast, Heather had taken her morning run while Brian slept in her bed. He had returned the previous night after going home to take a nap. They had intended to go out for a late dinner, but Brian ended up picking up Chinese takeout and bringing it to Heather's house.

She had just finished mixing the batter and was about to heat the waffle maker when her phone rang. Fifteen minutes later, Brian joined Heather in the kitchen just as she was ending her phone call.

"Wow, you've been busy this morning," Brian said as he watched Heather pour batter into the hot waffle maker. Already dressed for work, he asked, "How was your run?"

"It was good. I'm going to jump in the shower after breakfast. Chris is picking me up this morning. It's his turn to drive."

Brian peeked into the bowl of batter. "Looks like you're making a lot of waffles. Anyone joining us?"

"No. I'm going to freeze what we don't eat."

Brian gave Heather a quick kiss on the cheek and a playful tug on her ponytail before walking over to the coffeepot. As he filled his mug, he said, "I'm picking up the chief this morning."

Heather glanced over at Brian. "He's going to work today?"

"He wants to come in for a couple of hours. He has another week before he can drive. I told him I'd pick him up."

A few minutes later, Heather lifted the top of the waffle maker and removed the waffle. She set it on a plate and handed it to Brian. While pouring more batter into the waffle maker, she said, "I talked to Danielle this morning." Heather told Brian what had gone on at Marlow House after she had left the night before and then said, "She and Walt slept in their bedroom last night with the twins. He moved the portable cribs up there. Marie and Eva stayed for the night, too."

"Did anything happen?"

"Whatever it is, it likes to knock on walls."

"That must make for a restful night's sleep."

Heather shrugged. "The weird thing, it always knocks when the twins are already waking up to be fed."

"That's the weird thing? This is all weird."

"One of the weird things."

Brian sat at the kitchen table and poured syrup on his waffle. "So they really feel this might be energy and not a ghost?"

"Eva says we're all energy. Sometimes I like to surf for ghost hunters and look for the fake ones. Spoiler alert, most of them are fake. Anyway, one talked about objects being haunted. He said it wasn't a ghost per se, nothing with a soul or spirit, but just the energy of some negative event, lingering and attached to the object."

"Sounds like what Eva is saying."

Heather shrugged. "I guess. But if that's true for whatever's going on over at Marlow House, I wasted a good rant after that bookend tried attacking me. It had no idea what I was saying."

Brian chuckled and then said, "Since our experience at witch mountain, I've gone online and done some reading myself on the paranormal. I read about poltergeists and how some claim it's a ghost, while others say it's energy from a living person."

Heather giggled. "Witch mountain?"

Brian shrugged and took a bite of waffle.

"Danielle also told me she talked to Lily this morning. I guess Ian went over to Kelly's and told her Walt wasn't responsible for what happened in the nursery."

Brian looked up from his plate. "What did he say it was?"

"He told her they didn't know."

BRIAN HELPED the chief get into the passenger seat of the car. He then took the chief's walker, folded it shut, and placed it in the back seat.

"Thanks for picking me up," the chief told Brian after they were underway.

"No problem."

"So, anything exciting going on?" the chief asked.

Brian laughed.

The chief turned to Brian and frowned. "What?"

"Have you talked to Walt or Danielle lately?"

"Not for a few days. Why?"

Brian then told the chief what had gone on at Marlow House over the weekend.

The chief leaned back in the seat, now looking out the front windshield. "None of the mediums could see who it was?"

"Not even Marie and Eva. But like I said, Eva wonders if it's not a ghost, but energy from trauma."

The chief shook his head. "June Bartley might be right when she says Beach Drive is cursed."

"At the moment, she's convinced Walt and Danielle are playing tricks on her. Not sure if Ian is going to talk to his mother like he did to Kelly."

"I'm curious what Kelly is going to say to Joe," the chief said.

"I'm considering saying something to Joe myself."

The chief turned again to look at Brian. "Really?"

"Thinking about it. So, anything new with you? Maybe a good-looking physical therapist?"

The chief leaned back in the seat again. "I suppose some would call my physical therapist good looking. But he's not my type."

Brian laughed.

"Fred Lyons called me on Friday. He was checking up on things."

"I wonder how he's enjoying having Bowman's wife and kids living with him. When I think about Bowman, I still can't wrap my head around the fact he not only had an affair with my wife, he killed her." Brian shook his head at the idea as he steered the car down the road.

"I'm sorry, Brian. Especially because I didn't put my foot down and tell Fred I didn't want to hire his brother-in-law. I wasn't thrilled with Bowman ten years ago. But it all happened so fast."

"I don't blame you. I imagine Fred regrets it too."

"Oh, he does. Especially since it doesn't look as if his sister-in-law and nephews plan to leave."

"And the fact Bowman took off with his coin collection. That must hurt. And didn't he put up the bail money?"

"Yes. And to make it even worse, from what Fred told me, Bowman's wife believes her husband is innocent. Her sons think their father is going to come back after he proves his innocence."

"And that's why he disappeared and stole from family?" Brian gave a snort.

"Until Bowman took off, Fred seemed to believe he was innocent, too. They need to be in therapy. The whole family needs therapy." The chief let out a sigh and shifted in the seat to give his healing leg more room.

"GOOD MORNING," Brian greeted Joe when he walked into the Frederickport police station break room on Monday morning.

Joe, who stood at the counter, pouring himself a cup of coffee, turned to Brian. "Morning."

"I didn't expect to see you here this early. Didn't you get off late last night?" Brian walked to the coffeepot.

"Yes. Our schedules are so messed up right now. By the time I got home last night, Kelly was sound asleep. She was still sleeping when I left this morning."

"Speaking of schedules, or the reason they're messed up right now, the chief's here. I gave him a ride to the station this morning."

Coffee cup in hand, Joe turned to face Brian, who poured himself a cup of coffee. "I wanted to ask you something."

"Sure. What?" Now holding a full cup of coffee, Brian turned to Joe.

"Did you know Walt was going to pull that trick? You said nothing yesterday."

"Well, you didn't really give anyone a chance to respond. You just took off." Brian cupped the warm mug of coffee between his hands.

"Kelly was really upset."

"Yeah, I saw that." Brian sipped his coffee.

"She felt like everyone was making fun of her. I just sort of figured it was a practical joke. But Kelly's pretty sensitive when it comes to her brother and his relationship with his friends. She feels excluded. That's why I wondered if you and Heather knew Walt planned to do that."

"Walt did nothing." Watching for Joe's reaction, Brian took another sip of coffee.

"What do you mean?"

"Walt didn't make the chair rock. He didn't throw the stuffed animals. They have no clue what the hell is going on in the nursery. That's why they were downstairs with the babies. Strange things started happening in the nursery on Saturday."

"Oh please. No way." Joe rolled his eyes. "You're saying Marlow House is haunted?"

"Not sure what to think. No one does. None of us knows what is going on."

The sound of a walker being pushed down the hallway toward the break room interrupted their conversation. Both officers looked to the open doorway and watched as the chief shuffled into the room.

"Hey, Chief, how are you doing?" Joe greeted him.

"Hanging in there. Any more coffee?"

"Sit down, and I'll pour you some." Brian set his cup on the table and went to get a mug for the chief.

"So what's going on?" the chief asked as he sat down at the table.

"Brian's trying to convince me ghosts haunt Marlow House," Joe said with a snort.

"I said nothing about ghosts. I said we don't know what's going on." Brian carried a cup of coffee to the chief.

"Yeah, Brian told me what happened at Marlow House this weekend. Can't imagine dealing with something like that."

Joe looked at the chief. "They know what happened. Walt and his magic tricks."

The chief accepted the cup of coffee Brian handed him. He then looked at Joe. "While that would be a nice, neat explanation, I just got off the phone with Danielle. It wasn't Walt. While Walt might have some impressive magic tricks, what you saw in the nursery wasn't a magic show. They don't know what it was. In fact, both Ian and Walt are busy researching poltergeists and other paranormal phenomena."

"Ghosts aren't real," Joe scoffed.

"No one said it was a ghost," Brian said. "Perhaps it's some strange magnetic force caused by the weather. Who knows?"

Joe frowned at Brian. "You're serious, aren't you?"

"I am." Brian took another drink of coffee.

Joe stared at Brian for a moment. Finally, he said, "There is only one problem with what you say."

Brian arched his brows. "What's that?"

"No way would a new mother stay in a house where things start flying and rocking on their own. Danielle would pack up those two babies and be out of that house so fast."

Brian exchanged a silent glance with the chief before answering. He looked back at Joe and said, "As you know, Danielle claimed to have experiences with the supernatural when she was a child. She won't react how you might expect Kelly to react in a similar situation."

FOURTEEN

W alt and Danielle had a much better night's rest on Sunday evening than they had the previous night. They had left the quilt downstairs in the living room and brought the twins back up to the nursery, as there had been no activity in the babies' room since Walt had taken the quilt downstairs to show Millie.

Marie and Eva offered to stay for the evening, with Marie watching over the babies in the nursery, and Eva wandering the house, on alert for paranormal activity. Late into the night, Marie noticed Addison waking up and glanced at the clock and realized it was almost time for the babies to nurse. Marie was just about to take Addison to Danielle when she heard knocking on the wall between the nursery and Walt and Danielle's bedroom. She soon discovered it was not the new parents knocking. Aside from the knocking when the babies woke from hunger, all was relatively quiet in Marlow House on Sunday night.

The next morning, Danielle pumped milk several times and put the bottles in the refrigerator so there would be something to feed the babies if she and Lily didn't get back in time for their next feeding.

They planned for Danielle to drive this morning, although Lily hadn't walked over yet. Connor was staying home with his father. Before Lily arrived, Danielle wanted to say goodbye to Walt. When she got to the second floor, she peeked in the nursery first and found her babies floating around the room, asleep.

When Marie noticed Danielle standing in the doorway with a concerned look on her face, she said, "Don't worry, dear. I would normally give them an illusion that I am carrying them so they wouldn't think they were flying, But I didn't send them off until they were both asleep."

Danielle glanced to the window and noticed the open blinds, but she said nothing about the neighbors possibly seeing the babies flying. Instead, she said, "I'm going to run up and say goodbye to Walt. Lily should be here in a minute."

"Okay. Don't worry. Walt and I've got this!"

Danielle grinned. "Thanks, Marie." She then looked at her babies, who floated peacefully around the nursery in slumber. "Mommy loves you, Addison and Jack," Danielle whispered before turning from the room and heading up to the attic office.

"I'm going to be leaving in a couple of minutes," Danielle told Walt when she walked into the office. Walt, who sat at his desk in front of the computer, turned to Danielle. "Don't worry about anything. Marie and I've got this."

"That's pretty much what Marie just said. I put two bottles in the refrigerator. But please be careful when you warm them up. Test the milk on your wrist before you give it to them."

Walt grinned at Danielle. "Yes, Little Mama."

"Oh, and you might want to go down and shut the blinds in the nursery. Marie has our sleeping babies floating around the room like two planets and she's the sun. The blinds are wide open, and I don't think we need our neighbors seeing that. I was going to suggest Marie close the blinds when I was down there, but I didn't want her to break concentration and drop the babies."

Walt chuckled. "I doubt that would happen, at least not with Addison and Jack. That falls in the category of spirits not being able to harm an innocent—either intentionally or unintentionally."

"YOU WILL NOT BELIEVE THIS," Lily said as she and Danielle left through the kitchen door and headed to the garage twenty minutes later. "Kelly's helping Ian research poltergeist and paranormal phenomena."

"Really? Is she at your house?"

"No. She's doing it from her place."

After they got into Danielle's car and headed for Adam Nichols's office, Danielle told Lily about the knocking during the night.

"And that was the only thing that happened?" Lily asked.

"Yes. So weird."

"This makes me wonder, is this poltergeist activity?" Lily said.

"Why do you say that?"

"Think about it. There are people who believe poltergeist activity is nothing more than energy coming from a living person. Typically, it's from a teenager or preteen, but why not energy from infants whose father can harness his energy in a similar way? Knocking right when they're waking up, and want to eat, it could be their way of saying, hey Mom, we're hungry in here."

"What about the other stuff? The throwing things, the rocking, and the stuffed animals in the cribs?" Danielle asked.

"The stuffed animals in the crib, an easy one. They obviously wanted the stuffed animals. And the throwing stuff and rocking. Maybe they're just learning how this energy thing works."

Danielle let out a deep sigh, and for a few minutes both women considered the recent events and possible causes. Finally, Danielle glanced briefly at Lily and asked, "Did Kelly say anything to Joe about her discussion with Ian?"

"Not yet. Ian talked to her this morning. Joe got home last night after she fell asleep and left for work before she woke up. Ian sorta backtracked with her about wanting her to keep this from Joe."

"How come?"

Leaning back in the seat, Lily stared out the side window and watched the neighborhood go by. "Ian realized there was no reason for Kelly to keep this from Joe. It's not like he told Kelly about Walt, or Eva and Marie. He's not asking her to believe something. He's simply sharing with her something that none of us understands. Something that both she and Joe have already experienced. It's not like he's trying to convince her he saw things flying around in the nursery. She saw that herself. And so did Joe."

"You have a point. I guess we've all gotten into a habit of coming up with excuses for paranormal activity. Things that none of us control."

"Yes, but sometimes it's unavoidable," Lily said with a snicker. "Like when someone sees your babies flying around through the nursery window."

Danielle cringed. "You saw that?"

Lily giggled. "Yes, right before someone closed the blinds. When I was walking over to your house this morning. Anyway, sometimes it's necessary to come up with an explanation that's easier to digest, as opposed to getting into a long drawn-out explanation of how Marie's ghost stuck around after she died, and sometimes she likes to babysit."

Danielle glanced briefly over to Lily. "By the way, sorry I've hijacked your babysitter."

Lily shrugged. "No problem. Connor's playing with some toys in the living room while Ian sits on the couch with his laptop, doing his own research. If June wasn't pissed at all of us right now, Ian would ask her to watch Connor for a while, but he's not ready to sit down and have that talk with his mom."

"If you think about it, until Joe came up with his theory, June was already on board with the notion of a haunting at Marlow House."

"True, but I wasn't talking about that. I was talking about his mother going back on the tangent about how Beach Drive is cursed, and we all need to move."

———

ADAM'S ASSISTANT, Leslie, greeted Danielle and Lily when they walked into the front offices of Frederickport Vacation Properties.

Leslie let Adam know Danielle and Lily were there to see him, and then told them they could go on back.

"Surprised to see you two. Who's watching the kids?" Adam asked when Lily and Danielle walked into his office. He stood briefly and motioned for them to sit down on the two chairs facing his desk.

"Their fathers," Danielle said as she waited for Lily to choose a chair before she sat down.

"Together?" Adam asked.

"You mean are Walt and Ian together with the kids?" Lily asked as she sat down. "No. Ian's at home with Connor, and Walt's at Marlow House with the babies."

Adam sat back down behind his desk, facing Lily and Danielle. "Wow, brave of Walt babysitting two infants all alone."

Lily rolled her eyes. "It's not babysitting if a father is doing it. It's called parenting."

Adam let out a sigh and sat back in his chair. "You sound like Mel. Either way, sounds terrifying to me. So tell me, to what do I owe this visit?"

"Remember that quilt I showed you? The one Lily bought me from the estate sale?" Danielle asked Adam.

"Sure. You called it a twin quilt? Funny, Carla mentioned the quilt yesterday when Mel and I were at Pier Café." Adam glanced to Lily. "She told us you showed it to her when you and Kelly stopped by the diner last weekend."

Lily nodded. "Yes. After Kelly and I went thrifting, we stopped to get something to eat. What did she say about it?"

Adam shrugged. "She didn't understand why anyone would get rid of a homemade quilt."

"We're actually trying to learn about the quilt's history," Danielle said.

"How do you plan to do that?" Adam asked.

"When I told you where Lily got it, you mentioned you were going to be listing the house from the estate," Danielle reminded him. "We'd like to talk to the trustee, executor, whatever. Didn't you say the one who was listing the property was a Beckett?"

"Well, yes. But not sure what Scott Beckett can tell you about the quilt. He never lived in the house. And it obviously wasn't an heirloom."

"Why do you say that?" Danielle asked.

"The house belonged to Scott's aunt. And before that, his grandparents, and it was built by his great-grandparents. The aunt, who was never married, left the house to her nieces and nephews. Scott told me she had a list of heirlooms to be distributed to the nieces and nephews. If that quilt was sold at the estate sale, I have to believe it wasn't an heirloom. Plus, if it was made for twins, the Becketts didn't have any twins."

"We'd like to at least ask him if he knows anything about it. Could you contact him and see if he's willing to talk to us?" Danielle asked.

Adam chuckled.

Danielle frowned. "What's funny?"

"I can't even imagine how much—well—how tied down you are these days. And Lily." Adam turned to Lily. "Pretty soon Lily's going to have her hands full too. But here you are, spending your free time away from your kids, trying to track down the history of a second-hand blanket. I'd think you two would get your nails done, have a massage, or go to the movies."

"Not sure about the nails or movie, but the massage sounds good." Danielle flashed Adam a grin.

"But if this is how you want to spend your time, who am I to judge?" Adam chuckled again. "But you don't need me to call him. You can ask him yourself. He owns the Beckett's Gas Stop over on the other side of town."

"Oh, that Beckett!" Lily said.

Adam nodded. "He's probably there now. He usually takes the weekends off to be with his family. I'm not really violating any client confidentiality by sending you over there, since you told me you bought the quilt at the Beckett estate. You can just go ask him, and you don't need to tell him I filled in the blanks for you."

FIFTEEN

Danielle pulled up in front of the convenience store of Beckett's Gas Stop and parked the Flex. A few minutes later, she and Lily walked into the store and looked around. There was one man behind the counter, waiting on a woman, while a customer wandered down the candy aisle.

Danielle and Lily walked over to the counter and waited for the man to finish waiting on the customer. When the woman walked away, the man behind the counter turned a smile at Danielle and Lily. The first thing Danielle noticed was his name tag. It didn't say Scott Beckett.

"Morning, ladies, how can I help you?" he asked.

"We were wondering if Scott Beckett might be here?" Danielle asked.

"If you're trying to sell something or need a donation, then I'm the person you need to talk to."

"No, we're not trying to sell anything. And we're not here to ask for a donation."

The man narrowed his eyes and studied Danielle for a moment before breaking into a smile and asking, "Hey, aren't you Danielle Marlow?"

Danielle smiled. "Yes, I am."

Nodding at himself for getting it right, the man said, "My wife and I attended your open house when you first opened your bed-and-breakfast. Hey, didn't you just have twins or something? I heard you had them at Adam Nichols's house."

"Yes. They came a little early during the baby shower."

The man shook his head and chuckled. "Dang. I was with my wife when we had our son, and I can't imagine her having to do that at home and not in the hospital. And with twins! Wow." He flashed both Danielle and Lily a smile and said, "If you want to talk to Scott, you can catch him around back. He's washing his truck."

"Thanks."

"And congratulations." He turned to Lily and added, "And congratulations to you, too. But try to make it to the hospital. Don't do it at home like your friend." He gave her a wink.

Lily giggled. "I will definitely follow that advice."

THEY FOUND Scott Beckett behind the convenience store, drying off his truck with a chamois. His back was to Danielle and Lily as they approached the vehicle.

"Scott Beckett?" Danielle called out when they were about six feet from him.

Scott, a tall, muscular man in his forties, with sandy, closely cropped hair, stopped drying off his truck and turned to face Danielle and Lily. He flashed the two women a smile and said, "Guilty. How can I help you?"

"Hi. I'm Danielle Marlow, and this is my friend Lily Bartley."

Still holding the damp chamois in his hand, Scott arched his brows. "Danielle Marlow from Marlow House?"

Danielle grinned. "Now it's my turn to plead guilty."

He looked over to Lily and said, "I assume you're the Lily Bartley who also lives on Beach Drive, married to Jon Altar? I mean Ian Bartley?"

Lily grinned. "You know who we are?"

Scott shrugged. "I am a huge fan of your husband, and everyone in town knows about Marlow House and Danielle Marlow."

Danielle cringed. "They do?"

Scott grinned at Danielle. "Well, you've made Frederickport more interesting since you moved to town. So tell me, what can I help you ladies with?"

Danielle pulled her cellphone from her back pocket, opened the picture app to an image of the quilt, and handed it to Scott. Before accepting the phone, Scott tossed the chamois into the back of his truck, dried his hands off on the side of his denims, and took the iPhone. He looked at the photo while Danielle said, "Lily bought that quilt at your family's estate sale last weekend. And we wondered if you could tell us anything about it."

Scott handed the phone back to Danielle and gave a shrug. "Sorry, the only thing I can tell you about the quilt, my aunt Pamela didn't like it. She's the one who recently passed away, and I'm the executor of her estate. She gave me a list of heirlooms to give my cousins, and it wasn't on the list."

"So that's why you think she didn't like it?" Danielle asked.

"I visited her in the hospital a couple of days before she passed. She told me about the list of heirlooms she wanted to give to my cousins, and said the list was with the lawyer. Aunt Pamela also mentioned the quilt. She described it. Told me I would find it in the attic, and she said not to give it to my cousins or keep it. She said I should throw it away."

"Throw it away?" Lily asked. "But you didn't."

Scott shrugged. "My wife saw the quilt and said it would be a shame to throw it away. She convinced me I could honor my aunt's wishes by not keeping it in the family, but to include it in the estate sale. And it's not like I'm going against the trust, because she never had the attorney write up anything about the quilt." Scott paused, took a breath, and then said, "I guess that sounds bad. Here is the thing: I really had no kind of relationship with my aunt. I didn't even have much of a relationship with my grandparents. Both died when I was a teenager. And when I was a little kid, we rarely went over there, which sounds odd, considering we lived in the same town."

"But your aunt left you as executor?" Danielle asked.

Scott nodded. "Yeah. She called me up one day out of the blue, asked if I could come over to talk to her. I had seen her a few times over the years, but she liked her privacy. My father would periodically reach out to her, but she always made some excuse why she couldn't see him. Anyway, I visited her that day, and she told me she intended to leave her estate to her nieces and nephews, and since I was the only one who lived in town, she wanted me to be the executor."

"Why do you think your aunt wanted you to throw the quilt away?" Danielle asked.

"I have no idea."

"I've heard there were no twins in your family. Is it possible one of your aunts or uncles was a twin, but the other twin didn't survive? Is that why the quilt had such bad memories?" Danielle asked.

"I never said it had bad memories. I just said she didn't seem to like it. But no, there are no twins on that side of the family. Not even ones who didn't survive."

"I guess there is no way to find out where that quilt came from or who made it." Danielle sounded disappointed.

"I suppose you could talk to Iris Farmer," Scott suggested. "She might know."

"Who is Iris Farmer?" Danielle asked.

"She used to be my grandparents' housekeeper. Worked for them for as long as I can remember. She stayed on after they passed away and worked for my aunt. But she retired about ten years ago. Last I heard, she lives at Seaside Village. Moved there after she broke her hip."

"HOW ARE YOU DOING?" Lily asked Danielle when they drove up to Seaside Village and parked.

Danielle turned off the ignition and looked at Lily. "What do you mean?"

Lily glanced at Danielle's bustline and arched a brow. "I remember how it was when I nursed Connor. Leaving him for a few hours and worrying my milk was going to drop at any minute. And you have been nursing for two! I still can't believe how you've been able to do that."

Danielle glanced briefly to her breasts. "So far, I'm okay. But I pumped right before we left. Yet after we're done here, I think we should go home."

"IT'S KINDA strange coming in here again," Lily said as they stepped through the front entrance of Seaside Village. A little over three years prior, Marie Nichols had been murdered at Seaside Village when she had been a patient at the facility. The murderer had also tried to kill Danielle. But the woman responsible had been arrested, and new management had taken over the facility.

After entering the building, they walked over to the nurses' station, and Danielle noticed a familiar face, SeAnne Eason. SeAnne had been working at the care home during Marie's murder.

"Danielle, hello," SeAnne greeted her.

"Hi, SeAnne. I was wondering if we could talk to one of your residents. Iris Farmer?"

SeAnne glanced toward the lounge area and then looked back at Danielle. "I didn't know you and Iris were friends."

"We're kinda friends of friends," Danielle explained.

SeAnne turned and pointed to a woman sitting in a wheelchair, reading a book in the lounge area. "She's over there reading. But you need to sign in first."

"MS. FARMER?" Danielle called out hesitantly when she was about five feet from the elderly woman in the wheelchair. Iris looked up from her book. Danielle stepped closer and introduced herself and Lily.

Five minutes later, Lily and Danielle sat on the loveseat next to Iris, who remained in the wheelchair, her book now closed.

"Of course, I remember that quilt," Iris told them. "When Mrs. Beckett gave it to Miss Pamela for her dolls, I was surprised."

Danielle frowned. "Surprised?"

"Yes. It was a beautiful quilt, obviously handmade. Didn't look like it had been used. Seemed silly to give something like that to a child to play with. But Miss Pamela loved it. Most of her toys and clothes were hand-me-downs from her siblings. She loved that quilt. Until she didn't." Iris gave a snort.

"What do you mean?" Lily asked.

"Miss Pamela liked to play with her baby dolls, and she'd arrange them on the quilt like they were playing with each other. But then one day I found it wadded up and shoved in the trash can. I thought she might have spilled something on it. Stained it. But no, I pulled it from the trash, and there was nothing wrong with it. I showed it to Mrs. Beckett."

"She threw it away? Why?" Lily asked.

"That's what her mama wanted to know. She asked Miss Pamela, who said she didn't want it anymore. And Mrs. Becket said that's fine, but there was no reason to throw a perfectly good quilt away. She had me wash it and put it in the linen closet. But the next week, I found it shoved in the trash can again. This time, in the bin by the side of the garage."

"Wow, she really didn't like it," Danielle muttered.

"She was always an odd child. I didn't want to get Mrs. Beckett all upset, so I washed it again and put it in the attic. I said nothing to Miss Pamela about it, but I told her mother I had moved the quilt up to the attic to free up space in the linen closet. She was okay with that."

"Pamela never knew you kept it?"

"Funny thing. I was still working for Miss Pamela after her parents passed on. Right before my seventieth birthday, I told her I would be retiring. I just couldn't keep house anymore. She threw me a little birthday retirement party. I use the term party lightly. It was just the two of us. Miss Pamela always kept to herself. We were reminiscing about the years I worked for her family. The topic of the quilt came up, and I mentioned how I had found it, but didn't tell her mother. When I told her I had taken it to the attic and imagined it was still there, I thought she would be amused."

"But she wasn't?" Danielle asked.

Iris shook her head. "No, she turned white as a ghost and muttered something like *that explains a lot.*"

"What did she mean?" Lily asked.

Iris shook her head. "I don't know. Like I said, she was always an odd girl. I think if she could have, she would have gone up to the attic, gotten the quilt, and shoved it in the trash can again."

"What do you mean, if she could have?" Danielle asked.

"She had some health issues that made walking upstairs virtually impossible. For the last five years I worked for her, she never went to the second floor, much less to the attic."

"Do you have any idea where Mrs. Beckett got the quilt to begin with? I'd love to know who made it," Danielle asked.

"Mrs. Beckett's friend Gemma gave it to her. I don't remember Gemma's last name. She wasn't married when she gave the quilt to Mrs. Beckett. And I don't remember the name of the man she married. I remember he had twins. They were about two years old at the time they married. I remember thinking, *I wonder if she regrets giving the quilt away, since she's now a stepmother to twins.*"

"Did Gemma make the quilt?" Lily asked.

"I have no idea."

SIXTEEN

When Danielle and Lily returned to Marlow House early Monday afternoon, Lily headed back across the street. Danielle stepped into the kitchen as Walt walked in to get the filled baby bottles she had left in the refrigerator that morning.

"Hey, you're back. Good timing." Walt dropped a quick kiss on Danielle's lips. "Did you find out anything?"

"I found out who gave the quilt to the Becketts. That's about it."

"I was just coming to get the bottles and warm them up. Marie has both of the babies in the parlor with her. I'm assuming you would rather nurse."

"Yes. Definitely." Danielle moved the bottles to the freezer, washed her hands in the kitchen sink, and followed Walt to the parlor.

Less than fifteen minutes later, Danielle sat on the sofa with the nursing babies, while Walt sat next to her, and Marie perched in the chair facing them. Once Danielle had the babies settled down, she told Marie and Walt about her and Lily's morning.

Marie cringed. "Poor Iris, living in that horrid care home."

"It looks like they've recently remodeled the place. Plus, it didn't smell like urine and Lysol like when you were there. Not to mention it's under entirely new management. But some of the same staff is there. We saw SeAnne Eason. Oh, and we had to sign in. I don't remember doing that when you were there."

"I still wouldn't want to live there," Marie said.

"Were you good friends with Iris?" Danielle asked.

Marie shook her head. "No, not really. I knew her, but I wouldn't call us friends. She worked for Ansel and Alice Beckett for years. They were Scott Beckett's grandparents. Ansel and I attended school together, and Alice was much younger than Ansel and me. Not long after they married, she started having babies. One right after another. My son, Warren, was a friend with their son, Georgie. They were in Scouts together. That's really the only reason I remember, because I never really cared for Ansel when we were in school together."

"Iris told us Alice's friend, someone name Gemma, gave her the quilt. She didn't know if Gemma made it," Danielle said.

"Oh, that would be Gemma Francas. She moved to town when Warren was a freshman. I remember, because she paid Warren and Georgie Beckett to help her move some boxes when she moved into her house."

"And she wasn't married or anything when she first moved to town?" Danielle asked.

"No. She was a single woman, on her own. From what I understand, she met Alice when she first moved in, and she was looking for help to move some boxes. That's how Warren and Georgie got hired."

"Was Francas her maiden name? Or the name of the man she married?" Danielle asked.

"The man she married, Dan Francas."

"What happened to Dan Francas's first wife? From what Iris told us, when Gemma married him, he had two babies, twins. Was he a widower?" Danielle asked.

"No. I'm not sure what happened there. Dan Francas and his first wife moved here a couple of months before Gemma showed up. I remember they stayed at Elenore Percy's house while Elenore was in Florida visiting her sister. As I recall, the Francases were having a house built, and it wasn't finished yet. I'd heard they had twins, but never saw the wife around town or the babies. I assume because she was busy at home taking care of them. Then someone said his wife had to leave to take care of a sick family member, and Gemma, who had just moved to town, started helping Dan with the babies while he worked."

"So what happened to the wife?" Walt asked.

Marie shrugged. "She never came back. It took him a couple of years to get a divorce. At least, that was the rumor."

"She just left her babies?" Danielle glanced down at the infants who had just fallen asleep at her bosom. She couldn't imagine such a thing.

"I always assumed it was postpartum depression. Imagine dealing with postpartum depression while trying to care for not just one newborn, but two," Marie said.

"The mother never came back?" Danielle muttered.

"She may have, but I'm not sure one way or the other. I wasn't friends with Gemma or Dan."

"How was Gemma supporting herself before she started taking care of the babies?" Danielle asked. "A single woman, moving to town alone. Was she renting? Did she buy the house?"

"Again, I was not friends with Gemma. But someone at church said Gemma was living on an inheritance from her parents."

"Any chance Gemma is still alive?" Danielle asked.

"She was still around when I passed. And I assume I would have known if she's since moved on, considering news like that is typically the hot topic when I stop by the cemetery and visit with those who haven't moved on. But Dan passed away about twenty years ago. Gemma never remarried. She's always been a recluse. Never leaves her house."

"Sounds like Pamela Beckett," Danielle said.

"I suppose they're a little alike," Marie mused. "Although I never thought about it before. Neither one was very sociable. Homebodies."

"What happened to the twins?" Danielle asked.

"I just know they don't live in Frederickport anymore. I never really knew them. They were much younger than Warren, yet older than my grandsons, so they didn't go to school with any of them. I imagine they're in their mid-forties by now. When their father, Dan Francas, passed away, one of my friends attended his funeral and mentioned that neither of the daughters came to the service. Apparently, they had both left town after they graduated from high school and never returned. Not even for their father's funeral."

————————

DOWN AT THE POLICE STATION, Joe Morelli was having a difficult time accepting what Brian had told him. Even the chief seemed to accept the notion that paranormal activity and not Walt's magic tricks might be responsible for what he'd witnessed at Marlow House. But what he found more confusing was the cavalier attitude both men displayed when discussing the possibility.

Because the chief would only be at the office for a few hours, there was no time to discuss the matter with him in private—without Brian present. So when the chief was ready to leave, needing a ride to physical therapy before going home, Joe offered to drive him.

Once the two were in the police car and on their way to the chief's appointment, Joe glanced briefly at him before asking, "Do you seriously believe in ghosts? Or whatever Brian suggests made things move at Marlow House?"

Before answering, the chief took a deep breath and stretched his legs, wincing a bit from the pain. "Joe, there are lots of things in this world we don't understand. I have seen things, experienced things, that don't have what you call a logical explanation. Things I have never shared with you."

Joe frowned, his hands firmly on the steering wheel as he looked down the road. "Are you saying you've seen ghosts?"

"Hmm. No. I'm not saying I've ever seen a ghost. But the things I've witnessed, well, I don't need to share them with you. Because it's not important for me to make you believe or find explanations for things I've experienced in my life. Those are my life lessons. And the conclusions I've drawn are mine. I suppose what you witnessed at Marlow House is your life lesson. It's up to you to come to terms with what you witnessed with your own eyes. And I suspect, knowing you, you'll want to find your own logical explanation, one that works for you."

"Chief, you're being awful cryptic. Not to mention how nonchalant you are with all this. If nothing else, I'd expect you to tell me I was imagining things over at Marlow House."

"So you, Kelly, June, not to mention Walt and Heather, were all imagining the same thing? And weren't Lily and Ian there too?"

"Honestly, Chief, I'm not sure what I find more unbelievable, the fact I witnessed flying stuffed animals over at Marlow House or the fact both you and Brian are calmly accepting a theory that paranormal activity is behind what we witnessed, and not some elaborate hoax."

"Walt and Danielle have their hands full learning how to be parents, not just to one newborn, but two. They really don't have the time, or I suspect the interest or energy, to be practical jokers."

"That's another thing. I can't imagine having something like that happening under my roof with my wife and newborns without immediately moving out."

"As Brian reminded you, Danielle claims to have had experiences with the paranormal. And if you'll recall, Heather has made similar claims. While the activity might be considered terrifying to some, I suspect with Danielle, she finds it more annoying. Paranormal activity is disruptive and scares people. But there doesn't seem to be any evidence to suggest it's lethal."

"And you believe it's possible paranormal activity is behind what happened at Marlow House?" Joe asked.

"You're the one who saw flying stuffed animals. You tell me."

SEVENTEEN

Adam Nichols sat behind his desk on Monday afternoon, going through the notes he'd jotted down on the legal pad while waiting for Bill Jones to arrive. He was just turning to a fresh piece of paper when Bill walked into the office. Bill wore what he typically wore when working: faded denims, a blue work shirt and work boots. There was always a pack of cigarettes shoved in his shirt pocket.

Adam and Bill had been friends since high school. As a local handyman, Bill didn't work only for Adam, yet he took care of most of Adam's properties.

"So what do we need to do?" Bill asked as he plopped down in a chair facing the desk, his legs man-spread with the heel of his right work boot resting atop his left knee as he leaned back.

Adam tossed the notebook and pen on the desktop and looked at Bill. "It looks like I'm listing the Crawford property on Beach Drive."

"You talking about the tunnel house?"

Adam nodded. "They're getting a divorce."

"I'm not surprised." Bill reached for his cigarettes and then remembered he couldn't smoke in Adam's office, so he dropped his hand back to the chair's armrest.

"I didn't realize you knew them."

"I don't. But I've seen him at the Gray Whale a few times. And he wasn't with his wife, if you get what I mean. But hey, good for you. Right? Nice commission."

"I guess." Adam slumped back in the chair.

"Oh, I get it. You're worried about the tunnel? They never closed it up completely, did they?"

"No. They didn't. I'm trying to figure out how to handle it."

"Is that why you want me to go over with you? I'm assuming that's the listing we're going to."

"Yeah, that's the one. I also want to see if the place needs any work, since the owners have vacated the premises and want me to handle everything."

"How did you get the listing? Ahh, never mind. Their neighbor suggested you?" Bill gave a snort.

"Yeah. Chris recommended me to Mia Crawford. I talked to her husband right before I called you, and he told me to send him the contract. But first, I need to go over there and do a CMA. Neither one of them is there. Mia was supposed to be back in a week, but the soon-to-be-ex tells me she told him she's taken a brief detour to Hawaii, and don't expect her to come back. She said she will handle everything via email, and to sell the house furnished, for all she cares, just to send her half of the proceeds."

"Wow. What does he say?"

Adam shrugged. "Pretty much the same."

Bill stood. "Let's go check it out. I assume you have the key?"

"Yeah. Mia gave it to me when she stopped in the office."

ADAM SAT in the passenger seat of Bill's truck as they drove to the Crawford house. Bill motioned behind him and said, "I've got one of your signs in the back of the truck. Should we put it up when we get there?"

"No. Not until I have the listing signed by both parties."

They turned down Beach Drive. Bill glanced briefly to Marlow House as they passed by. "How're the new parents handling twins?"

"They seem to be much better than I'd be doing."

"You and Mel still not planning to have any kids?" Bill pulled into the Crawford driveway.

"No. Mel says I'm as much of a kid as she can handle."

They both laughed.

After Bill parked the truck and turned off the ignition, they both unbuckled their seatbelts and got out of the vehicle, each holding a notepad. Adam nodded to the side door of the driveway. "Mia told me to use that one. She said the deadbolt sticks on the front door. That's one thing I'll need you to look at."

They walked toward the side door while Adam dug his right hand into his pants pocket, looking for the key Mia had given him. When they got to the door, Bill absently reached for the doorknob, giving it a turn without waiting for Adam to try the key. He didn't expect the door to open. When it did, they both paused a moment and looked at each other.

"It wasn't locked?" Adam asked.

"Obviously not." Bill pushed the door all the way open, but he didn't enter. Instead, he called out, "Hello? Hello? Is anyone here?"

A few moments later, they hesitantly entered the house, and with silent agreement, they moved through each room, looking for intruders or squatters. Ten minutes later, after giving the house a thorough walk through, Adam said, "It looks like Mia forgot to lock the door when she left."

"Fortunately, we were the only ones to find it unlocked."

"She was obviously in a rush to get to Hawaii," Adam said with a snort. "Let's see what needs to be done before we put it on the market." Adam headed in one direction while Bill went in another, each jotting notes on their pads of paper when finding something that needed to be addressed before listing the house.

Fifteen minutes later, both men ended up in the kitchen. Adam walked to the refrigerator and pulled open its door. It was empty aside from a carton of milk and half a dozen eggs. Adam reached for the carton of milk and found it empty. He looked at Bill. "Want some eggs?"

Bill shrugged. "Sure. Why not?"

Adam left the refrigerator door open after he removed the empty carton of milk and tossed it in the kitchen trash can, while Bill removed the carton of eggs and set them on the counter before closing the refrigerator door. Adam opened its freezer and found it empty.

"Well, that was easy," Adam said when shutting the freezer door. He then walked to the pantry and looked inside. It was practically empty, too. "The way Mia talked, I expected to find a bunch of food I needed to get rid of. I suspect she knew she wouldn't be back when I talked to her the first time."

When they finished going through the kitchen and determined what might need repair, they headed to the living room so Bill could check out how the Crawfords had secured the door leading into the tunnel.

"Mia said it's behind the bookshelf," Adam said when they entered the living room. Adam walked right to the bookshelf yet paused, momentarily distracted by the books.

"What are you looking at?" Bill asked.

Adam reached out and absently moved his fingertips over the spines of several books while reading their titles. Adam shrugged and turned to Bill. "Mel always says you can tell a lot about a person by the books they have."

"So what do the Crawfords' books tell you about them?" Bill asked.

"One of them enjoys reading romance. I suspect it was Mia."

"Oh, I'm not sure about that. Her husband seemed to enjoy romance when I saw him at the Gray Whale." Bill then added with a snort, "At least smutty romance."

"Considering some of these titles, they could be Austin's books."

Bill chuckled and said, "Let's move this bookshelf so we can look behind it."

"Think we can just slide it down? Or do we need to remove the books?"

"Let's try sliding it," Bill suggested.

Together, Bill and Adam leaned into one side of the bookshelf and shoved it down about three feet along the wall, exposing the metal door covering the tunnel entrance.

Bill reached for the metal door and swung it open, revealing a dark cavity. "I thought I read in the paper that the Crawfords or the city blocked both entrances to the tunnel."

"They did," Adam said. "But Mia told me Austin took the bolts out when some of his friends were visiting and he wanted to show them the tunnel. He never put them back."

Bill peeked his head inside the entrance and couldn't see anything for the darkness. "I wish I had a flashlight."

"Use the one on your phone," Adam suggested.

Bill turned on his flashlight app, and the next minute they both peeked in while Bill directed the beam of light from his cellphone into the tunnel's opening. "I can't see anything, and if I drop this thing in there, I'm going to kill you."

"Why are you going to kill me?" Adam asked, stepping back from the opening.

Bill pulled his phone from the tunnel entrance, turned off the flashlight app, and shoved his phone in his back pocket. "It was your idea."

"Well, you didn't drop it. But we're going to have to see about bolting that up again. I can't have agents showing the property and then have some kid climb in the tunnel and get lost."

"I'm not sure they could get lost. From what I understand, it only goes to Marlow House, and I imagine they still have their end blocked off," Bill reminded him.

"Still, that thing is damn creepy."

"I have to agree with you there."

Adam shut the metal door and then asked Bill to help him shove the bookcase back in place.

"Why don't we just leave it? I have to come back and bolt it down, anyway."

Adam shook his head. "No. Until it's bolted shut, I'd rather keep it hidden by the bookshelf. The last thing I need is someone to realize the house is empty. Have them break in and discover the tunnel entrance and go exploring."

"Then let's hope that if someone breaks in, it's not someone who already knows about the tunnel, because that bookshelf will not stop them."

HE WALKED ALONE down the beach, the moonlight breaking the darkness. When he arrived at the house, he moved between two bushes onto the driveway and headed for the side door. But when he tried the doorknob a few moments later, he found it locked. It wasn't unexpected. He assumed this would happen when the Realtor came to list the property. From his back pocket, he removed the credit card he had gotten from the boy and used it to unlock the door. Once inside, he walked through the house and then moved to the kitchen. After opening the refrigerator door, he cursed when he saw the eggs gone. "Damn, I knew I should have moved those, too."

EIGHTEEN

On Tuesday afternoon, Marie Nichols took a break from babysitting and spirit watching to check in on her grandson, Adam, leaving Eva at Marlow House with Walt and Danielle. When Marie arrived at Frederickport Vacation Properties, she found Adam and Melony getting into Melony's car. Marie wondered where they were going and why Melony wasn't at her office in Portland.

Marie joined the pair in the car and sat quietly in the back seat, eavesdropping. From their conversation, she pieced together that they were on their way to Pier Café to have lunch and that Melony had taken the week off. Marie joined them for lunch.

At the café, Marie sat next to Adam on his side of the booth while Melony sat on the opposite side. Right after they all sat down, Carla brought iced water to their table, took their drink order, and left the table.

"Oh, I forgot to tell you. I saw Danielle and Lily yesterday," Adam told Melony. "They stopped by the office."

"Just the two of them?"

"Yeah. Lily, wow, she looks really uncomfortable."

"And she has two more months." Melony picked up her glass of iced water.

Adam cringed. "I don't envy women having to go through that. And Danielle. Wow."

About to take a sip of water, Mel paused and looked over at Adam. "Wow, what?"

"Oh, come on, you've seen her. She looks like she should work at Hooters."

"Adam!" Melony scolded before taking a sip of water.

"Mel, she is majorly stacked now! I'd like to see her in a bikini."

"Adam Nichols, that is a totally inappropriate thing to say," Marie scolded right before grabbing hold of his left earlobe and giving it a violent twist and pull.

Adam let out a squeal in pain, briefly drawing the attention of the other diners, while he quickly clasped a hand over his injured earlobe.

Setting her glass on the table, Melony frowned at Adam. "What is wrong with you?"

Hesitantly, Adam moved his hand from the injured ear, leaned over the table toward Melony, and turned his head slightly to show her his ear. "Did something bite me?"

Narrowing her eyes, Melony leaned over the table and examined Adam's left earlobe. "Well, it is red, but there's no bite mark." She looked down at his shirt. "I don't see any bugs on you."

Adam rubbed his earlobe and leaned back in the booth. "It reminded me of my grandma."

"Marie?"

Adam nodded. "Yeah. When I was little and did something naughty—"

"Which was probably all the time," Melony snarked before he finished his sentence.

Adam rolled his eyes. "Whatever. Anyway, she never hit me or slapped me, not like my parents did. But when she'd get pissed with me, she would grab hold of my earlobe and give it a twist and a yank." He rubbed his ear one last time and dropped his hand back to the table.

"Well, maybe it was your grandma, and she came back because she heard your sexist crack about Danielle," Melony teased.

"What? I said nothing bad. Just saying the truth."

"Of course Danielle's bustier now." Melony rolled her eyes. "She's a nursing mother, you idiot. And she's nursing for two."

Before Adam could respond, Joe and Kelly Morelli walked by their booth and stopped to say hello.

"Are you guys following us?" Melony teased. "You showed up the last time we were here."

Joe laughed. "It seems that way."

"We haven't ordered yet. You want to sit with us?" Adam offered.

"Drat, I'm going to have to move again," Marie grumbled, remembering the same thing had happened on Sunday. Instead of finding another place to sit, Marie returned to Marlow House, leaving her grandson and his wife to have lunch with Kelly and Joe without her.

Carla showed up with Adam's and Melony's drinks by the time Adam moved to Melony's side of the booth, and Joe and Kelly sat down next to each other. Since they already knew what they wanted to eat, Carla took their orders and then left to get Joe's and Kelly's sodas.

After Carla brought Kelly's and Joe's drinks and left again, Adam told Joe and Kelly about Danielle and Lily stopping by his office on Monday, without mentioning his observation involving Danielle's increased bust size. He told them about Danielle's interest in exploring the history of the quilt Lily had given her, which sounded like a boring way for them to spend their few free hours.

"It's not as boring as you think," Kelly told them as she picked up her soda.

"Oh please, don't start, Kelly," Joe groaned.

Kelly sipped from her straw, set the glass back on the table, and looked at Joe. "You saw it yourself."

"What are you guys talking about?" Adam asked.

Kelly told Melony and Adam what had happened since they had last seen them on Sunday. She ended by saying, "We all wonder if the quilt is the key to everything. From what we've discovered, sometimes the negative energy of an event attaches itself to an object, like the quilt. And this all started around the time Lily gave Danielle the quilt. So not a haunting, but trapped energy."

Joe groaned again and looked at Kelly. "Yeah, what you discovered on some website. And anyone can make a website."

Melony looked at Joe. "Kelly just told us you saw the rocking chair rocking on its own, and all the stuffed animals flew across the room. Did that not happen?"

Joe shifted uncomfortably in the booth seat and shrugged. "Yeah, but, well, there has to be a logical explanation."

"What, that Walt's the next David Copperfield?" Adam asked with a snort.

"David Copperfield performs some pretty convincing magic tricks," Joe reminded him. "And I can't believe you think this could be anything but a great trick."

"Like Brian and the chief?" Kelly asked Joe. She then told Adam and Melony what the chief and Brian had said to Joe regarding the incident.

When Kelly was done, Joe said, "I don't think you should have told them all that. After all, the chief shared that with me in confidence, and I don't think he wants it to get out that he believes in paranormal mumbo-jumbo."

"Don't worry about us," Mel told Joe. "Eddy and I go back a long way. And as we told you the other day, Adam and I have seen things."

ACROSS THE DINER, Robyn Lyons sat down at a table with her sister and two nephews. The server working the shift with Carla brought the table iced water, took their drink orders, and then left them to look over the menu.

"I have no business going out to lunch," Debbie muttered as she looked over the menu.

"Oh, Debbie, I've got this," Robyn insisted.

Debbie let out a sigh, closed the menu, and set it on the table. "You've already done so much."

Robyn grinned at Debbie. "Don't be silly. What are sisters for?"

Fifteen minutes later, after their drinks had been served and food orders taken, Eric and Zack sat quietly at the table, playing on their tablets. Their mother hadn't let them bring their earbuds to the restaurant, and she wouldn't let them turn the volume up, so they had to play games that didn't require sound.

"Life really isn't fair," Robyn mused.

"That's for sure." Debbie picked up her water and took a drink.

Robyn slumped back in her chair. "You remember Marlow House?"

"Yeah, it's a B and B now, right?" Debbie asked.

"Yes, but they aren't open right now because she just had her babies." Robyn paused a moment and glanced briefly at her nephews and then back to her sister. "She had twins. Anyway, she inherited that house. So it's paid for. I told you about the gold coins and the Missing Thorndike."

"Yes. Does she still have them?" Debbie asked.

"She does, and I think that's the stupid thing. She has them sitting in a safe-deposit box at the local bank. They're worth a fortune. She doesn't need the money. I heard she also inherited a fortune from her cousin. It's just unfair. She should sell those things and do something with that money to help people. It's such a waste. If someone cleaned out her safe-deposit box, she would never miss it."

"I agree. Life's not fair," Debbie muttered.

Zack looked up from his tablet. "What gold coins?"

"Nothing that concerns you," Debbie told him.

"Are you talking about Marlow House with the secret tunnel?" Eric asked.

Robyn smiled at Eric. "Your uncle told me you boys got a sneak peek at the tunnel exhibit at the museum."

"What about the gold coins?" Zack asked again.

Robyn looked at Zack. "They were old gold coins that were found hidden in a house across the street from Marlow House, under some floorboards. They belonged to Walt Marlow, who used to live at Marlow House years ago. Danielle Marlow, who now lives in the house, well, they determined the coins belong to her. And she keeps them in the local bank."

"Too bad she doesn't keep them at Marlow House," Eric said under his breath.

———

"LET'S GO SEE THE HOUSE," Kelly told Joe. Adam had just told Kelly and Joe how he was listing the Crawford house, and that he was taking Melony over to look at it after lunch. When Melony saw Kelly perk up when Adam mentioned the listing, she suggested they join them.

"I've already seen the house," Joe said. "And we can't afford it."

"Aw, come on, don't be a party poop," Kelly nagged.

"We're going over there anyway," Melony told Joe. "I'm curious to see what the Crawfords did inside the house. I heard they made a lot of changes."

"Oh, that's right, you...umm..." Kelly didn't finish her sentence.

Melony smiled at Kelly. "It's okay." The previous owner, Pete Rogers, had been good friends of Melony's parents until he had murdered Melony's mother and tried to kill Melony.

———

BILL HAD FIXED the front-door deadbolt before they left the house the previous day, so Adam unlocked the front door at the Crawfords' house to let them all in.

"The place hasn't been cleaned yet," Adam explained as he opened the door for Melony, Joe, and Kelly to enter.

As they walked through the house, Kelly asked Melony, "It doesn't bother you walking through this house?"

She shrugged. "Not really. Like I said, I kind of wondered what changes the Crawfords made. When I was a kid, we used to have cookouts here. It's always weird to think about those days because there were some wonderful memories. But as we get older, we learn people aren't who we think they are, and that can go for our parents too."

While Melony and Kelly walked through the bedrooms together, Adam took Joe into the living room and was telling him how Bill planned to bolt the metal door to the tunnel shut. Joe had already been in the tunnel and was familiar with both entrances. As Adam discussed the tunnel with Joe, he paused a moment at the bookshelf and stopped talking.

Noticing Adam's sudden silence, Joe asked, "What's wrong?"

Adam pointed to the bookshelf. "The books. Someone moved them. The romance books are on the bottom shelf now."

NINETEEN

I nstead of going directly to Marlow House, Marie took a brief detour and stopped in at where Gemma Francas had lived before Marie's death. She found Gemma still alive and living in the home she had shared with her husband.

By the time Marie returned to Marlow House, the sun was setting, and Walt and Danielle were in the kitchen, having dinner.

"Where are the little ones?" Marie asked when she appeared in the kitchen.

"Upstairs in the nursery with Eva. She's singing to them; she has a lovely voice," Danielle said.

Marie nodded. "She does."

"You spent a lot of time with Adam this afternoon. Did you pick up any interesting gossip while eavesdropping?" Danielle grinned mischievously.

Marie waved her hand dismissively and took a seat at the table. "Oh, I wasn't with him for that long. Melony has taken the week off, and the two had lunch at Pier Café. I love that boy, yet I don't know how Melony keeps from whacking him over the head with a cast-iron skillet, considering some things that pop out of his mouth."

"Probably because she's a criminal attorney and knows it's not wise to represent herself," Walt said with a chuckle.

"What did he say?" Danielle asked.

"Oh, it doesn't matter. But after I left them, I stopped at Gemma Francas's place. She still lives in the same house. You should go over there tomorrow and see what she knows about the quilt."

"Walt and I were just talking about that."

"Has there been any activity since I've been gone?" Marie asked.

"Just the knocking. I have to admit, it's actually kind of helpful." Danielle shrugged. "Although, now when I hear knocking, my milk drops, even if it's someone at the front door."

"I suppose that's better than objects flying around the nursery," Marie said.

"I'll give Lily a call and see if she wants to go over there with me," Danielle said.

"By the way, when I was at Gemma's, I had a look around her house. It was very interesting."

"Interesting how?" Walt asked.

"Well, if you think about it, she raised her stepdaughters for most of their lives. She was really the only mother they ever had. Yet there isn't a single picture of them in the house. While they no longer live in Frederickport, they could very well be parents now, even grandparents. And if so, she has no pictures of grandchildren displayed."

"Some people aren't into family photos," Danielle suggested.

Marie shook her head. "No. There were pictures around the house of her husband, Dan. Pictures of the two of them. There were even pictures on the wall of what I have to assume were her or Dan's parents or grandparents. But nothing of Dan's girls. And if they have children or grandchildren, no pictures of them either."

AFTER DANIELLE'S shower that night, she went into the nursery to feed the babies. Marie and Eva had gone downstairs to chat, giving Walt and Danielle some alone time with Addison and Jack. But the moment Danielle stepped into the nursery, she saw the twins' quilt again draped over one rocker, no longer downstairs in the living room.

She paused a moment in the doorway and looked over to Walt, his back to her as he changed one of the babies' diapers. "Walt? Why did you bring the quilt back upstairs?"

Walt turned to face Danielle. "What are you talking about?"

Danielle pointed to the quilt. He looked at it and frowned.

A moment later, Walt took the quilt back downstairs and promptly returned without it. "Marie said she didn't bring it up here. And we know Eva can't."

"Wonderful," Danielle said dryly as she picked up Addison.

DANIELLE OPENED her eyes and stood in a bedroom she had never seen before. Rose-patterned paper covered the walls, and pink lace curtains hung across the room's only window. She glanced around, observing the collection of bedroom furniture and the two baby cribs. It looked as if someone had come in and pushed all the bedroom furniture against a wall to make room for the cribs.

Confused, Danielle walked to the cribs and looked in one and was startled to find a sleeping infant. Dressed in a pink sleeping gown, the baby had shoved its tiny, clenched fist into its mouth, and Danielle could hear the suckling sound, as if the baby nursed. She walked to the second crib and found another baby, identically dressed. Red fuzz covered both infants' heads, a stark contrast to the dark hair both Addison and Jack had been born with.

Knowing she did not belong here, Danielle moved toward the open doorway and looked out into the hallway. She was no longer at Marlow House, but she didn't know where she was or how she had gotten here.

Danielle rushed down the hallway and started down the stairs but paused. She couldn't just leave the babies alone.

"Hello? Is anyone here?" she called out. No one answered. She continued down the stairs and started walking through the first floor. Danielle wanted to leave the house, but she couldn't abandon the babies.

"Hello?" she called out again. When she didn't get a response, Danielle moved through the first floor of the house, looking through the kitchen, living room, and what looked like a sitting room. Deciding to check on the babies, Danielle ran back upstairs. But when she reached the top of the stairs, she heard voices on the first floor.

She turned around and called out, "Hello?" The next moment she felt a hand shove the center of her back, sending Danielle tumbling down the stairs onto the floor below.

Danielle sat upright in bed, let out a scream, and opened her eyes.

Walt, who had been sleeping next to her, bolted upright.

"SO YOU ACTUALLY SCREAMED IN your sleep and woke up Walt?" Lily asked Danielle as the two of them drove to Gemma Francas's house.

"Yes. Poor Walt. I think I scared the crap out of him." Danielle looked down the road, her hands firmly clutching the steering wheel.

"Is this a house your brain just made up, or did it look like one you've been in before?" Lily asked.

"Wasn't familiar. But aside from the cribs, it was like a house you would expect a little old spinster lady to live in, like from one of the old movies my mom used to watch. Definitely no man touches in that house."

"Could it have been a dream hop?" Lily asked.

"One thing about dream hops, I always sorta know it's a dream. But in this one, I didn't realize I was dreaming."

"What do you think it means? Dreams always mean something."

"It could mean you're having twins," Danielle teased.

"Oh, shut up! Why would you say that?"

"Well, those twins in the dream definitely weren't my babies. But by their hair color, they could be yours."

"Oh hush, or when we get to Gemma Francas's house, I'm going to knock even if she has a doorbell."

Danielle laughed. "Please don't do that. I promise I'll behave."

Lily sat back in her seat and patted her baby belly. "I wonder who pushed you down the stairs."

Danielle shrugged. "Maybe my subconscious was telling me it was time to wake up."

WHEN DANIELLE STOOD with Lily on the front porch of Gemma Francas's house, she was grateful the home had a working doorbell. It was going to be awkward enough convincing a stranger to talk to them, and she didn't need her blouse getting soaked with breastmilk.

Gemma recognized Danielle from a photograph she had seen in the local newspaper, and she was curious why Danielle Marlow wanted to talk to her. She invited Danielle and Lily inside, took them to her living room, and insisted on serving them tea.

Gemma had left Lily and Danielle alone in the living room to get the tea when Lily whispered, "This is the house, isn't it?"

Danielle frowned at Lily. "What house?"

"The one from your dream!"

Danielle chuckled. "No. Sorry to disappoint you. It looks nothing like the house in the dream. And you didn't notice? This isn't a two-story house."

"Oh, that's right." Disappointed, Lily slumped back in the chair.

Gemma returned a few minutes later, carrying a tray with a plate of cookies and three glasses of tea. Danielle stood up to help her with the tray, but Gemma told her to sit down, that she was fine. The next moment, she set the tray on the coffee table.

After handing both her guests a glass of tea and a napkin with a cookie, Gemma asked what they wanted to talk to her about.

"This is a little wild," Danielle began. "You see, I recently had twins."

Gemma nodded. "Yes, I read about it in the newspaper. Congratulations. Although, I read how they came early at your baby shower, and you didn't make it to the hospital. That must have been terrifying."

"Well, it kinda happened fast. I didn't really have time to think about it. Anyway, my friend Lily here went to an estate sale last week and bought me a quilt for my babies. It's unique. And I would love to know who made it."

Danielle pulled out her phone and found the photograph she had taken of the quilt. She handed the phone to Gemma while saying, "I was told you were the one who gave the quilt to Alice Beckett. Lily bought the quilt at the Beckett estate sale."

Now holding Danielle's cellphone in her hand, Gemma froze a moment before looking down at the phone. She glanced briefly at the picture and then quickly handed the cellphone back to Danielle.

"Do you remember it?" Danielle asked.

Gemma nodded silently.

"Umm, can you tell me something about it? Who made it? Who was it made for?"

Gemma closed her eyes for a minute and then opened them again and looked at Danielle and Lily. She absently licked her lips before saying, "My husband's first wife, Betsy, made it."

"For her twins?" Danielle asked.

"Why would you give it away?" Lily blurted. She instantly regretted asking so bluntly.

Gemma settled back in her chair and folded her hands together on her lap. In a soft voice she said, "My husband Dan, Betsy, and I, we all grew up together. Dan and Betsy moved to Frederickport right after their twins were born. I moved here too. After all, Betsy and I were best friends."

Danielle set the glass of tea she had been holding back on the tray without taking her eyes off Gemma, listening to what she had to say.

"Unfortunately, Betsy changed after the babies were born. Wasn't interested in them."

"Postpartum depression?" Lily asked.

"I assume so. One day I came to visit Betsy, and she told me she no longer wanted this life. That she didn't want to be married or a mother. I couldn't believe what she was saying. I stood quietly as she folded the quilt she had made for her babies, set it on the kitchen table, and then removed her wedding ring and set it on the quilt. She just left. Walked out of the house. Someone picked her up. But I don't know who it was. I only know that it was a man."

"She just abandoned her babies?" Lily muttered.

Gemma nodded. "After she left, I had to stay with the babies. I couldn't leave them all alone. I considered calling Dan, but I wasn't sure what to tell him. So I just waited for him to come home from work while trying to figure out how to tell him what Betsy said."

"I can't imagine having to give someone that news," Danielle said.

"After I told him, he was utterly broken. I ended up helping Dan with the babies since he had to work. Eventually he was able to get a divorce, and well, Dan and I had spent so much time together, we had both lost someone we once cared about. I suppose it's not that surprising. We fell in love, and we eventually got married."

"Did you ever consider keeping the quilt for the twins? Something to have from their mother?" Danielle asked.

Gemma smiled sadly. "It was actually Dan who wanted the quilt gone. Whenever he looked at it, it was like a knife in his heart. A couple of weeks after Betsy left, he told me to get rid of it. I took it home with me that night. It was still in my car the next morning when I stopped by Alice's house to pick up some eggs. She walked them out to my car and saw the quilt and admired it. I told her it belonged to a friend who no longer wanted it, and I told her she was welcome to it. She was happy to take it."

TWENTY

On Wednesday evening, Connor sat on Marie's lap in the nursery of Marlow House while she read him a book, and Eva watched over the infants, who slept in their cribs. Downstairs, the mediums of Beach Drive, along with Lily, Ian, and Brian, sat in the living room, discussing what they now referred to as a poltergeist. One thing they all agreed on was that they couldn't come to an agreement on how to define poltergeist, which made sense to them, since they had no definitive answer to what was going on at Marlow House.

Brian and Heather had picked up food at Beach Taco, and the group now sat around the living room, plates of food in hand, discussing what Danielle and Lily had learned about the quilt.

"It's sounding more and more like negative energy," Heather said. "Not a haunting in the sense of a shy ghost, but some bad mojo wrapped up in the quilt."

Brian, about to take a bite of his taco, paused a moment and looked at Heather. "How do you figure that?"

Heather shrugged. "Think about it. This Betsy person put all this love in the quilt, and then hormones flip an evil switch, and she ditches her family. She had to have been conflicted. The energy from all her negative feelings got sewn into that quilt."

"I'm not so sure about the negative energy getting sewn into the quilt. From what Gemma told us, Betsy made the quilt when she was pregnant. It was after her babies were born, and after the quilt was made, that she seemed to change. But I agree in that the quilt was probably a likely target for the negative energy. If that's really what's going on," Danielle said.

"You think it's something else?" Chris asked.

"I don't know." Danielle leaned back in the sofa, a half-eaten burrito in her hand and, under it, a paper plate on her lap. "I guess it's hard for me to wrap my head around the fact she never came back after the roller coaster of the postpartum depression subsided. Although, it can last for years, especially if left untreated."

"She obviously got in touch with her husband sometime," Chris said.

"Why do you say that?" Danielle asked.

"If he remarried two years later, they must have gotten a divorce. I would have to assume that meant they had some contact."

"Who do you think the guy she left with was?" Heather asked. "Some boyfriend?"

Danielle shook her head. "I doubt that. When did she have time to meet someone? She probably arranged a driver."

"I don't think they had Uber back then," Ian teased.

"What do we do now?" Lily asked. "Bury the quilt?"

"Yeah, and have it reappear, like it showed up in the nursery last night after we left it downstairs?" Danielle asked.

Chris glanced around the living room. "Where is the quilt now?"

"I put it in the basement in a trunk. Hopefully, it will stay put," Walt said.

"Are the walls still knocking?" Chris asked.

"Only when Addison and Jack are hungry," Danielle said.

"What's the plan now?" Brian asked.

"A plan would be nice," Danielle groaned.

"I'm sorry, Danielle. I wish I had never gone to that estate sale," Lily said.

By the time Danielle went to bed that night, they had resolved nothing regarding the annoying poltergeist. Ian told them he would see if he could find out what happened to Betsy. Danielle was also curious about what happened to their twins.

"WE'VE GOT to figure this out," Danielle told Walt after she snuggled up to him later that night under the blankets in their bed. "We can't expect Marie and Eva to spend all of their time here."

"They have an eternity," Walt teased.

Danielle giggled. "You know what I mean."

Walt wrapped his arms around Danielle tighter and pulled her close. "I do." He let out a sigh. "This is not how I imagined we would spend our early weeks of parenthood."

"Me either. I really thought Eva would figure this thing out by now."

Walt dropped a kiss on Danielle's lips. "We're going to work this out. But for now, I want you to get some sleep."

"I'll try not to yell in my sleep tonight."

Walt chuckled. "Yes, that would be nice. I love you."

"I love you too, Walt."

They both closed their eyes and drifted off to sleep.

Danielle opened her eyes and found herself back in the bedroom with the two cribs and the rose-patterned wallpaper. She remembered being in this room before, but she couldn't remember when that had been, or who lived in the house.

Confused, Danielle glanced around the room before moving closer to the cribs. She leaned over one crib and looked inside and saw a sleeping baby, and then peeked into the second crib, finding another sleeping infant. She wasn't surprised to find them, yet she didn't know whom they belonged to.

"I shouldn't be here," Danielle whispered to herself, overcome with a sense of dread. Turning from the cribs, she rushed from the room into the hallway and then abruptly stopped. She almost called out to see who was there to take care of the babies, but she instinctively understood that would be dangerous. Instead, she needed to get out of the house and find help.

Danielle rushed to the staircase, clutched the handrail, and started down the steps, careful not to make any noise. She had only taken three steps when something hit her in the back, and she tumbled down the stairs, head over feet, until she landed, facedown, on the floor.

She screamed, but no sound came out of her mouth. Danielle tried to speak, but she could not form words. She tried to move, but she felt paralyzed. She had landed on what looked like a large throw rug covering the wood floor.

Something, someone, grabbed hold of her ankles and lifted her legs up several feet from the floor. They dragged her backwards, shifting her body and then dropping her. The next moment she felt herself being rolled up into the carpet and then dragged backwards along the floor.

From one end of the carpet rolled around her body, she could see the staircase, which she had just been pushed down. Someone was pulling her away from the staircase, dragging her across the floor. The carpet rolled around her made her think of a straitjacket, holding her arms immobile along the sides of her body. She had been in this house before. They were taking her to the kitchen.

The monster dragging her across the kitchen floor stopped a moment, and she heard a door open. Her carpet prison no longer slid easily across the wood floor, but now bumped and slapped her body along what felt like dirt and rocks. She watched as she was pulled backwards from the kitchen door leading to the backyard.

Once again, she tried to scream, but she remained mute, locked inside herself and the rolled-up carpet. She watched as the house seemed to disappear, and her captor dragged her by a red barn with a large white *J* painted above its closed barn doors.

Finally, the monster stopped dragging her and twirled the rolled-up carpet—with her in it—around, giving her a view of where she had been taken. It looked like the entrance of a root cellar, or at least like pictures she had seen of root cellars.

She watched as its doors opened. Someone shoved her toward the opening, and then the carpet unfurled, spitting her out, landing her in a dark, earthy cavern. Whoever had been moving her stepped into the root cellar with her and rolled her body farther into the space until finally she hit a cool dirt wall. She opened her mouth to scream, but dirt filled her mouth as someone covered her with loose soil.

AS DANIELLE WAS JUST WAKING up from her nightmare, two young boys across town hadn't yet fallen asleep. Instead, they had helped a man sneak into their garage apartment without their mother, aunt or uncle seeing. Their mother was in the shower and assumed her sons had already fallen asleep. What she didn't know, her sons were hiding someone in her bedroom.

Wearing her robe and a towel wrapped around her freshly washed hair, Debbie stepped out of the bathroom and looked into the living room. The hide-a-bed had been pulled out, and she could see both of her sons tucked under the covers. She turned and headed for the bedroom. As she opened the door to her bedroom, she could swear she heard her sons giggling.

She paused for a moment, looked back into the living room, and said, "You boys need to go to sleep. No playing around."

"Yes, Mom," they chorused before suppressing more giggles.

She turned her back to her sons, opened her bedroom door, stepped inside the room, and shut the door behind her. The next moment, someone grabbed her from behind, held a hand over her mouth, and whispered, "Deb, don't scream. It's me. Clay."

Clay released hold of his wife, and the next moment Debbie twirled around, threw her arms around her husband, and sobbed.

DEBBIE AND CLAY snuggled under the blankets in the dark bedroom. They had been talking for hours. Clay told her where he had been, how he had run into their sons after they had broken into the Crawford house.

Debbie told him how she had been spending her time; she told him of Fred's change of attitude and how he seemed resentful having her and the boys stay with them. She recounted conversations she had had with her sister, including a recent one about the gold coins and the Missing Thorndike, and how both she and her sister felt it unfair, how some people seemed to have everything handed to them. Debbie only recounted that conversation after Clay told her about the tunnel and opening the locked door leading into the Marlows' basement.

Their conversation shifted to his current troubles with the law, and Debbie said, "I never doubted your innocence."

Clay kissed his wife's forehead. "The boys told me you knew I was innocent. Until then, I wasn't sure."

"Of course I believe you. I knew about your affair with Camilla. But I also knew you wanted to end it. You made a mistake, and you chose me and the boys. That's all that mattered. There was no reason for you to kill that woman. Heather Donovan killed her."

"Unfortunately, no one will believe me now. Not after I ran off."

Debbie held Clay tighter. "You didn't have a choice. Not the way the police department is in this town. It's ridiculous the control Edward MacDonald has on the city council. Since your arrest, I see it more clearly. But you shouldn't have come back, Clay. It's too dangerous."

"Everyone assumes I'm in Canada by now. I can't leave you and the boys."

"I should be furious at the boys for stealing those keys and breaking into the house, but I'm glad they did, because it brought you back to me."

"Our boys are smart, Deb."

"Like their daddy."

Clay chuckled.

"I love you, Clay! But what are we going to do?"

"You need to trust me, Deb. But that means you need to promise not to say anything to your sister about me being here."

"I won't tell her. I promise. While Robyn has been great, super supportive, she would say something to Fred if I told her you were here. And Fred would call the police. He's pretty pissed you took his coins."

"Yeah, I probably shouldn't have done that. But I panicked."

"I understand."

"But I have a plan. You've given me some ideas tonight on how to get us some money. Enough that you and the boys can leave this place, and I'll meet up with you. You need to trust me, Deb. Can you trust me?"

TWENTY-ONE

"At least I didn't scream and wake you up last night," Danielle told Walt on Thursday morning after she finished recounting her most recent nightmare. They sat together at the kitchen table, eating breakfast. Before coming downstairs that morning, they had put each baby in his or her infant carrier. Both carriers now sat on the kitchen table while each infant, wide awake, cooed softly, their tiny hands inside scratch mittens, which they waved randomly and shoved in tiny mouths.

"It's no surprise you're having nightmares, considering what's been going on," Walt said. "And speaking of what's been going on around here, how are we going to handle Joanne? What do we want to say to her?"

Their housekeeper, Joanne Johnson, was returning from her vacation and planning to come back to work tomorrow.

Danielle groaned. "I totally forgot about Joanne."

They both sat in silence for a few minutes, finishing their breakfast and deciding what they wanted to tell Joanne when she came in for work the next day.

Danielle absently ran her fingers over Addison's mitten-clad hands. She gave a sigh before saying, "The only thing we can tell her, the truth. After all, Joe, Kelly, and June have all seen it. Joe and Kelly already told Adam and Mel. It's sort of funny."

Walt arched his brows. "I'm surprised you're describing it as funny. That's the last thing I would expect you to say regarding this situation."

Danielle shrugged. "Since most people won't believe things mediums can see and hear, it seems we're always making up stories to explain something that happened. Like when Heather told Brian about seeing Camilla, and he told Joe, only to find out later it was Camilla's ghost Heather saw. Heather couldn't come out and tell Joe the truth. But in this case, the nonbelievers have witnessed it, and none of the mediums know much more than they do about what's happening."

Walt picked up his cup of coffee. "I understand what you mean."

"I also suspect Joe's response from now on won't be that much different from Ian's initial one."

About to take a drink of his coffee, Walt paused. "In what way?"

"When Ian looked through the kitchen window and saw objects floating around the room, he, like Joe, assumed it was nothing but a trick. We told Ian the truth. But that didn't change Ian's mind back then. I suspect Joe is still convinced you're responsible for what happened upstairs, and he's waiting for someone to fess up and say it was all a hoax."

Walt took a drink of his coffee and set his cup on the table. "You're probably right. But it sounds like Kelly no longer holds me responsible."

"I wonder if Ian's told his mother yet, or she still thinks it was you doing some magic trick."

"If Ian hasn't, I imagine Kelly has."

Danielle let out a deep sigh. "We all need to get out of the house for a while and clear our heads."

"We could go for a drive with Addison and Jack. They're too young to take in a restaurant, but we could make a picnic lunch and stop at one of the beach parks."

Danielle considered Walt's suggestion a moment, shook her

head, and said, "That sounds like a lot of work. And it's still too cold to eat outside with them. And I really don't want to sit in a car and eat."

"Then what do you want to do?"

"Well, we could go to the chief's house. He hasn't met Addison and Jack yet. I can call him and see if he's home and up to visitors. The boys are still in school, so if he's home, he'll probably be alone. Not like we're taking the twins out to a restaurant to be exposed to a bunch of strangers. It would be like when our friends come to visit us here."

DANIELLE CALLED the chief and asked him if he was up to a visit. He told Danielle he would love to meet the newest residents on Beach Drive, and that he would be home the rest of the day.

Danielle soon learned that visiting a friend with the twins, even with Walt's help, proved to be as much work and hassle as she had imagined throwing a picnic together might be. She was grateful she didn't have trouble nursing because that would mean packing up bottles and formula, along with the random assortment of baby paraphernalia she and Walt had loaded into the Flex before heading over to the chief's house.

When filling her diaper bag, she wasn't sure how many diapers she might need for their visit. While the twins often slept for hours with no diaper change, once Jack had filled four diapers within an hour. And what if they both did that at the same time? Danielle tossed several boxes of disposable diapers in the back of the car. That prompted her to add additional receiving blankets and changes of clothing. Before leaving Marlow House, she had dressed each baby in one of the adorable outfits her ex-mother-in-law, Madeline Saunders, had sent her for a baby gift. But she worried Jack and Addison wouldn't be comfortable in the outfits for an extended period, so she tossed in a comfy sleeper for each one and added two spares.

By the time they set out for their outing, Walt said, "I didn't realize we were spending the weekend at Edward's."

When they arrived at the MacDonalds' home, the only thing they took inside was a diaper bag—which Danielle had repacked twice while standing in the chief's driveway—and two infant carriers, each carrying a baby.

Chief MacDonald soon proved he hadn't forgotten how to hold a baby, and the first thirty minutes of their visit they exchanged oohs and ahhs, and the conversation focused primarily on the challenges of taking care of not just one, but two newborns.

Not long after their arrival, the babies demanded to be fed, and soon Danielle was sitting on the chief's loveseat, nursing the twins, while a receiving blanket provided her some modesty. The topic of conversation shifted to the unexplained paranormal activity at Marlow House. MacDonald told Walt and Danielle what he had said to Joe about the matter.

"How did he take it?" Danielle asked.

"What seemed to bother him most was your and Walt's reaction. Which is why he assumed it had all been some magic trick. He couldn't imagine either of you would stay under that roof while unexplained paranormal activities were going on—not with the babies."

"He has a point," Walt said.

"If it weren't for Eva and Marie, we probably wouldn't still be there," Danielle added.

They discussed the topic for a few more minutes before moving on to Danielle's recent nightmares. She described each dream, and when she finished, she noticed the chief's odd expression.

"Chief?" Danielle asked. "What is it?"

"You said there was a red barn with a large J on it?" MacDonald asked.

Danielle frowned. "Yes. Why?"

"And there was a root cellar?" the chief asked.

"The door didn't go into the building. It was against a dirt mound and opened up to a hole in the ground. I assumed it was a root cellar. But it was a dream, so who knows, perhaps the doors led to an alternate reality, but I woke up too soon."

"No, it was a root cellar. And I suspect it wasn't a regular dream," the chief said.

"It wasn't a dream hop. If that's what you're suggesting. I didn't realize I was sleeping, not even the second time when I was standing in the same room. I had a sense of déjà vu. Yet it didn't dawn on me I hadn't actually been in that room before. I had only dreamt about it."

"Edward, what is it?" Walt asked.

The chief turned to Walt. "Your wife has described something I saw when I first moved to Frederickport."

Danielle frowned at the chief. "What are you talking about?"

The chief took a deep breath, raised his footrest higher, exhaled, and settled back in the recliner. "I had just started working at the Frederickport Police Department. It was before Eddy was born. There was a house on the east side of town owned by Bud Jameson. The wife had passed away years earlier, and they never had kids. He lived at that house for years by himself. He was a recluse. At least, that's what Brian told me. I never met the man."

"Jameson? Does this have something to do with the *J* on the barn?" Danielle asked.

The chief nodded. "Yes. There was a red barn with a white *J* painted above the barn doors. Anyway, Old Man Jameson, as Brian called him, had passed away from old age about a month before I moved here. They didn't find his body for a couple of weeks."

Danielle wrinkled her nose. "Eww."

"But after they found him, his attorney hired someone to clean up the place so they could list it. Under the terms of his will, the property was to be sold, and the proceeds were to go to some charity. He didn't have any relatives."

"Sounds more like a coincidence. A barn with a *J*," Danielle said. "Perhaps the *J* in my dream was for another name. I know several Johnsons but can't remember any Jamesons."

The chief looked at Danielle. "When they were cleaning up the property, they found an abandoned root cellar. They didn't find any food stored inside, but they found the remains of a woman, who, by the condition of her remains, looked as if she had been there for years. Someone had buried her along the back wall of the root cellar."

"Bud Jameson was a murderer?" Danielle asked.

The chief shrugged. "Someone murdered her. They smashed in her skull. We could never identify the remains. There were no reported missing women of her approximate age and estimated time of death, that we could find in the area. After talking to some people who remembered Bud Jameson, they said his wife was timid, and a few claimed he liked to slap her around. But did he murder the woman we found? We don't know."

"How old was this woman?" Walt asked.

"Twenties or early thirties. She had been in that root cellar for years. It remains a cold case."

"How did the neighbors respond?" Danielle asked. "Did they have any theories on who she might be?"

The chief shook his head. "His neighbor to his right hadn't lived there that long, and the previous owner had passed away. The neighbor on the other side had moved into a care home and, by that time, couldn't remember her own name. So they were of no help. We ran articles in the newspaper; it was on the news. But we never got a response."

"There wasn't a roll of carpet in the root cellar, was there?" Danielle asked.

The chief smiled. "No. No carpet."

"Was there a DNA test?" Danielle asked.

"Yes, but nothing came of it. It's a cold case."

"Where is she buried now?" Danielle asked. "Or was she cremated?"

"She's buried at the local cemetery. In fact, the attorney handling the Jameson estate paid for her burial from the estate."

Walt arched his brows. "Does this mean the attorney felt Jameson was responsible?"

TWENTY-TWO

Adam Nichols sat at his desk, surfing through the local MLS listings on his computer, when Bill Jones walked into his office.

"You're working hard," Bill snarked as he took a seat on one chair facing Adam.

Adam looked up from his computer and took his right hand off his mouse and absently picked up a pen. "Seeing if anything interesting has come on the market."

"And?"

Adam leaned back in his office chair, his right hand still holding the pen. "A couple of things, but overpriced. So what's up?"

"I stopped by to ask when you want me to make the rest of the repairs over at the tunnel house."

Adam cringed. "Can you call it the Crawford house?"

"Why? I bet if you list it as the tunnel house, every agent in town will make an appointment to show the property."

"I'd rather have someone show it to one approved buyer than a hundred lookie-loos who end up stomping through the house with dirty shoes and no intention to buy."

"It's possible a couple of those lookie-loos might want to buy a house with a secret tunnel to Marlow House and you end up with a bidding war."

"Yeah, right," Adam scoffed.

"So when do you want me to do the work?"

Adam tossed the pen back on the desktop and sat up straighter. "I'm still waiting for the Crawfords to sign the listing agreement. At the moment, they're arguing with each other over the listing price, and I don't want to spend money making repairs if they decide not to list the property."

"Why wouldn't they list it?"

Adam shrugged. "Who knows, all this arguing over the price might rekindle something in their relationship. Chris once told me, when he first met them, they were arguing. Fighting could be their thing."

"Okay, call me when you're ready for me to go over there." Bill stood up, but Adam asked him to sit down for a moment.

"What?" Bill sat back down.

"I wanted to say moving those books around was a good joke. You had me going there for a few minutes."

Bill frowned. "What are you talking about?"

Adam chuckled. "You know what I'm talking about. The books on the bookshelf over at the Crawford house."

"Uh, no. I have no clue what you're talking about."

"Are you saying you didn't reorganize the books on the shelves over there?"

"Why would I do that?"

"It had to be you. After we were there, I took Mel and a couple to look at the house, and the romance books that were on the top shelf had moved."

Bill shook his head again. "And when did I do this? When was I alone in the living room after we pushed the bookcase back in place?"

Adam frowned while considering Bill's question. "Umm, you came back later?"

"And how did I get in? You haven't given me a key yet."

"Then who moved the books around in the bookcase?" Adam asked.

"It wasn't me. Ghosts?" Bill snickered.

Adam leaned back in the office chair, staring at Bill. He was right. Bill hadn't been alone with the bookcase after they had moved it, and he didn't have a key to the house.

"Speaking of ghosts…" Adam then told Bill what Joe and Kelly had told him and Mel.

Bill stared at Adam. "We never talk about it. But I remember that croquet set in Marlow House's attic." Not long after Danielle moved to Frederickport, Bill and Adam had broken into Marlow House, looking for the Missing Thorndike, which had been rumored to be hidden somewhere in the house.

After entering the attic while looking for the necklace, some invisible force had chased them away by throwing wooden croquet balls their way. Later, Adam convinced himself that someone had rigged the old croquet set to a remote control device. Bill never bought into that theory, yet pretended to accept it, and pushed the incident to the back of his mind.

"What are you suggesting?" Adam asked.

"There is something about that house. We've both experienced it. We pretend it didn't happen. But stuffed animals flying across the room isn't much different from what we experienced. Although not as painful."

"That crossed my mind when Joe and Kelly told us what they saw."

Bill considered Adam's words before saying, "There's a tunnel from Marlow House's basement to the Crawford house. Maybe our ghost followed the tunnel over and, instead of throwing the books, rearranged them?"

Adam arched his brows. "Our ghost?"

AT MARLOW HOUSE, Walt and Danielle had just returned from Chief MacDonald's. They found Eva and Marie in the living room, waiting for them.

"How did the babies do?" Marie asked.

"They were great. Slept most of the time. How was it here? Any activity?" Danielle asked as she and Walt walked into the living room, each carrying a baby carrier with a sleeping infant.

Marie immediately relieved Danielle of one carrier while Walt continued to handle the other one, gently setting them both next to the sofa.

"It's been silent," Eva said.

"The chief told us something interesting." Danielle told Marie and Eva about the body found in the root cellar years earlier.

"Oh, I remember that. Not that it had been found in a root cellar, only that it had been found buried on the property," Marie told them. "I'm fairly certain they never identified the remains."

"No, they didn't. But I have to wonder if this has something to do with what's going on here," Danielle said.

"How?" Eva asked.

"In both dreams there were twins, twin girls. At least, I assume they were girls, since they wore pink. Betsy made that quilt for her twin daughters," Danielle said.

"Considering you recently had twins, and the fact you're trying to learn more about the woman who made a quilt for her twin girls, it doesn't sound unusual to dream about twins," Eva pointed out.

Danielle shook her head. "I was probably wrong about the dreams not being dream hops. It's true, at the time I assumed they were regular dreams, but I can vividly remember each one. I typically forget a dream not long after I wake up, and even if I can still remember it hours later, it's more of a vague recollection."

"And who brought you into this dream hop?" Marie asked.

Danielle shrugged. "I don't know."

"Did you see the quilt in the dream?" Marie asked.

Danielle shook her head. "No."

"And now that Edward has told you about the body found in the root cellar, you think that is some way connected to the dream where you're pushed into a root cellar?" Marie asked.

"In my dream, there was a *J* on the barn I saw. And according to the chief, there was a *J* on the Jameson barn." Danielle let out a sigh. "Or it's a coincidence, and they were just dreams. Like you said, considering all that's been going on, it's no surprise I'm dreaming about twins."

ADAM PULLED up in front of the Crawford house and parked. He sat in his car for a few minutes, staring at the front door before getting out of the vehicle. He walked up to the front door and paused a moment before unlocking it and walking inside. Instead of shutting the door behind him, he left it slightly ajar.

He walked through the house, and everything looked as it had during his last visit. But when he came to the bookshelf, he froze. Once again, someone had reorganized the books. Adam stared dumbly at the bookshelf and then slowly took his cellphone from his pocket, turned on his camera app, and aimed the phone at the bookshelf, preparing to take a picture to document the placement of the books.

"Hey!" a voice called out. Adam startled, his hands flew upwards, and he tossed his cellphone into the air. Adam turned abruptly while fumbling to catch his phone. He saw Chris standing by the entry hall, and his cellphone landed on the floor.

"Dang, I didn't mean to scare you," Chris said.

Adam took a deep breath, exhaled, and then leaned down and picked his phone up off the floor and looked at it. The screen hadn't broken. "Umm, that's okay. You just startled me." Adam glanced back at the bookshelf.

Chris narrowed his eyes at Adam. "What's going on?"

Adam glanced from the bookshelf to Chris. "Can we go to your house and talk?"

"Sure."

Adam quickly snapped a picture of the bookshelf and then hurried with Chris from the house, locking the door behind him.

"YOU JUST GET HOME FROM WORK?" Adam asked Chris as they walked over to Chris's house.

"Yeah. I saw your car; figured I'd come say hi. I didn't mean to scare you like that."

"It's okay." Adam didn't sound convincing.

When they walked into the house, Chris offered Adam a beer. A few minutes later, the two men sat in the living room, each drinking a cold beer.

"So what's up?" Chris asked.

Adam sipped his beer, looked Chris in his eyes, and asked, "Do you believe in ghosts?"

Chris grinned. He hadn't expected that question. "Actually, yeah, I do."

"I do too." Adam took a swig of the beer.

"So, did you see a ghost or something? Or did you think I was a ghost when I walked in?"

Adam took another swig of beer before telling Chris about the books, about the croquet set, and about what Joe and Kelly had seen at Marlow House. When he was done, Chris said, "I was there when all that happened with Joe and Kelly."

"So what do you think is going on?"

Chris shrugged. "I know Joe's convinced Walt did one of his magic tricks. But he didn't. Walt and Danielle are as stumped as everyone. One theory, it's not ghosts, but negative energy."

"Kelly mentioned that."

"Some people theorize negative energy can attach to an object. Or perhaps it's more accurate to say the energy from a traumatic event. Right before all this started happening, Lily gave Danielle an old quilt she bought at an estate sale."

Adam nodded. "Kelly also mentioned the quilt."

"The strange things started happening after Lily gave it to Danielle. One theory, the quilt holds the energy from some traumatic event."

"And that's why Danielle wants to find out about the quilt's history."

Chris nodded. "Yes."

"Seems kind of far-fetched. Strange things happened to me at Marlow House long before Danielle received the quilt."

"Yes, but those things you experienced at Marlow House stopped happening a long time ago. About the same time we stopped smelling cigar smoke."

Adam stared at Chris for a moment. Finally, he said, "Are you suggesting there was a ghost that haunted Marlow House, but it isn't there anymore?"

Chris smiled. "Yes. I believe he moved on. After all, isn't a ghost just a spirit on this plane who hasn't moved on?"

Adam shrugged. "Umm, I suppose."

"Because of a few things that have happened, they believe it's connected to the quilt."

"If they think it's the quilt, why don't they just burn the damn thing?" Adam asked.

"That's been suggested. But will that destroy the negative energy, or just move it to another object?"

"Where is the quilt now?"

"I heard Walt moved it to a trunk in the basement."

"The basement? If you think about it, the basement is connected to the Crawford house. Is this energy coming through the tunnel and rearranging the books?" Adam asked.

TWENTY-THREE

W alt's telekinetic powers, along with Marie's help, made it easy to take what they had brought to the chief's house back upstairs to the nursery, minus any of the receiving blankets or clothing that needed to go to the laundry room. While Walt and Marie took the items upstairs, Danielle stayed in the living room, chatting with Eva while nursing the babies. Addison and Jack finished nursing and fell asleep before Walt and Marie returned to the living room.

When they came downstairs, they brought with them the two portable cribs. Danielle looked confused. "Why did you bring those downstairs? I was going to take the babies upstairs in a minute and put them down to sleep in their cribs."

"Yes. That was the plan," Walt said as he helped place the portable cribs in the living room. "But when Marie and I got up there, the quilt had returned."

"Didn't you lock it in a trunk in the basement?" Danielle asked.

"Apparently, the quilt can pick locks." Walt walked over to Danielle, picked up Addison, and carried her over to a portable crib.

"Did you leave it up there?" Danielle asked.

"I suggested he leave it in the nursery," Marie said. "The babies can sleep with you tonight. We can take the portable cribs back upstairs when you're ready to go to bed. I'm curious what sort of activity might take place in the nursery if the quilt's up there again instead of in the basement."

"Probably the same. It wasn't in the basement that long." Still sitting on the sofa, Danielle handed Jack to Walt, who placed the sleeping baby in the empty portable crib.

Danielle's cellphone buzzed. She leaned over to the coffee table, picked up the phone, read the message, and looked up to Walt and said, "Ian's sending me some information he found on Betsy Francas." A minute later, she opened the files Ian had sent, along with some notes.

Walt took a seat next to Danielle on the sofa, while Marie and Eva each sat on a chair facing them. They sat quietly, watching Danielle while she read the files Ian had sent over.

Finally, Danielle let out a sigh and said, "Well, I guess I was wrong." She dropped her hand, clutching the cellphone in her lap.

"Wrong about what?" Walt asked.

"I wondered if the woman the chief told us about was Betsy. She was a young woman, about Betsy's age."

"That could describe countless murder victims," Walt reminded.

"Yes. But also, I dreamt about the murdered woman—kinda—and the twins in the same dreams."

"Now you say you were wrong?" Marie asked. "Why?"

Danielle nodded and lifted her phone off her lap. She looked at the screen again. "Ian did some searching on Betsy Francas. During his search, he came across an obituary for Betsy's father. In the obituary, which was written in 1995, Betsy's father, who was named Hector Burr, was survived by his son, Hector Burr Jr., daughter Betsy Francas, and granddaughters, Karen and Jillian Francas. It lists some other surviving relatives, but you get my point. Betsy was alive at the time of her father's death, and that was just a few years before they found that woman's remains in the root cellar. And according to the chief, that woman had been in the root cellar a lot longer than a couple of years."

"Are you sure it's the same Betsy?" Eva asked.

"Yes. Ian also found a birth announcement for the twins when they lived in Vancouver, Washington. Which is where Gemma told us they all moved from. The parents were listed as Betsy and Dan Francas. And the twins have the same names as the granddaughters listed in the obituary. Plus, the year matches when the twins were born."

AFTER DINNER ON THURSDAY NIGHT, Walt and Danielle headed upstairs and together bathed the twins. When they brought them downstairs, they found Heather and Brian waiting for them in the living room.

"Marie told us to come on in," Heather explained when Walt and Danielle walked into the living room, each carrying a swaddled baby.

"Since when do you have to be told?" Walt teased.

Brian chuckled.

Heather ignored Walt's comment and walked closer to him and Danielle to have a closer look at the babies. "Can I hold one?"

"Did you wash your hands?" Walt asked.

Brian chuckled again. "The minute we walked in the kitchen, Heather went straight to the sink and washed her hands."

Heather shrugged. "Walt's been training me."

Danielle handed Addison to Heather, who gently and lovingly held the bundle, cooing down at the baby.

"We just got back from dinner and wanted to stop by and see how it's been going. And if you've figured out if you have a new ghost," Brian said.

Marie and Eva excused themselves to go upstairs to the nursery while Danielle remained on the sofa with Walt and Jack, and Heather sat down on a chair, holding Addison, and Brian sat in the chair next to her.

When they finished catching Heather and Brian up on what they knew regarding the matter, Heather said, "If Betsy is alive, you need to track her down and see if she can shed some light on what's going on. Assuming all this is really being caused by negative energy attached to the quilt."

Brian looked at Heather and rolled his eyes. "And exactly how do you do that? Find the woman and say, hey, we have a quilt you made, and it's making things fly around. Any idea why that's happening?"

"If only it were that simple," Walt said. "But, if there's some truth that a traumatic event can generate negative energy and attach to an object, maybe Betsy can give us some insight into what was happening back then. Of course, the traumatic event could also be the fact she abandoned her babies."

"Then what?" Brian asked. "We already know she abandoned her babies. If that's the traumatic event, what do you do now?"

"Eva and I have talked about this," Danielle said. "Perhaps the negative energy is a tool used by the Universe to get our attention. To help us right a wrong—or bring some resolution."

"What kind of resolution?" Brian asked.

Heather had been staring down at Addison, examining every inch of her petite, perfectly formed features while listening to the conversation. She looked up and said, "It's possible the Universe wants you to bring Betsy and her daughters together. Betsy put a lot of love into that quilt. To me, that says she was looking forward to the birth of her daughters. I have to believe postpartum depression initially drove her away."

"If she was mentioned in that obituary, then who's to say she hasn't since been reunited with her daughters?" Brian asked.

"The second wife said Betsy never returned," Danielle said.

"What were the girls' names?" Brian asked.

"Karen and Jillian Francas," Danielle said.

"Oh, yes. the Francas twins. I remember them." Brian grinned.

Heather looked over at Brian. "You do?"

Brian nodded. "Yes. I pulled them over a few times when they were in high school. They liked to drive their daddy's car fast. It also explains a lot. I had no idea Mrs. Francas wasn't their mother. Not a nice thing to say, but she was rather a frumpy woman. Reminded me of a toad."

Heather scowled at Brian. "You're right. That is a horrible thing to say."

Ignoring Heather's reprimand, Brian continued, "They looked nothing like Mrs. Francas. Now I understand why. Of course, they didn't look like their father either."

"What color hair did they have?" Danielle asked.

Brian shrugged. "I wouldn't call them redheads, like Lily, and not blonde like Melony. In between the two. They were cute girls, but they were a little wild. I remember busting up a high school party once, and they had been drinking. We had to call their parents, and their mother—or I guess their stepmother—was furious."

"Brian could be right, and the girls got back with their mother after they graduated from high school," Danielle said. "We were told they didn't come back for their father's funeral. There was probably more going on between their parents than we know. And it sounds like Gemma had her hands full with her stepdaughters."

"But what does that mean for us and the quilt?" Walt asked.

"The energy isn't necessarily angry energy. It could be the love Betsy poured into the quilt, and it needs to find its way back to Betsy and her daughters. Much of what has happened hasn't been antagonistic toward us. The knocking, for example, it only happens right as Addison and Jack are waking up because they're hungry. It's like the energy wants them to be fed as soon as possible and not make them wait. Or the stuffed animals put in the cribs," Danielle explained.

"What about the stuffed animals thrown at June or Joe?" Walt asked.

"Or the bookend that almost hit me?" Heather asked.

Danielle shrugged. "Possibly the energy saw you as a threat to the babies?"

"You can look kind of scary." Brian grinned at Heather.

"You're lucky I'm holding Addison. Or I would show you how scary I can be." Heather looked from Brian to Danielle and added, "You're suggesting energy has a mind?"

Danielle shrugged. "Eva always tells us we're all made up of energy. Thoughts from the source? Maybe on autopilot?"

Heather shook her head. "I'm confused."

"One way to find out, contact someone from the family," Brian suggested. "Something in the article might help us contact a family member."

"One of the screenshots Ian sent me was on the uncle. He owns an art store in Vancouver. We could contact him and see if he can tell us where his sister is," Danielle said.

"If you already have an address for him, why not send him the quilt with a note for him to pass it on to his sister or nieces?" Brian suggested. "Sounds a lot quicker."

"And if we're wrong?" Danielle asked. "I'd hate to send that quilt on to them and then they experience what we have, and it would be worse for them because they would not understand what's going on."

"To be fair, we don't understand what's going on either," Walt reminded Danielle. "Anyway, I suspect sending the quilt off on a hunch might not be much different from burning it. Whatever energy that's there might attach itself to another object."

"Basically, you're saying there is no solution to this," Brian said.

Danielle shook her head. "No. I doubt that's true. We just need to learn as much as we can, and something will come to us. The Universe always has a plan."

"Chris and I are going to Vancouver next week. I might be able to talk him into going tomorrow instead. And when we're there, we could stop in the uncle's art store and see if we can find out where his sister or his nieces are," Heather suggested.

"What would you say to him?" Brian asked.

Heather shrugged. "I don't know. But Danielle can help me come up with something. She's good at that. It's just too bad Betsy didn't have a sister instead of a brother."

Brian frowned at Heather. "Why do you say that?"

Walt chuckled. "I know."

Brian looked at Walt. "Why would it help if Betsy had a sister instead of a brother?"

Walt grinned at Brian. "Because Heather will have Chris with her. Think about it for a minute."

TWENTY-FOUR

C hris picked Heather up for work on Friday morning. When she opened the passenger door and he saw she didn't have her calico cat with her, he asked, "Leaving Bella home today?"

"Yep." As Heather climbed into the car, Hunny, who was sitting in the back seat, stuck her nose between the seats to say hello.

"Hi, Hunny," Heather greeted while leaning over to kiss Hunny's nose. "You sure look like you're doing better." Heather shut the car door and began putting on her seatbelt.

"She is." Chris drove the car away from the sidewalk in front of Heather's house and headed to the office.

They discussed Hunny for a few more minutes, and then Heather asked, "Why don't we go to Vancouver today instead of next week?"

"Why do you want to go today?"

Heather told Chris about her and Brian's conversation at Marlow House the night before. "We can stop at the brother's art store. I looked up the address last night."

"What are you going to say to him?" Chris asked.

"Danielle suggested I stick as close to the truth as possible. I can tell him a friend of mine bought a quilt at a thrift store, and she found out his sister made it. And we wondered if she had any other quilts she wanted to sell. At first, we considered saying something like Danielle wanted to return the quilt to his sister, but it might be a bad idea."

"Yeah. I can understand not wanting to make an offer to give the quilt away until we have a better idea of what's going on."

"Brian keeps saying we should burn it."

Chris chuckled and then said, "The quilt also has Adam a little shook."

Heather frowned. "Why?"

Chris told Heather about how he had run into Adam at Crawford's house and their discussion involving the bookshelf.

Heather scrunched up her nose. "I don't really see that happening. This thing, whatever it is, likes to throw things and knock on walls. Make chairs rock on their own. I don't see it moving down the street, through the tunnel, and then, what, reorganizing a bookshelf?"

"I agree. I told Adam it sounds like Mia gave one of the neighbors a key, and that neighbor is borrowing her books and then putting them back in the wrong place."

"Did Adam say any books were missing? Or new ones added?"

Chris shrugged. "No. But that doesn't mean some weren't."

"If books go missing or a new one shows up, I agree it's probably someone Mia gave a key to. But I don't see a neighbor or—what are we calling this thing? Energy?—coming into someone's home to rearrange book shelves."

"It could be someone pranking Adam," Chris suggested.

"And then there are Joe and Kelly..."

Chris glanced briefly at Heather. "What about Joe and Kelly?"

"Brian says Joe's still convinced this is an elaborate hoax by Walt, but Kelly no longer thinks Walt has anything to do with it. In fact, she told her mother it wasn't Walt."

"What did June say about that?"

"In one way, she's taking it better than Joe, in that she no longer blames Walt. So she's no longer annoyed at everyone. But she's also back on her *sell your Beach Drive house* kick."

"That's rich. I wonder what she would do if she learned the property they purchased was probably one of the most haunted pieces of real estate in Frederickport."

"True, but those spirits have moved on. We just need to get this thing—whatever it is—to move on, too. By the way, Kelly's helping Ian research paranormal activity, and I guess it's bugging the hell out of Joe. He's been ranting about it at work, according to Brian."

CHRIS AGREED to drive with Heather to Vancouver on Friday instead of waiting for next week. Before they left, they dropped Hunny off at Marlow House. Once they reached Vancouver, they stopped at the art store first. Hopefully, Betsy's brother would be at the store. If not, they would stop by again before heading back to Frederickport.

When they walked into the art store, there were several customers milling around, and one employee behind the counter—a woman.

Heather glanced around. "Oh crud, he doesn't seem to be here."

"He could be in the back?" Chris suggested.

Heather nudged Chris. "Go ask the girl behind the counter if he's here."

CINDY MURPHY HAD BEEN KEEPING a close eye on the girls lingering at the bead display. She had to wonder why they weren't in school, but then remembered some schools were already out for the summer.

She heard the bell to the front door ring and glanced over as a woman walked into the store. The first thought that popped into her head was, *I didn't know Goth was still a thing.* But then her gaze shifted to the woman's companion, and whatever had been in her mind was replaced by something else.

Cindy couldn't help but stare. She felt ridiculously breathless, like that time she had been a freshman in high school and had gone to her first concert with her friends to see her idol and had made an utter fool of herself, with her jumping up and down, screaming, the tears. Cindy wanted to do that now.

Instead, she took a deep breath and forced a smile as the couple approached the counter. He had to be someone famous. A movie star?

"Hello," he greeted her.

Cindy told herself to get it together. "Hi. How can I help you?" After she asked, she wanted to suggest some ways she would love to help him. But first, they needed to get rid of his friend. *Please let it just be a friend*, Cindy prayed.

"I'm looking for Hector Burr?" the yummy man asked her.

"Hector?" Cindy didn't consider for a moment not telling this beautiful man where he could find Hector. "Hector's next door at the coffee shop." Cindy immediately regretted telling him that. Not that she felt bad about telling him where to find Hector, even though Hector would prefer she simply take the man's name and number and get back with him when and if he wanted to. Cindy cursed herself for not asking for that contact info, not because it was what Hector would prefer, but then she would have the yummy man's name and phone number.

"Thank you," the man said. Cindy groaned as she watched the handsome stranger turn and walk away with his companion.

WHEN HEATHER and Chris walked into the coffee shop next door, they had a pretty good idea which customer was Hector Burr. They guessed it was the man sitting alone at one table, wearing a colorful shirt just like the one worn by the woman behind the counter at the art store.

They walked to the man's table, and Heather said, "Hector Burr?"

The man looked up from the newspaper he was reading. "Yes?"

"Sorry to bother you," Heather said. "My name is Heather Donovan, and this is Chris Johnson. We were wondering if we could have five minutes of your time? We need to ask you a question about your sister."

Hector frowned at Heather. "Betsy?"

Heather nodded. "Yes."

"We're from Frederickport," Chris added, in hopes Hector might be more inclined to talk to them since Betsy had once lived in Frederickport.

Hector took a deep breath and said, "Sure." He pointed to the empty chairs.

"If you don't mind, I'm going to grab Heather and me some coffee and a roll. We just drove in from Frederickport, and after we talk to you, we have a number of errands to run."

Hector nodded.

"Can I get you anything?" Chris offered.

Hector shook his head. "Umm, no. I'm fine."

Heather sat down while Chris went to get them some coffee. "As Chris explained, we live in Frederickport. After I told a friend of mine that we were coming to Vancouver today, she asked me if I would stop at your art store and ask you a question for her."

Hector's frown deepened. "You said this was about my sister?"

"It is. You see, someone gave my friend a quilt. It was from an estate sale. My friend loves it, and she wondered if the person who made it had any other quilts they wanted to sell. Your sister was the one who made the quilt."

Hector leaned back in the chair. "What does this quilt look like?"

"Umm...it's a baby quilt."

"What's the pattern? The theme? Ducks? Teddy bears? Rainbows?"

"Twins."

Hector silently stared at Heather for a moment. Finally, he said, "I wondered what happened to that quilt."

"What did your sister say happened to it?" Heather asked.

Before he could answer the question, Chris returned to the table, carrying two coffees and an assortment of muffins and donuts, which he set in the center of the table and told Hector and Heather to help themselves.

Hector thanked Chris for the offer and looked back at Heather. "As for your question, I have been estranged from my sister for years. I have no idea where she is."

"Oh. But you're familiar with the quilt?"

Hector nodded. "Betsy always liked to sew. She started making baby quilts in high school, and she'd sell them. It's possible your friend could stumble across another quilt she made. But I don't know where. That was a long time ago. The quilt your friend has was the only one Betsy made for herself. I always wondered what happened to it. I asked Karen and Jillian about it once, but they don't remember seeing it. Dan probably got rid of it. Can't say I blame him."

"Your nieces?" Heather asked.

"Yes. Twins. I remember when Betsy made it. She seemed so excited about her pregnancy, but she ended up being just like our mother. She didn't stick around to raise her kids. Of course, I should probably give Mom a little more credit. She stuck around until I was five and Betsy was four. Betsy didn't even stick around until her girls had their first birthday."

"Postpartum depression?" Heather asked.

Hector scoffed. "No. Mom didn't have postpartum depression. She took off with another man, started a new family. I guess she liked them better than us, considering she raised the kids she had with him."

"That's what Betsy did? She didn't leave from postpartum depression?" Heather asked.

Hector shook his head. "No. According to Dan, she seemed perfectly fine after the babies were born. She didn't act depressed. He said she seemed happy. Dan didn't realize she was probably happy to no longer be pregnant so she could hook up with her boyfriend, just like our mother."

"I guess you weren't very close to your sister?" Heather asked.

"We were once."

"Do you see your nieces?" Heather asked.

"If you're suggesting your friend give the quilt to my nieces so they can have something from their mom, don't. It would only hurt them."

"You have a relationship with them?" Heather asked.

Chris sat quietly and listened as Heather kept asking one question after another, and Hector kept answering them. He expected the man to tell Heather it was none of her business, but it was obvious Hector had a lot of pent-up anger toward his sister, and talking to a stranger about her seemed to be what he needed.

"Somewhat. I hadn't seen them for years. Dan contacted me after Betsy took off. I suspected he hoped I would know where she was. I saw the girls a couple of times over the next few years, but after he married Gemma, I couldn't deal with it. Gemma was a bitch. I never liked her."

"From what my friend told me, Gemma was the one who told her who made the quilt. Gemma claimed she and your sister were good friends."

Hector nodded. "Yes. She and Gemma grew up together. They were best friends since preschool."

TWENTY-FIVE

Joanne Johnson almost didn't attend her favorite aunt's eightieth birthday party because Danielle had given birth just the week before, and Joanne figured the new parents needed her help. But when Danielle learned of the surprise birthday party, she insisted Joanne attend, reminding her of the importance of family. Then, instead of experiencing guilt for considering taking off a week to attend the party, Joanne felt guilt for almost letting her part-time job take precedence over her aunt's special day.

If anyone could make Joanne feel guilty for not appreciating her family, it was Danielle. After all, not long after Danielle moved into Marlow House, she'd lost her last remaining family member when someone murdered her cousin. But now, Danielle had a new family with Walt and the twins and her close-knit friends in Frederickport. She even had a new cousin in Melony Nichols, although only by marriage.

While Joanne enjoyed her recent getaway, she looked forward to returning home and to Marlow House. Joanne was grateful Danielle had kept her on after she inherited the estate, although taking care of Marlow House differed from when Danielle's great-aunt, Brianna Boatman, had owned the property.

Brianna had never lived at Marlow House, so it had remained locked up for decades, since the murder of its previous occupant, Walt Marlow. Brianna's attorney had hired Joanne to come over to the house once a week to keep the dust and dirt away, wash the windows, flush the toilets, make sure there were no broken pipes, keep vermin away, and let him know if anything needed to be repaired.

A common question asked by Joanne's friends and acquaintances was, "Aren't you ever afraid to go over there alone? Isn't it creepy?"

It was a fair question, considering many in town said Marlow House's previous resident haunted the premises. Joanne secretly shared that belief, yet it never frightened her. While Joanne could never claim to have seen the ghost of Marlow House, she sensed his presence in countless ways—the distinct scent of cigar smoke, the random closing of doors, bric-à-brac mysteriously moving from one location to another. Although she had never actually seen the items move by themselves.

Joanne had gotten into a habit of talking to Walt Marlow when she came over to do her weekly chores. Sometimes she imagined she could hear him answering her. After Danielle moved into the house, she no longer held her one-sided conversations with Walt unless it was in the library when she dusted his portrait and no one was around.

Strangely, not long after Walt's distant cousin came to visit, she stopped noticing the scent of a cigar. She took an immediate dislike to the cousin, and after his accident, when he moved into Marlow House, demanding to be called Walt and insisting he had amnesia, her dislike intensified. To be fair to the cousin, his real name had been Walter Clint Marlow—yet he had previously gone by his middle name.

But then something happened. Clint, now Walt, apologized to her for his previous behavior. It wasn't the apology that eventually won her over, but his transformation and how he treated Danielle and everyone around him.

While Joanne would never admit it to anyone, sometimes she

imagined Walt Marlow had replaced Clint Marlow—the Walt Marlow from the portrait in the library. Of course, she recognized it was all a fanciful notion; after all, she wasn't crazy.

WALT STOOD at the living room window looking outside at the street, his back to Danielle, who sat in one recliner reading a book. Their babies each sat in an infant seat on the floor, while Danielle's cat, Max, weaved in and out of the seats, taking it upon himself to stand guard over the newest residents of Marlow House. Upstairs in the nursery, Marie and Eva took turns watching for any sign of paranormal activity.

"Joanne just pulled up," Walt announced before turning around to face Danielle.

Danielle closed her book and set it on her lap. "I had hoped we'd have this resolved before she returned."

Walt shrugged. "Even if it had been, it wouldn't be a secret considering how many non-mediums and nonbelievers witnessed the activity."

"True, but then she would just say everyone's imagination got the best of them."

They heard the front door open and shut and then the sound of footsteps coming down the entrance hall. A few moments later, Joanne peeked into the living room, and when she saw Walt and Danielle, she walked all the way into the room.

"Welcome home," Danielle greeted. "Did you have a good time?"

"Hello, Joanne," Walt said as he walked to the chair next to Danielle and sat down.

"Thank you. Yes, and I'm glad I went. It was nice seeing everyone, and my aunt enjoyed her party."

"I'm glad you had a good time," Danielle said.

Joanne walked over to the twins, smiling down at the pair yet raising her brow over the cat's proximity to the newborns. She looked over at Walt and Danielle and asked, "How has everything been going here? These two seem quite content sitting here watching Max."

"They sleep a lot, and fortunately they haven't had issues like colic. Knock wood. We haven't had to walk them to sleep. Just feeding them seems to do the trick," Danielle said.

Joanne smiled at Danielle. "That's wonderful, because getting sufficient sleep is important for all of you. Well, I'll start the laundry and—"

"First," Danielle interrupted, "we need to talk to you."

Furrowing her brows, Joanne glanced from Danielle to Walt, back to Walt. "Is something wrong?"

"Why don't you sit down?" Walt motioned to the sofa across from them. "But first, this isn't about you. It's about something that happened at Marlow House while you were gone, and you should know."

Now curious, Joanne walked to the sofa and sat down, facing Walt and Danielle.

JOANNE SAT QUIETLY on the sofa, her hands folded on her lap while Walt and Danielle finished telling her all that had happened since June first witnessed the rocking chair moving on its own in the nursery, along with their theories on what might be behind the strange events.

"Is that all?" Joanne asked, suppressing a smile.

Danielle frowned at Joanne. "Don't you believe us?"

Joanne looked up at Danielle, seemingly startled at the question. "Oh, no. I do. I don't necessarily agree with your theories about what's behind it. But I don't doubt it happened."

"Do you have a theory?" Walt asked, eyeing Joanne curiously.

Joanne looked sheepishly at Walt. "It might sound kind of crazy."

Walt chuckled. "After what's been going on here? What's your theory?"

"It's Walt Marlow."

"You agree with Joe?" Danielle asked.

"Oh, no! I didn't mean that. I'm talking about the other Walt Marlow. It's no secret many people in town used to say Marlow House was haunted. I'm talking about before you moved in. I've cleaned this house for years. And while I never engaged in the haunted gossip that sometimes surrounded Marlow House, I, well, I've seen things, experienced things when I would come over here. I never mentioned it before, but I always felt Walt Marlow—the other one—haunted Marlow House."

Walt arched his brow. "Really? I'm curious. What have you experienced?"

Joanne grinned. "I don't feel so foolish sharing this now, considering what's happened since I've been gone. But let's see, there was the cigar, of course; you all smelled that."

"Anything else?" Danielle asked.

"Yes. When I would come over here to clean, before you moved in, doors would sometimes shut on their own. I used to tell myself it was probably from a draft. But other things would happen, like once I moved a figurine off the mantel to dust, but I got distracted, left to do something, and when I came back, the figurine was already back on the mantel. I hadn't put it there. But someone did. I often wondered if it was Walt Marlow."

"Anything else?" Walt asked.

"Well, I never saw him. But sometimes I heard him."

Danielle frowned. "What did he say?"

"Sometimes, when I was dusting something breakable, I swore a man's voice would say, '*Be careful with that.*'"

"And you think that's who is doing this now?" Danielle asked.

"Yes. Although, after I stopped smelling the cigar smoke, I wondered if his spirit had moved on after Clint—Walt—moved in. But clearly, he hasn't. I assume with all the extra activity around here, a door closing by itself is something I might miss now."

"That's an interesting theory," Danielle stammered.

Joanne stood up. "Well, unless there is nothing else, I probably should get started."

Danielle and Walt sat in silence as Joanne fairly skipped from the room. When she was out of earshot, Danielle said, "She thinks it's you. Not you exactly, but your ghost."

"I have to say, I didn't expect that response."

Danielle looked at Walt. "I thought you never moved objects until after I moved in?"

Walt shrugged. "I must have. At the time, I thought I was alive, so I didn't even think about it."

Danielle slumped back in the chair.

MARIE SAT in a rocking chair in Marlow House's nursery, contemplating what she might want to do after Eva returned to take over for her. She considered stopping across the street to see Connor, and then going over to Adam's office before returning to Marlow House for the evening.

"Joanne's here," Eva announced when she appeared in the room, sans the fanfare of snowflakes, glitter, or flower petals. "Her car's parked out front."

"I wonder if they're having the talk."

Eva sat down in the empty rocking chair. "I imagine they are. Walt said they planned to do it as soon as she arrived."

"I wonder how that's going. Perhaps I'll pop on down to the living room and listen in."

Eva held up her hand, signaling for Marie to be quiet so she could listen. After a moment, she said, "Someone's coming."

The door to the nursery opened, and Joanne walked into the room. The two spirits silently watched Joanne, who stared Eva's way.

"Why is she looking at me like that?" Eva asked.

"She's not looking at you, dear. She can't see you. My guess, she's looking at the quilt." The quilt hung on the back of the rocker where Eva sat.

Joanne glanced around the room and called out, "Walt? Are you here?"

Marie frowned. "Does she think Walt's hiding up here?"

Joanne looked back toward Eva.

"She's staring at me again."

Eva and Marie watched as Joanne approached Eva, stopping short of stepping on her toes. Joanne reached out, moved her hands through Eva's head, and took hold of the quilt, pulling it from the rocker. Eva leapt from the chair.

Joanne held up the quilt to examine. "Beautiful. Impressive needlework. Adorable appliques. But not haunted, or whatever they called it. So silly."

Joanne carefully refolded the quilt and placed it over the back of the rocker. She looked around the room again. "Walt, show me if you're here."

The next moment, the stuffed elephant flew across the room, aimed at Joanne's face. The housekeeper reached up in time to catch the stuffed animal before it hit her. Now laughing, Joanne clutched the soft elephant to her chest and cried, "I knew it was you!"

TWENTY-SIX

Both Danielle and Walt had kept Marlow House tidy throughout the week, but Danielle had to admit she appreciated the feel of her home after a thorough cleaning by Joanne.

Heather had called Danielle on her way back to Marlow House, giving her a brief recap of what had happened in Vancouver. It was then decided the mediums, along with Lily, Ian, and Brian, would come over to Marlow House for dinner and to update everyone on what they had learned. Chris volunteered to bring burgers.

Heather and Brian arrived at Marlow House first, followed by Chris. While Brian helped Chris bring in the burgers and fries and set them on the buffet in the dining room, Ian and Lily walked over from across the street.

"Where's Connor?" Heather, who was helping Danielle bring out the napkins and plates to the dining room, asked Lily when she and Ian walked in the house.

"John was over with some guys working today," Lily began. "June came over right before they left to check out the progress. She overheard me say something to Ian about coming over here tonight. June about freaked. Insisted she watch Connor over at her house while we're here. I suspect she's afraid of a demon possession."

"She's not afraid you and Ian might get possessed?" Danielle teased.

"Mom's given up on us. She's trying to save her grandson." Ian grinned and shut the door behind him. As soon as he shut the door, Sadie came charging through the doggie door, almost knocking Ian down.

"Hey, slow down!" Ian laughed as Sadie rushed to greet Hunny, who had just walked into the kitchen from the hallway. Sadie and Hunny ignored Ian, and Sadie slipped back outside through the pet door, Hunny right behind her.

AFTER GRABBING their burgers and fries, the friends headed to the living room to eat and discuss the recent events. Danielle started first, telling them about Joanne's reaction to what they had been calling the poltergeist.

"So she's always assumed the house was haunted?" Brian asked.

Danielle shrugged. "I guess."

"And she's not afraid?" Ian asked.

"Not from what Marie told us. And I am starting to suspect our housekeeper has a major crush on my husband. At least his ghost."

They all laughed.

"But she actually heard him?" Lily asked.

"That's not so surprising," Chris said. "I just find it interesting Walt was moving objects for longer than we assumed."

A few minutes later, Heather told them what they had learned in Vancouver. "I felt sorry for the brother. He's never been married. His mother obviously messed up his head when she deserted him, and then his sister did the same thing to her kids. Poor guy needs a good therapist."

Brian looked at Heather. "He told you all that?"

Chris laughed. "No, not all of it. But Heather asked him a lot of personal questions. He just kept answering them. I was waiting for him to tell her it was none of her business. But he never did."

Heather shrugged. "I was curious. Anyway, the only reason they mentioned Betsy's name in her father's obit was because whoever wrote it assumed she was still alive, not that they knew it."

"Before her father died, didn't he ever wonder where his daughter was all those years?" Lily asked.

"The father had been in a memory care home for years," Chris explained. "He had no idea what was going on, and his son just assumed his sister not only skipped out on her kids and husband but left him to deal with their father."

They discussed the visit to Vancouver a bit more, but then shifted the conversation when Lily said, "Ian did some more research today. When he wasn't helping his dad."

"Did you find out anything?" Chris asked.

Ian looked over at Chris. "We all assumed that before Gemma and Dan got married, Dan and Betsy divorced. After I found that obit, I figured that was additional proof she had resurfaced after she took off."

"Her brother told us the last time he saw his sister was right before she and Dan moved to Frederickport," Heather said.

"I couldn't find any records that showed Dan and Betsy ever divorced, or that Gemma and Dan got married," Ian explained. "I checked with Oregon Vital Records and Certificates, and I never found a marriage certificate for Dan and Gemma."

"They could have gotten married in Vancouver?" Heather suggested.

"I checked Washington State too. I found nothing for Dan and Gemma, but I found the marriage certificate for Betsy and Dan. But no record of divorce. I also searched for any death records for Betsy. She could very well have passed away by now, but nothing came up."

"I can understand why Joanne doesn't accept our quilt theory," Danielle said. "Considering her experiences at Marlow House before I arrived."

"Joanne could be right, and it has nothing to do with the quilt or Betsy's family," Lily said.

"But I keep going back to that dream and how I can still remember it. Those babies had strawberry blonde hair. And Brian said Betsy's daughters were strawberry blondes. It has to mean something."

"I remember someone else with that hair color," Brian asked.

Heather looked at Brian. "Who?"

"I had forgotten all about it until Danielle mentioned that dream. The body we found on the Jamesons' property, she had long reddish blonde hair. Or as Danielle calls it, strawberry blonde."

"I imagine after being there that long, you couldn't tell what she looked like," Heather said.

Brian shook his head. "No."

"Was my original hunch correct?" Danielle asked. "Betsy was murdered? But why were they at the Jamesons' house?"

"Didn't you say someone pushed you down the stairs in your dream?" Brian asked.

Danielle frowned. "Yes, why?"

"The Jameson house doesn't have a second floor. Neither does the house Dan raised his daughters in, and from what I remember hearing, he and his first wife, Betsy, built that house. Plus, it's on the other side of town from the Jameson place."

"But Betsy wasn't living in that house when she disappeared," Danielle said. "Marie said they were building a house here and staying somewhere else while their house was being finished."

"Whose house were they staying at?" Brian asked.

"I'll have to ask Marie the name. I don't remember. She said something about the woman visiting her sister in Florida, so she let them stay in her house." Danielle stood up.

"Where are you going?" Walt asked.

"I'm going upstairs to ask Marie the name of the woman who lent Betsy and Dan her house." Danielle rushed from the living room before anyone could respond.

When Danielle returned five minutes later, Lily asked, "What did Marie say?"

Danielle stood in the doorway, looking at her friends. "They were staying at Elenore Percy's house. And according to Marie, Elenore lived next door to the Jamesons."

RODNEY HEALY HAD NEVER BEEN to Frederickport, Oregon, but his business associate Clay Bowman had called him this morning and told him about a unique opportunity he couldn't pass up and he needed to come immediately, because they had a narrow window to pull it off.

Rodney was fully aware of Clay's recent predicament. He had read about it in the newspaper, and according to one news report, Clay had jumped bail, and some speculated he was now in Canada.

While Rodney was not in the habit of answering calls from unknown phone numbers, the text message from an unknown number, one with a unique word, one used only by Clay when he wanted to pass some information on to Rodney, caught his attention. Information that would help Rodney facilitate a profitable heist. Of course, Rodney always paid Clay a generous finder's fee.

Minutes after receiving the text message, the call came in, and Rodney answered it. Clay apologized for the short notice, but promised there was enough time to pull it off as long as Rodney came immediately to Frederickport. Once he arrived, Clay would explain everything.

Rodney used his GPS to find Frederickport Pier and headed down Beach Drive. He drove slowly down the dark street, checking out the neighborhood, and passed an old Victorian-like house on his left, noticing its front window blinds wide open, the room's interior well lit and people inside. He continued driving down the street until he reached the pier.

After parking, Rodney got out of his vehicle and followed the instructions Clay had given him. He was to walk under the pier and head north until he passed a certain number of houses. When he reached a specific house, he was to walk through the bushes to the house's driveway and then go on to the side door off the driveway. It would be unlocked.

Rodney stayed in the shadows as he walked down the beach; fortunately, none of the houses facing his way had their blinds open.

When he came to the bushes Clay had described, he stepped through them onto the driveway.

The house was dark, but he could see the back door Clay had described. He walked to the door, reached for the doorknob, and found it unlocked, as promised. Hesitantly, he opened it and stepped into the dark house.

"Glad you could make it, Rodney."

RODNEY STOOD in the tunnel with Clay, dumbfounded by what surrounded him. Lanterns along the tunnel's wall lit the way, with several large coolers shoved against one tunnel wall. According to Clay, the coolers held food.

"I got all that stuff from the house we were just in," Clay explained. "The owners are gone, but the Realtor is getting ready to list the place. That's why we must move fast."

"You said the tunnel leads to that big Victorian house I passed on the way to the pier?"

Clay nodded. "Yes. The only people who live there are Walt and Danielle Marlow. They had twins about three weeks ago."

"There were a bunch of people in the house when I drove by earlier."

"Yeah, well, they'll be gone late tonight. We need to work out the details over the weekend so we can be prepared to move on Monday night. It has to be on a weekday, when the bank is open."

"What does this have to do with bank hours?"

"Danielle Marlow has a freaking fortune in gold coins and gems in her safe-deposit box at the local bank. We need her to go to the bank, empty her safe-deposit box, and bring it all home and wait for further instructions. Of course, we won't call to give her instructions. We'll simply enter through the tunnel and take it."

"How are we going to get her to clean out her safe-deposit box in the first place?"

"Haven't you figured it out yet? I said she had two infants. We get in the house in the middle of the night through the tunnel, unlock the front door so they assume someone entered that way, and then take one kid out through the tunnel. As far as they're concerned, the tunnel is all locked up and no one can access it. So no one will look here. They won't have any idea we're in their tunnel waiting for them."

"How do we get one baby out of the house without the parents knowing? Babies tend to cry, especially if you wake them up in the middle of the night. Sounds like for this plan to work, the parents need to find the baby missing after we already have it in the tunnel."

"I have a couple of ideas. That's one thing we need to work out over the weekend."

"How about when we get the loot? Do you have any ideas about that?"

"No reason to hurt the kid. But I say we take mom and dad down to the tunnel and let this be their final resting place. We don't need any witnesses."

TWENTY-SEVEN

The portable cribs sat against a far wall in Walt and Danielle's bedroom, and they no longer obstructed Danielle's view of the bed from where she sat at her vanity. While brushing her hair, she looked in the mirror, and instead of watching her own reflection, she watched her husband's. Walt lounged on the mattress, partially sitting up while leaning against one elbow, wearing pajama bottoms, his chest bare. Wide awake, both Addison and Jack lay on the mattress with their father, with tiny feet and hands in motion. Danielle smiled at how Walt gazed down at the pair, his voice soft as he talked to them.

Can it get any better than this? Then Danielle remembered and chuckled.

Walt looked up from the bed to his wife, her back to him as she sat at the vanity, brushing her long, dark hair. "What's funny?"

Danielle set her brush down and turned around on the bench, now facing Walt. "Watching you with them, I asked myself, does it get any better than this?"

Walt smiled at her. "Why is that funny?"

Danielle nodded her head toward the nursery. "Because in that moment I had forgotten about our poltergeist—or whatever it is."

"Whatever it is, it doesn't seem as antagonistic as we initially worried it might be."

"True. I don't feel this energy means any harm to Addison or Jack."

Danielle's cellphone rang. She stood up, and Walt reached for her phone on the nightstand. He handed it to Danielle when she reached the bed. Danielle glanced at the phone. "It's Heather."

After Danielle answered the phone, Heather said, "Have you had breakfast yet?"

"No. I'm just getting dressed. We're still upstairs in our bedroom. But just fed the twins, and they're awake and happy, playing with their dad on the bed." Still standing while holding the phone to her ear, Danielle flashed Walt a smile.

"Playing? How does a baby their age play?" Heather asked.

"They don't run around a lot, that's for sure."

"Ha, ha. Anyway, I'm calling because last night you seemed convinced Betsy was the murdered woman found at the Jameson place, and you said we needed to talk to the chief about it. I wanted to let you know Brian is picking up the chief this morning and taking him to breakfast at Pier Café, and he wondered if you and Walt wanted to meet them there."

"We'd love to, but I want to wait a few more weeks before I take the twins out in public."

"If Marie is still there, how about I come over and watch the babies with her, and you and Walt get out of the house together? You can have breakfast there. It would be good for you. And you can tell the chief your thoughts."

"Are you sure?" Danielle asked.

"Hey, if there's a problem, I can give you guys a call, and you can be back home in a couple of minutes. I'll be fine with Marie there."

WALT AND DANIELLE walked to Pier Café on Saturday. The brisk morning temperature hovered in the mid-fifties, with a clear sky overhead. A warm jacket and knit cap kept Danielle warm as she and Walt walked hand in hand toward the pier.

"It feels kind of weird, leaving the babies," Danielle said.

"You left them the other day when you were with Lily," Walt reminded her.

"True. But you were with them."

Walt let go of Danielle's hand and wrapped his arm around her shoulder, pulling her close while they continued down the street. "Heather has Marie and Eva, so if they need us, Eva can be at the café in seconds, and I trust both Heather and Marie."

WALT AND DANIELLE sat in the booth with Brian and the chief. The server had just taken their order and filled their coffee mugs before walking away.

"Where's Carla?" Danielle asked no one in particular.

"She's not working today," Brian said.

"I can't remember ever having another server here." Danielle picked up her coffee and took a drink.

"Brian told me you may know the identity of the woman found at the Jamesons' place," the chief said.

Danielle told him why she believed the woman was Betsy Francas, and then added, "You said nothing came of the DNA results. Which only means none of her close relatives have their DNA on file. But all you have to do is get her brother's DNA."

"I can't very well go to the brother and ask for his DNA based on a dream you had," the chief reminded her.

"But his sister has been missing for years. No one has seen her."

"You don't know that for certain," the chief corrected. "From what I understand, Heather and Chris only spoke to one member of her family."

"But she was staying next door to where you found the body. The right gender, age, and hair color," Danielle argued.

"There is no connection between Betsy Francas and Jameson or Jameson's neighbor."

"But Marie——" Danielle began, only to be cut off by the chief.

"But Marie said they stayed with Elenore Percy. The woman's been dead for years. The house has changed hands, and there is no way to prove they stayed there unless we can find someone who remembers. Someone other than a ghost."

"It's possible her brother remembers where they stayed," Danielle said. "I'm sure Gemma Francas knows. She was there back then."

"Gemma claimed a man picked her up that day after she left her wedding ring on the quilt. But if they found her body next door, does that mean Gemma lied?" Walt asked.

"Either that, or Betsy returned for some reason. Maybe even to get the babies. Her husband was there. They fought, and he dragged the body next door to the old root cellar. I don't think Gemma lied about Betsy leaving that day, because that would mean she killed Betsy. And I don't believe Gemma is strong enough to drag a body next door and hide it in a root cellar," Danielle said.

"It's possible Gemma covered up for Dan and made up the story about Betsy leaving with a man. After all, they did eventually marry, so obviously she had feelings for him," Brian suggested.

"I suppose we can speculate on motive and possible suspects all day long, but first we need to get a positive identification of the victim. Let me think about how I might move forward on this," the chief said. "I don't doubt anything you're saying, but I can't go to Betsy's brother and ask for a DNA sample until I have more to offer him."

"I understand. How about if we can find someone—a living person—who remembers where Betsy and Dan first lived when they moved to town? And once we have that connection, all you need is more proof that no one has seen Betsy since she left Frederickport. Just because no one filed a missing person report on her doesn't mean she isn't a missing person," Danielle said.

The chief nodded. "When we found the body, we searched matches from women who had gone missing during the estimated timeframe of the murder. None matched. But if we can find information to show Betsy hasn't been seen since she left town, coupled with the knowledge she was staying next door to where the body was found, yes, with that I wouldn't have a problem asking her brother for a DNA test."

Danielle absently ran a finger over the rim of her water glass while listening to the chief. When he finished talking, she looked up and said, "Something was said about Betsy's twins leaving town after they graduated and never coming back. Marie said they didn't even go to their father's funeral. And the brother told Heather he stopped visiting them because he couldn't stand Gemma. I wonder what happened in that family. It might give us more insight into what happened back then."

"You could start by talking to someone who knew the twins in high school. Don't teenage girls confide in their friends?" Brian asked.

Danielle looked to Brian. "I have no idea who might have known the Francas twins back then."

"I do." Brian smiled.

"Who?" Danielle asked.

"Remember when I told you about that party I busted when the Francas twins were in high school?"

"Yes."

"Jesse Mills, she works at the nursery on the weekends. Jesse grew up here, and I'm pretty sure she used to hang out with the twins, because that party was at her house. You could start there."

"Oh, so you want me to do your police work?" Danielle teased.

"You'd probably have more luck talking to her than me," Brian said. "She still holds a grudge about that bust. I think she missed prom because of it."

DANIELLE DIDN'T GO DIRECTLY to the nursery after leaving the diner. She first went home with Walt, and after feeding the babies, she and Heather left for the nursery, leaving Walt at home.

They found Jesse Mills outside in the rose section. She was about the right age to have gone to school with the twins, but it was her name tag that gave her away.

"Hi, I'm Danielle Marlow," Danielle introduced herself to Jesse. "I was hoping I could talk to you for a minute."

Instead of responding to Danielle, Jesse looked at Heather. "I recognize you. You date that jerk Brian Henderson."

Heather grinned. "Yeah, Danielle used to say he was a jerk, too."

Jesse looked back at Danielle. "Used to?" She gave a shrug and then asked, "So what do you need?"

"It's kind of a strange question, actually. You see, I was given a vintage baby quilt, and I've recently learned who it was originally made for, and I'm wondering if I should see if they want it, but someone said offering it to them might be a bad idea and bring up all sorts of bad memories, so I thought I should talk to someone who knew them, and you're the only one I could find."

Jesse stared blankly at Danielle. "Uh, yeah. It is a strange question. Kind of confusing, too."

"Do you know Karen and Jillian Francas?" Heather blurted.

Jesse turned to Heather. "Yes. I do. I haven't seen them for ten years or more, but we were good friends in high school. Why?"

"I have a quilt that their mother made them, and I'm wondering if I should try getting it back to them," Danielle explained.

"That bitch Gemma? If you want it burned, then go ahead, send it to them," Jesse said with a snort.

"No, actually, their birth mother made it. Gemma was their stepmother," Danielle corrected.

Jesse nodded. "Yeah, Karen told me she was their stepmom. But even if the quilt was made by their bio mom, they'd probably still burn it. She abandoned them and left them with their father and bitch stepmom."

"What was bitchy about her?" Heather asked. "What did she do?"

Jesse shrugged. "I always thought Gemma was the stereotypical Disney stepmom villain, just not attractive. I think part of the problem, they looked just like their real mom. Of course, they didn't know that by looking at pictures. Their father burned anything that once belonged to their mother, including any photos of her. But Gemma loved to tell the girls they would never amount to anything because they were losers just like their mother, adding that they even looked exactly like her. She'd also tell them they weren't lovable, that even their real mother had to get away from them."

"Wow. Did their father know what his wife said to them?" Danielle asked.

"He was always working, never home. And when he was home, if they tried to complain about her, he would tell them it was between them and their mother, and they had to work it out. But she was never their mother, and he was never much of a father. He left all the parenting to his wife, who clearly hated those girls. Minute they turned eighteen, they were out of there. I can't say I blame them."

TWENTY-EIGHT

Danielle and Heather sat in Danielle's car in front of the nursery. Danielle had just put the key in the ignition and was about to fasten her seatbelt when she asked Heather, "Would you mind if we stopped one more place?"

"Where do you want to go?"

"I'd like to talk to Gemma again. See if she can tell me where Betsy and Dan lived when they first moved to town."

"Is that a good idea? What if she's the one who knocked off her friend to get Dan?"

"I doubt she's the one who dragged me across the yard."

Heather rolled her eyes. "Danielle, that was a dream. As far as you know, Gemma told Betsy she wanted to show her a cool root cellar she found next door, and when they went to look at it, Gemma knocked her over the head, Betsy fell in the root cellar, and she rolled her far into the cellar and covered her with dirt."

Danielle looked over at Heather. "You've been giving this some thought, haven't you?"

Heather shrugged. "She had the motive. I know she claimed to be good friends with Betsy, but she moved in pretty quick on her husband. And Betsy's brother sure didn't like her. Of course, he wasn't too fond of his sister, either. Maybe they were both bitches. Sometimes they run in packs, you know."

Danielle giggled. "Like mean girls?"

"Exactly."

"Well, I'll be careful how I question her, and I'm confident we can both take her."

"I'll go with you, but I'm going to call Brian and tell him where we're going, and you call Walt." Heather pulled her cellphone from her purse.

WHEN DANIELLE PULLED her car up in front of Gemma's house, they saw the woman outside, pulling weeds from her flower bed. Gemma sat on a garden stool, wearing long denims, a flannel shirt, garden gloves, and a straw hat, her back facing Danielle and Heather as they walked into the yard.

Gemma didn't notice the women approaching. Sitting on the stool, she leaned over and pulled weeds from the ground before tossing them in a pile.

"Hello, Mrs. Francas," Danielle greeted her.

Gemma sat upright and turned around quickly. With the tip of one gloved finger, she shoved the front brim of her hat up to get a better view. "Danielle Marlow? You're back again?"

"Sorry to bother you, but I have a quick question," Danielle said as she and Heather approached.

Gemma remained sitting on the stool, but now faced the two women. She pulled off her gloves and tossed them on the ground. "What can I help you with?"

Danielle motioned to Heather. "This is my friend Heather, Heather Donovan."

Gemma gave Heather a nod and looked back at Danielle.

"It's about that quilt," Danielle began. "I was wondering if rather than keep it, I should return it to your stepdaughters. After all, it was made for them."

185

Gemma shrugged. "I doubt they would even care. They've never been particularly interested in that sort of thing."

"Perhaps you could ask them the next time you talk to them?" Danielle asked. "The only reason I question keeping it, I lost my parents when I was in college, and if I found out my mother made a quilt especially for me, and it was out there, I would really want to have it."

"I doubt I'll be talking to the girls anytime soon. When I said they weren't particularly interested in that sort of thing, I meant anything that had to do with family. The girls broke their poor father's heart, just leaving town and never coming to visit. They didn't even bother attending his funeral. Such selfish girls. What do they say? The apple doesn't fall far from the tree."

"Oh, I'm sorry," Danielle stammered.

"And they never knew Betsy. I seriously don't think they would care. If you like the quilt, go ahead and keep it. After all, your friend bought it for you. It's yours."

"I suppose you know them better than anyone." Danielle paused and looked around the yard. "Your yard is beautiful. I love all your flowers."

Gemma smiled at Danielle. "Thank you. I planted everything in this yard. Dan had the house built for him and Betsy, and he moved into it just two months after she ran off. When we got married almost two years later and I moved in, he had done nothing to the yard. He hadn't planted a single flower."

"You did a beautiful job. I don't have much of a green thumb." Danielle smiled at Gemma. "Your flowers remind me of my dear friend Marie Nichols. She loved to garden. Did you know Marie?"

"Just who she was."

"Did you go to church with her?" Danielle asked.

"No." Gemma casually mentioned the church she attended with her husband and added, "But I stopped going after Dan died. I was never much of a church person before I married Dan. But it seemed to be important to him."

"Well, anyway, you have a beautiful yard. Your husband was lucky you have such a green thumb."

"Thank you."

Danielle smiled sweetly. "Where did your husband live while his house was being built?"

Gemma stared blankly at Danielle a few moments before answering, "A friend of one of his relatives let him stay at her house while she was out of town."

"In this neighborhood?" Danielle asked.

Gemma shook her head. "No."

"Where was the house?" Danielle persisted.

Gemma frowned. "Why are you asking?"

Danielle shrugged. "No particular reason. I was just curious."

"Well, I don't remember where it was. That was a long time ago. Over forty years." Gemma leaned over and picked up her garden gloves off the ground. She started pulling them on. "I need to finish weeding this flowerbed. But I really don't think the girls would be interested in the quilt. Just keep it."

"SHE'S LYING," Heather said as they drove back to Marlow House. "She knows where that house is."

"I agree. If she knows Betsy was murdered and someone put her body in the neighbor's root cellar, she also knows it was found. I'm sure it was in all the newspapers back then. Which makes me wonder, what was said in the local newspaper when the body was found?"

Heather looked at Danielle. "What do you mean?"

"The chief said when they found the remains, they tried looking for young women who disappeared during a specific time frame. I wonder what they put in the paper. Did they say she had long strawberry blonde hair? Did they give an estimated age at the time of death?"

Heather leaned back in the seat and considered what Danielle had said. "If I had a friend who tells me she's leaving, and I never see her again, and they find a body next door to where I last saw her, a body with the same hair color and age, who died around the last time I saw my friend, I would be asking questions."

"They found the body after Dan died. Let's say he was responsible for Betsy's death," Danielle began. "Let's say Gemma had nothing to do with the murder. That she assumes Betsy is still alive, even though she has never seen her again. But then she reads about the body and starts wondering if Betsy came back, and in a fit of anger, Dan murdered his wife and buried her body. I can understand how Gemma wouldn't say anything. Especially if she loved him. That would be a horrible thing to have to acknowledge."

"I still think Gemma could be the murderer," Heather said. "If that's the case, then it's obvious why she said nothing when the body was found."

"And it is always possible no one murdered Betsy. Those may not be her remains, and she could be alive and well somewhere," Danielle reminded her. "Gemma claims she and Dan married after he divorced Betsy."

"Ian said he couldn't find anything about the divorce or on Dan's supposed second marriage. I was curious if a person could get a divorce in Oregon if their spouse just took off and disappeared and wasn't around to sign divorce papers. From what I read online, it looks like it might be possible with no-fault divorces, and it looks like Oregon had no-fault divorce when Betsy left. But don't quote me on that," Heather said.

"I was thinking about that, too. But I wonder if they would still have to show they tried to contact her. If one of them killed Betsy, I don't think they would want to draw attention to the fact that no one can find her."

"Gemma gave you the name of the church she and Dan attended. If they got married, I would assume they got married there. I wonder if Ian checked those records," Heather asked.

"I'll mention it to Ian."

"It would be easier if the chief would just ask Betsy's brother for his DNA," Heather grumbled.

"There is one thing I don't understand," Danielle said.

"What?"

"The vitriol Gemma spewed toward her stepdaughters. She raised those girls from the time they were infants." Danielle shook her head in disgust.

"I also found her attitude toward Betsy interesting. She claims—and Betsy's brother confirmed—that she had been close friends with Betsy for years. Can you imagine if after Lily had her baby, she experienced such extreme postpartum depression that she leaves, and not only don't you help her, but after she leaves, you hate not only her, but the baby she abandoned? Not even mentioning the fact of you marrying Ian if you weren't already married."

"There was obviously something more going on there. You told me Betsy's mother abandoned them, and the brother claimed it wasn't postpartum depression. I'm not sure about the mother, but I don't believe Betsy would abandon her babies unless she had postpartum depression. It doesn't matter what her mother did. When Betsy was pregnant, she made that quilt for them, and she made it with love. I can feel the love when I look at it."

TWENTY-NINE

M illie Samson walked into the museum's storage room on Saturday morning to find it had been reorganized. The last time she had been at the museum had been the previous Saturday, but she had left town for a few days to visit her cousin in Salem after one of the newer docents, Trish Bean, offered to fill in for the days Millie normally served as docent.

Millie stood speechless in the storage room, when she heard a voice behind her call out, "Surprise! What do you think?"

Millie turned around and found herself looking at Trish Bean. "Well?" Trish's grin broadened.

Millie waved her hand in a pointing gesture and asked, "Did you do this?"

"I did," Trish said proudly. "It was slow yesterday, and I didn't want to sit around. I wanted to surprise you and get this storage room in shape. It was so disorganized."

Millie stared dumbly at Trish, suddenly regretting ever encouraging the woman to docent for the museum. Millie wasn't just a docent, she was also a member of the historical society's board of directors, which oversaw the museum. Since Ben Smith's death, she had assumed more responsibility regarding the operation of the museum.

Trish attended church with Millie, and because of her outgoing nature and local knowledge, Millie assumed she would be a perfect docent. Trish hadn't been at the museum long enough to familiarize herself with the storage room, plus her docent duties did not extend to this section of the museum.

"Well, how does it look?" Trish asked again.

"Uh…I am a little surprised." Millie smiled weakly.

"Here, let me show you around. Everything was all jumbled up. No real organization. I put all the photographs in that box." Trish pointed to a cardboard storage box on a nearby shelf. While Trish prattled on, Millie noticed the display partitions shoved against one wall. She walked to one and pulled it out. Last week, photographs for the tunnel display had covered the partition.

Millie turned to Trish. "Where are all the pictures that were on here?"

"I put them in the photo box, of course." Trish pointed back up at the cardboard storage box on the shelf. "They were pinned on those partitions, and there weren't any labels or anything, so I figured we would have more room in here if we put all the photos in one box, and that way we can shove the partitions against the wall to free up floor space. If we left the photos on the partitions in this cramped space, they were going to get ruined."

Millie groaned. "We have been putting together the tunnel display for July. It took all day to organize those photos."

"I didn't know that." Which was true. Trish hadn't been at the museum when the staff had been working on the display, and she had only seen it after coming in to fill in for Millie.

"Where's the rest of the tunnel display?" Millie asked.

"Well, I can't really say for sure, since I've never heard about a tunnel display. You should tell docents these things. I was just trying to help." With a huff, Trish turned and left the storage room.

Millie spent the next few hours moving boxes around and trying to find the parts of the tunnel display Trish had shoved in random nooks and corners of the storage room. Meanwhile, Trish assisted visitors to the museum in the display area and the gift shop in the front of the building.

"I'M GOING HOME NOW," Trish told Millie when she walked back into the storage room on Saturday afternoon. "My replacement is here."

"Trish, when you were reorganizing the storage room, there was a small box on the back shelf right here." Millie pointed to the shelf. "It had two unusual-looking keys in it. Where did you put it?"

Trish shrugged. "I don't remember seeing them."

"They were there. I saw them last Saturday when I came in."

"Well, they're obviously here somewhere. I'm sure they didn't just walk out, and I didn't take them. I just don't remember. There was so much stuff in here, just all over the place. I'm sure I put them someplace safe. They're here."

"Here where?"

"You'll just have to look, I guess. But I have to leave now. And frankly, I really don't appreciate your attitude."

Millie arched her brows. "My attitude?"

"It's not like I'm even getting paid. This is a volunteer job. You're the one who kept telling me I should docent at the museum. But all you really want is free labor, and then you don't even appreciate it. You act like I did something wrong. I came in and covered for you while you took a vacation, and when you come back, you don't even thank me. I quit. I really don't need this."

Trish turned abruptly and marched out of the museum storage room, leaving Millie speechless.

MILLIE SAT in the gift shop, talking to the afternoon docent, who had been helping at the museum for much longer than Trish.

"I should have come in and checked on her yesterday. I had no idea she was going to do that."

Millie shrugged. "I suppose it's my fault. I know how Trish can be. But I need to find those keys."

"We'll find them. They're back there somewhere. The tunnel display doesn't open until a month and a half from now, so we have plenty of time to find where she put them."

Millie let out a sigh. "You're right. To be honest, I'm more upset about her taking all the photos off the display partitions."

RODNEY HAD CHECKED into a room at the Seahorse Motel on Friday evening, telling them he needed the room for him and his brother. On Saturday morning, Rodney left his supposed brother—Clay—in the room alone with the do-not-disturb sign on the door while he made a reconnaissance mission of Marlow House. This involved driving by several times and walking by twice.

When he returned to the motel room, he brought food for Clay and himself and, while eating, hooked his laptop up to the motel's Wi-Fi and went online to Marlow House's Bed and Breakfast's website, where they found interior photos. While the official website for the bed-and-breakfast didn't include a floor plan of Marlow House, they found another website, not affiliated with the Marlows, that had a floor plan.

Their motel room included a small circular table for two, where they both sat, looking at the laptop sitting on the tabletop while they ate lunch.

Rodney's right hand held a half-eaten burger. With that hand, he pointed to the floor plan they had just brought up on the laptop's screen. "When I looked in the window, I saw the babies were sleeping in there. They had cribs set up."

Clay frowned. "In the living room? How could you see all that from the sidewalk?"

"I walked up to the front door." Rodney chuckled. "Took me right by the window."

"Isn't that kind of risky? What if someone saw you?"

"No problem. I left a religious pamphlet I'd picked up by the front door. If anyone saw me, they would just assume I was out saving souls." Rodney laughed and took a bite of his burger. With food in his mouth, he said between chews, "They were like those small playpen things. I doubt they sleep there at night."

"It's nice and close to the basement." Clay pointed to the basement on the floor plan. "That would be a hell of a lot better than having to go upstairs to grab them."

"The parents left them for about an hour with one of their neighbors. A broad who walked over from a couple of houses up the street from their place." Rodney knew what the parents, Walt and Danielle, looked like because he had already gone online to find their pictures before leaving that morning.

"Did she have long black hair? Dress like she was going to a seance?" Clay asked.

"I guess."

"It was probably Heather Donovan. Did they leave her alone with the babies?"

"I didn't see anyone else in the house."

Clay laughed. "That would be perfect."

"What are you thinking?"

"There's no guarantee they're going to have her babysit again. I know she works during the week. But she could be plan A."

"Plan A, how?"

"If they have her babysit again and leave her in the house alone with them, we can go in through the tunnel, grab all of them."

"Why would we want to grab her?"

"I said that wrong. I don't want to grab Donovan. We can slip into the house by the tunnel and put a bullet through her head. And if she has that damn pit bull that belongs to her boss with her, we can kill it, too."

"You want her dead?"

"Why not? We're already planning to get rid of the Marlows. And it would be perfect. They'd get home, find Heather dead and the babies gone, front door open. They would understand we're serious and wouldn't call the cops. They would do anything to get their babies back. No idea they're in the tunnel."

"You don't like this Heather, do you?"

"You catch on quick."

"But what if this Heather doesn't watch the babies again? We can't wait around forever. You said yourself we need to move quick."

"I know. But getting Heather would be a bonus. She was the one responsible for getting me arrested and screwing up my life. But like I said, that's plan A. And yeah, it's a long shot. We also need a plan B."

"I have a plan B," Rodney said.

"What's that?"

Rodney shoved the last bite of burger in his mouth and used his shirtsleeve to wipe off his lips. After swallowing his food, he said, "The husband came back later, and that girl you love, Heather, took off with the mom. The father stayed in the kitchen for a long time and left the babies in the living room all alone, sleeping. He never checked on them."

"Interesting."

"Kitchen is on one side of the house; the basement is on the other side. And the living room, where they are letting those babies sleep during the day, looks closer to the basement than the kitchen. We can get from the living room to the basement faster than he can get from the kitchen to the living room."

Clay nodded. "I like that."

"And we only need one kid. But we can use the second one."

Clay frowned. "How so?"

Rodney pointed to the floor plan. "There's a bedroom downstairs. We could grab both of them and then leave one in the bedroom with the door open while we go to the basement with the second one. The baby we leave in the bedroom will probably start crying. When Marlow finds his kids missing, he'll hear the baby crying and see the front door open. He'll undoubtably go to the crying kid, giving us more time to get in the tunnel."

Clay considered that plan for a moment. "There's only one problem."

"What's that?"

"Shouldn't one of us be monitoring where Marlow is at all times?"

"Yes. We'll figure something out. But this is a good start. This is going to work."

THIRTY

When Danielle and Heather returned to Marlow House, they told Walt and Marie about their afternoon. The four sat in the living room while the babies slept nearby in the portable cribs.

"If you intend to look at the church Gemma and Dan attended for a record of their marriage, don't bother looking," Marie said. "Because you won't find it."

"Is that because they didn't get married in their church?" Danielle asked.

"Exactly. While we weren't friends, there was a bit of gossip after they first moved to town. I understand that after he got the job at the hospital, he purchased a house that was already under construction, but not finished yet, which is why they stayed at Elenore Percy's house for a couple of months. After his wife abandoned him and their newborns, he started going to a church my friend attended. I suspect he was looking for support."

"He certainly needed it," Danielle said.

"My friend told me there were a couple of ladies who were more than willing to step in and help him. After all, he had a good job, a brand-new house, and a ready-made family, which appeals to some women." Marie shrugged.

"But there was Gemma," Danielle said.

Marie nodded. "Yes, after a few months, she started going to church with him. He introduced her to everyone as an old family friend. And after a couple of years, they announced their marriage. My friend assumed they had their wedding in Vancouver, where they were both from. My friend mentioned they were private people, and after they married, they continued attending the church, but the husband wasn't very sociable after the marriage. The couple kept to themselves."

"Ian said he looked for their marriage records in Vancouver and found nothing," Heather reminded them.

LATER THAT EVENING, after Heather headed home and they had dinner, Danielle sat on the sofa in Marlow House's living room, with her feet propped up on the coffee table. Her thighs cradled Addison, who wore a unicorn-patterned cozy sleeper. Addison's tiny feet gently tapped against Danielle's belly as the back of her head rested on her mother's knees. The baby's tiny fingers wrapped around Danielle's thumbs as mother and daughter gazed into each other's eyes.

Walt sat next to Danielle, similarly holding his son. Faint gurgling sounds drifted up from the happy infants.

"It's adorable how you each have a baby to spoil," Marie said. She sat across from the sofa on a recliner.

"You know, they say you shouldn't hold babies all the time, that you'll spoil them. That you should let them cry," Danielle said before leaning down and kissing the top of Addison's brow.

"Oh, posh." Marie shook her head. "Give them all the love you want. You can never spoil a baby with love. And they grow up much too fast. Enjoy this time. Before you know it, they'll be all grown up, and you'll be asking yourself where the time has gone."

Danielle smiled up at Marie. "I realize how lucky we are. Walt and I have the luxury of enjoying this brief time with our babies. We don't have to worry about finding childcare so we can go to work. Or worry about making money to put a roof over our heads. We are so blessed."

"I am forever thankful for this amazing second chance," Walt muttered, his eyes still focused on his son.

Marie chuckled. "The only thing you two have to worry about is a pesky poltergeist."

"If we didn't have you and Eva, I'm not sure I'd feel this blessed right now," Danielle confessed. "Thank you, Marie. You have no idea how much we appreciate you and Eva."

Marie smiled. "I'm more than happy to help. And I know Eva feels the same way."

"Where is Eva?" Walt asked.

"She's still upstairs, determined to figure out what exactly is haunting the nursery. She sees this as a challenge," Marie said.

Danielle glanced down to Addison, sighed, and looked back up to Marie while Addison continued to hold tightly onto her thumbs. "Even if the chief asks Betsy's brother to give a DNA test and can prove she was murdered, there is no guarantee it will do anything about our poltergeist, or whatever it is."

SATURDAY NIGHT, Walt moved the portable cribs back upstairs, and once again the twins slept in their parents' bedroom instead of their nursery. The poltergeist hadn't thrown anything since throwing the stuffed animal at Joanne on Friday. But the knocking continued and was always timed perfectly for when the twins fussed from hunger.

On Sunday morning, Walt and Danielle woke up to clear blue skies and by midmorning realized they were experiencing unseasonably warm weather for May. Walt suggested they take a drive with the twins and even put the double stroller in the back of the Flex, should they decide to take the babies for a stroll while out.

"Where do you want to go?" Walt asked as he backed out of the driveway. Danielle sat in the passenger seat with the twins in the back seat in their car seats.

"This may seem weird, but I'd like to drive by and check out the Beckett house."

"Why?"

Danielle shrugged. "If this thing we're experiencing really is connected to the quilt, I guess I'd like to see where the quilt spent the last forty-five years."

"Do you have the address?" Walt asked.

"Yeah, hold on." Danielle pulled out her cellphone and looked up the address.

Ten minutes later, Walt pulled up to the front of the Beckett house in time to see Bill Jones putting up a For Sale sign for Adam. Walt parked a few feet from the sign. Bill turned around and noticed Walt and Danielle sitting in the now parked vehicle. Danielle got out of the car and walked to Bill, leaving Walt with the twins.

"Is Adam making you work on a Sunday?" Danielle teased.

"He called me this morning and told me he got the signed contract faxed to his office last night. Said if I was out this way, he'd appreciate if I could put up a sign. I was out this way, so…" Bill motioned to the house. "You interested?"

"No. I just, well, Lily bought me a quilt from the Beckett estate sale. I was just curious what the Beckett house looked like."

"Ahh, the haunted quilt." Bill chuckled.

Danielle arched her brows. "You heard?"

"Yes. Adam told me about it. We wonder if your ghost has come through the tunnel and is moving books around in the Crawford house."

"Wow, really? I didn't hear that."

Bill shrugged.

"And that doesn't sound crazy?"

Bill's gray eyes studied Danielle for a minute. Finally, he said, "Since you moved to town, crazy is kind of the normal."

Danielle laughed. "Well, I'm not sure how I feel about that."

Bill shrugged again and picked up his tools. "Hey, are your kids in the car with your husband?"

"Yes."

"Can I have a look? Can't get over the fact you had them at Adam's house. Like I said, crazy."

Danielle rolled her eyes, turned around, and motioned for Bill to follow her. He walked to Walt's side of the car, greeted him, and then peeked in the back window.

"Pretty cute," Bill said.

They chatted for a few minutes, and after Bill left and Danielle got back in the car, Walt looked up at the Beckett house. "Well, the good news, the house is still standing and has a roof."

"What do you mean by that?"

"It survived the quilt, so no reason we can't. Where to now? Have any request?"

"Yes, but this is an even weirder request, but it's so pretty out, and they have nice sidewalks and lots of flowers."

WALT DROVE the car into the cemetery parking lot, parked, and turned off the ignition. "I didn't expect we'd be trying out the stroller here for the first time."

"It's pretty, with nice walkways. And I'd kind of like to see Betsy's grave. The chief told me where to find it."

"You thinking her spirit might be lingering around?"

Danielle shrugged.

"Considering Eva and Marie frequent this place, if Betsy has been here for the last forty-five years or so, they would have run into her," Walt reminded her.

"True. But I still want to see it."

Ten minutes later, Walt had the double stroller out of the back of the car, set up, and both babies snugly inside. Together, Walt and Danielle pushed the stroller down the walkway.

"It's peaceful here. I used to hate coming to places like this," Danielle said.

It took them fifteen minutes to find Betsy's grave. It wasn't an unmarked grave in that it had a modest stone marker that said

Unknown Woman, along with the date the remains had been found. Danielle stood there a moment, looking down at the marker.

After a few moments of silence, Walt let out a sigh. "Okay, I'll say it. Betsy, Betsy Francas, are you here? If you are, we want to talk to you."

They stood there for a few more minutes in silence. Finally, Danielle said, "I doubt she's here."

Walt smiled. "I agree."

They headed back toward the parking lot but took another route. They had been walking for about five minutes when Danielle stopped abruptly and said, "Look. It's Pamela Beckett's grave."

Walt stopped by Danielle's side and looked down at the marker. He could tell by its condition it had been set recently.

"Hello, Pamela," Danielle told the marker. "We drove by your house a little while ago. It just got put on the market."

Neither Danielle nor Walt expected a response to Danielle's impromptu greeting, and both jumped back a few inches when a woman's apparition appeared before them while asking, "What were you doing at my house?"

Danielle's eyes widened at the sight. "Pamela?"

The spirit cocked her head slightly to the right and asked, "You can see me?"

"We both can," Walt said.

Pamela looked at Walt and frowned. "You're Walt Marlow."

"I am."

"You're something of a legend around here. I recognize you from your portrait. I saw it at the museum back when I could still get out a little."

"I'm surprised Eva and Marie didn't mention you were here," Danielle said.

"I've heard of them too, but I haven't seen them." Pamela shrugged.

"I have a question for you," Danielle asked.

"You never answered my question. Why were you at my house?"

"I wanted to see it because a friend of mine purchased a quilt for me from your estate sale."

Pamela stared at Danielle. "What quilt?"

"It was a baby quilt. Made for twins. As you can see, we have twins." Danielle motioned to the stroller.

Pamela shook her head. "No. You really need to get rid of that. I should have burned it years ago. I told them to get rid of it. They weren't supposed to sell it to anyone."

"What is wrong with the quilt?" Walt asked.

Pamela looked at Walt. "My mother gave it to me when I was a child. At first, I figured my brothers were playing tricks on me. It would move. It would never stay put. And if I took it into a room, the door would slam. I'd get in trouble for slamming doors. Sometimes doors would slam, and it wouldn't even be in the room. I tried to get rid of it, but it came back. You should get rid of it."

"Did it ever hurt anyone?" Walt asked.

Pamela frowned at Walt as if she didn't understand the question. "What do you mean, hurt anyone? It was a quilt. How could it hurt anyone?"

THIRTY-ONE

W hen Walt and Danielle left the cemetery, Danielle asked Walt to stop off at the mini-mart to pick up a bottle of water. After they arrived at the mini-mart, Walt stayed in the car with the babies while Danielle got out of the vehicle. After closing the door behind her, she looked back in the car through the open window.

"You want something to drink?" Danielle asked.

"See if they have any ginger ale."

Danielle wrinkled her nose. "Seriously? A ginger ale?"

Walt shrugged. "It was my favorite when I was a kid."

"What if they don't have any?"

"A cola, then."

"Want anything to eat?" Danielle asked.

"No, just a drink."

"Okay." Danielle turned from the car and headed into the mini-mart.

When she reached the cooler, she recognized a familiar face, Heather.

"Hey, how did you get away from the babies?" Heather greeted Danielle.

"Walt's in the car with them. We took a little drive, and I'm getting us something to drink. Thanks again for sitting with the twins today." Danielle didn't mention Pamela's ghost because she was afraid the man looking in the cooler nearby might overhear the conversation.

"Hey, no problem. Anytime I'm free, I'd be happy to help you out. And I was looking at the calendar on my phone a little while ago, and it reminded me your wedding anniversary is less than two weeks away." Heather was referring to the date Walt and Danielle had eloped, not the wedding they'd held at Marlow House nine months later. "I think it falls on a Friday. If you and Walt want to go out that night, I would be more than happy to babysit."

"That's really sweet of you. I'll talk to Walt about it."

"And if you want to go somewhere tomorrow, I'm free."

"Don't you work tomorrow?"

Heather shook her head. "No, Chris is going to be out of town for a couple of days. He's leaving tonight. He told me to take the next couple of days off."

"Is Hunny going with him?"

"Yep. So I'm free if you want me to babysit the twins tomorrow. Brian's working, so we won't be doing anything."

"That's super sweet, but with everything going on." Danielle glanced around, not wanting to say too much. The man lingering by the beer coolers finally made his choice and now stood in the aisle next to her, browsing through the snack foods. She looked back at Heather.

"That's why you need to get out. How about Pearl Cove's new Monday brunch?"

Danielle grinned. "Lily told me about it. I doubt it's as crowded as their Sunday brunch."

"I only mention it because tomorrow is Monday. I think you should go. With all that's been happening, it would be good for you and Walt. I'll come over in the morning if you want. Like I said, I'm free."

"Really?"

"Yep. Talk to Walt about it."

"HEATHER WAS IN THE STORE," Danielle said as she climbed into the passenger side of the car, carrying her purchases.

"I thought that was her car in the parking lot. I figured that's why you were taking so long."

Danielle glanced in the back seat. Both babies slept. She handed Walt his drink, set her bottle of water on her lap, shut her door, and started putting on her seatbelt. "Remember that new Monday brunch thing at Pearl Cove Lily was telling me about?"

Walt opened his drink. "Yes, what about it?"

Danielle picked up her bottle of water and opened it. "Want to go tomorrow? Heather offered to babysit; she has the day off. And with Marie and Eva there, the babies will be fine." Danielle took a drink of water while waiting for Walt's reaction.

He glanced in the back seat. He looked back at Danielle. "That would be nice."

The next moment Heather walked out of the store with a paper sack filled with her purchases and, behind her, the man Danielle had seen by the cooler. He, too, held a paper sack with purchases.

Danielle leaned out the window and yelled, "Hey, Heather, we'd like to take you up on your offer to babysit tomorrow morning."

Heather stopped walking and grinned at Danielle. "What time you want me to be there?"

Danielle glanced at Walt.

"How about nine?" Walt suggested.

Danielle looked back out the window. "How about nine?"

"I'll be there!"

BEFORE RETURNING TO MARLOW HOUSE, Danielle made one last request. She wanted to drive by the property the Jamesons once owned. According to Marie, it was located on the outskirts of Frederickport. Homes along that side of town were on larger parcels of land, some being an acre or more.

Walt turned down the street and parked between what had once been the Jamesons' house and the house that once belonged to Elenore Percy. A For Sale sign stood in front of the Jameson house. The chief had explained the house had been vacant for the last couple of years, and its current owner had torn down the barn before putting the property on the market. Danielle sat in the passenger side of the car, staring at the buildings behind the For Sale sign. Nothing looked familiar, and she assumed it was because, in her nightmare, she'd looked at it from a different angle.

Danielle glanced over to the two-story farm-style home Elenore Percy had once owned, and spied an American flag hanging from a flagpole mounted on the front of the house. It waved gently in the afternoon breeze. There was a car parked in the driveway, and a gray cat slept on the first step of the front porch. Like the Jameson property, the house that once belonged to Elenore Percy did not look familiar to Danielle, but she had only seen the inside of the house in her dream.

Danielle turned to Walt. "Do you mind if I walk down the side of the Jameson property where it borders the Percy house? I'll stay on the Jameson side since no one's there."

"Okay, but please stay where I can see you. Just in case."

Danielle arched her brows. "In case of what?"

"You never know what you might run into when walking around on a vacant piece of property."

Danielle unfastened her seatbelt. "Okay." She leaned over to Walt and dropped a quick kiss on his lips. "I'll stay where you can see me. And I'll only be a minute." She glanced in the back seat. "And those two should be waking up pretty soon, anyway. I'd like to get home before my milk drops."

Walt grinned at Danielle. "Where did the romance go?"

Danielle laughed.

SHE WONDERED if they came to look at the house, but only the woman got out of the car. Ever since they had put up the For Sale sign, more and more people had been stopping by, walking around, and a few made rude comments about her murder. They even made jokes about it, which she found insensitive.

Betsy hadn't always known she was dead. It had been dark where her killer had left her, and she hadn't seen her body when the root cellar door had slammed shut.

She didn't follow her killer, but stayed quiet in the darkness until she felt it was safe for her to leave. By the time she got the courage to escape the root cellar and sneak into the house where she had been staying prior to the attack, Dan was no longer there, nor were her daughters. Their cribs had been removed from their upstairs bedroom.

Not sure whom to trust, Betsy stayed in the house, but hid in the attic when Elenore returned. She remained in hiding until one day she looked out the attic window and spied police cars next door and decided she needed to go to the police and tell them someone had tried to kill her.

When she walked next door, none of the police officers would pay attention to her, as they were all busy looking down into the root cellar, its doors now wide open.

Curious, Betsy approached the root cellar and looked inside. Sunlight streamed in the once dark cavity, and she spied two police officers standing inside the cellar, looking down at something. Betsy moved closer until she stood between the two officers. She looked in utter horror at what had captured their attention.

Curled up on the dirt floor were decomposed human remains partially buried in dirt. She remembered reading once that your hair keeps growing after you die. Whoever this person had been now had long hair, a similar color to hers. One officer knelt down and, with a gloved hand, gently brushed away some of the dirt, exposing the blouse worn by the corpse.

Betsy recognized the blouse. She had made one just like it before she got pregnant. Later, she'd used the leftover fabric from the blouse in a quilt. In that moment, Betsy understood the truth. Her killer had been successful.

After the police removed what remained of her body from the

site, Betsy stayed. There was no other option because she didn't have any place to go. Perhaps the killer would return to the scene of the crime. Didn't someone once say the killer always returns to the scene of the crime? If she followed the killer, she might find her daughters.

Betsy continued watching the woman from a distance. But then the sounds of babies crying caught her attention. She instinctively knew those cries came not from one baby, but from two. The woman stopped, turned around, and glanced back toward the car she had come from. Instead of coming closer to where Betsy stood, the woman rushed back to the car.

After the woman got into the vehicle and drove off, the sound of the crying babies began to fade. Betsy stared at the vehicle as it drove away. One thought jumped out at Betsy. *My babies!*

Unable to resist, Betsy did something she hadn't done since they found her body. She left the property, following the faint cries of two babies.

THIRTY-TWO

Betsy stood outside Marlow House, looking through the living room window, the sun setting behind her. Each time someone from inside the house glanced her way, she stepped out of sight. Yet considering how the police had reacted when they discovered her body in the root cellar, she doubted living people could see her.

After following the couple's car to Marlow House, she had first perched high on a tree branch, affording her a clear view of the garage and side door into the house. The woman and man brought the two babies from the car to the house. Intense longing and grief welled up inside Betsy at the sight of the two infants.

When they disappeared into the house, she moved from the tree and peeked in the windows on the first floor. It was at the living room window where she found them again. They each changed a baby's diaper. It was then she realized these were not her babies. Mesmerized, she studied the couple.

Betsy couldn't remember Dan ever changing a diaper. After the diaper change, the woman sat on the sofa and nursed both babies. Betsy's mother hadn't nursed her. In her mother's time, baby formula companies discouraged women from breastfeeding. When Betsy became pregnant, she wanted to try breastfeeding, as many mothers her age began doing again. She tried, but she could not produce enough milk for one baby, much less two.

After nursing the babies, the woman placed them each in a crib, where they now slept. Betsy watched as the man and woman sat together on the sofa, each reading a book.

Betsy's eyes widened when something that resembled snow fell from the living room ceiling. Neither the man nor woman looked startled by this bizarre occurrence and simply glanced briefly to the ceiling. The next moment, two women appeared in the living room, standing before the sofa. One was an elderly woman and the other a younger woman who looked as if she came from the early 1900s.

"Ghosts?" Betsy muttered to herself. She had never seen a ghost before, yet she assumed that was what she now was. The man and woman seem unfazed by the sudden appearance of the two women and began talking to them. This confused her.

Betsy moved upwards, her feet leaving the ground, until she reached the windows of the second floor. She looked inside through the first window she came to and spied a bedroom with a fireplace. She moved over to the next window and looked inside. It was the babies' nursery.

Betsy's gaze fell on the two cribs, and she instantly thought of her daughters. She looked around the room and then froze. Her quilt, the one she had lovingly made while pregnant, was in the room. Someone had placed it over the back of a rocking chair. *Why is it here?* she wondered.

Without thinking, Betsy moved through the window into the room and stood before the rocking chairs. She reached out, her fingertips moving through the quilt. She closed her eyes. Anger and grief swelled up inside her. Betsy opened her eyes again and looked to the nursery doorway leading into the hallway. She moved toward it, floating instead of walking. She did not look back and didn't realize the quilt had moved from the rocker and now followed her.

BEFORE RETURNING to his motel room after going to the mini-mart, Rodney had stopped by the front office to tell them he and his brother would leave early in the morning, so he wanted to settle up now. Rodney had no intention of telling Clay he had, in essence, just checked out.

When he returned to the motel room, he found Clay sprawled out on one bed, television remote in hand, channel surfing. Rodney carried a grocery bag and several bags of food from a fast-food restaurant. He walked into the motel room, shut the door behind him, and headed for the small table. Clay turned off the television and tossed the remote on the bed as Rodney set the sacks on the table.

"Did you get some beer?" Clay asked.

In answer to the question, Rodney pulled two beers from one sack, tossed one to Clay, and sat down on a chair facing the beds. He opened his beer and looked at Clay. "You know that long shot you were talking about?"

Clay frowned. "What long shot?"

"Plan A." Rodney took a swig of beer and then told Clay what he had overheard at the mini-mart.

"Holy crap, are you kidding me?"

"She said her boss is going out of town tomorrow."

Clay frowned. "I wonder if he's leaving the dog with her."

"Is the dog's name Hunny?"

Clay nodded. "Yeah, that's the mutt's name."

"He's taking the dog with him. This means we need to go over to the house later tonight. You'll have to spend the night in the tunnel. After you get in, I'll close the door and move the bookshelf back just in case the Realtor shows up tomorrow. We can't have them walking in with the bookshelf pulled away from the wall."

"What are you going to do?" Clay asked.

"Since the walkie-talkies don't work in the tunnel, you'll need to be on the other side by nine." On Saturday, Rodney had purchased some walkie-talkies, which they had tried out in the tunnel on Saturday night. They had discovered the walkie-talkies did not work in the tunnel, yet they could get reception after leaving the tunnel on the Marlow side, just before the entrance to the Marlow House's basement. "Donovan is supposed to get there at nine, and I would expect the Marlows to leave within a half an hour after that. I'll be hanging out in the alley and will contact you as soon as the Marlows drive away. So you need to be out of the tunnel by then so you can use the walkie-talkie."

"Where you gonna sleep tonight?"

"I'll come back here and get up before sunrise and find a comfy place in the alley, out of sight, to hole up."

AFTER DARKNESS FELL, Rodney removed all his belongings from the motel room, along with a bag of trash. Clay didn't question Rodney when he left nothing behind, even though Clay believed Rodney would be returning there to sleep for the night. Clay understood whenever Rodney was doing a job, he wanted the freedom to take off if something went sideways. He also didn't want to leave his DNA in the room, which was why he always packed up his trash and disposed of it at another location.

Rodney drove into the parking lot under the pier, parked, and turned off his ignition. He removed the bag of trash from the back of his truck and put it in a nearby trash can. A few minutes later, he and Clay walked north up the beach, each carrying a fishing pole and tackle box. The fishing poles were for show, and the tackle boxes held items they needed for the job. When they reached the house, Clay quickly unlocked the back door using the credit card his son had taken from his wife. After unlocking the door, he handed the credit card to Rodney because Clay believed Rodney would need to unlock the door the next time.

They had left the fishing poles outside, hidden under the bushes along the property's western border, but they took the tackle boxes inside. Once in the living room, they slid the bookshelf over instead of bothering to remove the books like they had previously done. Rodney helped Clay climb inside the tunnel, and then handed Clay the tackle boxes after removing what he needed.

After shoving the bookcase back in place, Rodney smiled in satisfaction. He had no intention of ever seeing Clay Bowman again. His plan differed from Clay's. Instead of waiting for Danielle to return to Marlow House with the gold and necklace, he would wait for her in the garage. He planned to kill her, leave her body in the garage, and take off with a fortune before anyone realized what had happened. He didn't doubt they would eventually find Clay in the tunnel with Walt's and Heather's dead bodies and the missing infants.

Rodney had no plans to return to the motel. Instead, he intended to crash at the house, set the timer on his watch to wake up before sunrise, and be in the alley behind Marlow House before daybreak to hide in the bushes. He wasn't worried about leaving his truck in the pier parking lot overnight, as Clay had explained vehicles often parked overnight in the pier parking lot.

IT WASN'T the sunshine filling the bedroom that woke Rodney on Monday morning. It was the sound of someone slamming the front door shut. Rodney bolted up in bed and cursed to himself. He snatched his gun and walkie-talkie from the nightstand and rolled off the mattress to the floor, not wanting to be seen by whoever had just entered the house. He turned off the walkie-talkie. The last thing he needed was for Clay's voice to come blasting through its speaker and draw attention from whoever had just entered the house.

Rodney had slept on top of the bedspread fully clothed, so if someone looked in the bedroom, they would only notice him if they walked into the room. If necessary, he could use his gun.

He glanced at his watch; it was 8:10 a.m. He had overslept. Later, he would check his watch and discover he had set his alarm for p.m. instead of a.m.

Holding his gun in his right hand and leaving the walkie-talkie on the floor by the bed, Rodney crawled to the partially open doorway and looked out to the living room. A man stood in front of the bookshelf, his back to Rodney. The man wore jeans, work boots, a blue work shirt, and held a toolbox. The man set the toolbox on the floor and shoved the bookshelf to one side.

Rodney knew if the man opened the door to the tunnel, he would see the lights from Clay's lanterns. If that happened, Rodney would be forced to shoot the man.

To Rodney's surprise, the man did not open the door. Instead, he took out a cordless screwdriver and a handful of screws, which he screwed into the holes along the door's edge, locking the door shut. There was now no way for Clay to escape the tunnel without going through the Marlows' basement.

After securing the door shut, the man moved the bookshelf back to its original place, put his cordless screwdriver back in his toolbox, and left the house. Rodney crawled to the bedroom window and peeked out through the blinds. The man climbed into a work truck and then drove away.

Rodney slumped back against a wall and looked again at his watch. He didn't have that much time to get to the alleyway behind Marlow House, and now he couldn't do it under the cover of darkness.

He stood up, shoved his gun in his coat pocket, and picked up the walkie-talkie and turned it on. There was no static, and Rodney assumed Clay's walkie-talkie was still off. Time was running out.

THIRTY-THREE

R odney walked down Beach Drive carrying two fishing poles. He wore the same clothes he'd had on the night before, denims, a long-sleeved navy-blue T-shirt, and a dark gray, bulky down jacket, with a gray baseball hat and an old pair of black athletic work shoes. Before leaving the tunnel house, he had shoved his gun in one jacket pocket, with the walkie-talkie in the other.

On the other side of the street was Marlow House, with its front living room window blinds wide open. A man stood in the living room, but Rodney didn't want to stare or stop to get a better look, so he kept walking.

He had just passed Marlow House when he spied Heather Donovan on the other side of the street, walking from her house to Marlow House. At the mini-mart yesterday, he'd worn a black hoodie instead of the bulky jacket, and a different baseball hat, so he didn't think she would recognize him, plus he doubted she had even noticed him in the store.

Rodney glanced at his watch. It was almost nine. He should have been in the alley by now, but by the time the guy had finished bolting down the tunnel door, it had been past 8:30. And before Rodney could leave the house, he'd had to use the bathroom.

After he passed Heather's house, he crossed over to her side of the street and sprinted up to the road leading to the alley. A few minutes later, as he started down the alley, he spied the Marlows' Packard coming in his direction. Rodney stopped a moment and watched them drive by. Had they been in their other car, he wouldn't have stopped. But he imagined they were used to people stopping and staring at them when they drove that car. He thought it would have looked suspicious had he pretended to ignore it as it drove by. After a moment, he started back up the alley, looking for the hiding place he had previously staked out.

BETSY DIDN'T UNDERSTAND why her daughters' quilt was in this house, with these people. She still wasn't sure if they could see her if she showed herself, but she knew they saw the other two ghosts. At least, she assumed they were ghosts. She assumed she was a ghost. It was all too confusing.

One thing she knew, she missed her daughters and was drawn to the other twins, who now napped in the living room. Last night they had taken them upstairs to the parents' room to sleep. She wanted to get closer to the babies because she knew somehow they could make her feel closer to her own daughters.

This morning, they'd brought them back downstairs. She hid behind the door and listened as they talked about going out to breakfast and how someone named Heather would come over to watch them, along with Marie and Eva. She had already figured out those were the names of the other two ghosts.

This morning, the one called Eva mentioned the quilt was missing again, and she wondered if they were talking about her quilt. But then she found her quilt, no longer upstairs, but sitting on the floor by an open door. Curious, she wondered where the open doorway led. She moved through the doorway to investigate.

Betsy floated down the stairs to the basement, and to her surprise, a man stepped out from the darkness, holding a gun. He clearly could not see her. He held what looked like a small radio next to his right ear. A crackling sound came from the radio.

"Rodney, I'm in the basement," the man said into the radio.

"Heather's alone in the house. Don't drag this on. Find her and put a bullet in her head. Leave the ransom note we prepared on her body. Grab the babies before you do anything else. You need to get them in the tunnel as soon as possible, in case the parents come home early," a voice on the walkie-talkie said.

"You're kidnapping the babies!" Betsy roared. He didn't even flinch.

"I'm turning off the walkie-talkie," the man said into the device. "I don't need to warn Donovan that I'm here."

Betsy tried grabbing the gun from the man, but her hand slipped through his, and then he walked through her body.

Not willing to let what had happened to her happen to Heather, or let anyone harm the babies, Betsy floated up the stairs, reaching the landing on the first floor before he was halfway up the stairs.

A WOMAN'S scream caught the attention of Heather, Eva, and Marie. They had been in the living room with the babies, and all three moved quickly into the entry hall just in time to witness a woman's transparent apparition move down the entry hall from the basement, reminding Heather of an incoming tornado, with long strawberry blonde hair cascading around her body.

The apparition reached out her hands to Heather. "He plans to kill you! He's after the babies."

The next moment, Clay stepped into sight. He spied Heather and without hesitation aimed his gun in her direction. Marie's energy was primed to snatch the gun from his hand, but the quilt beat her to it, wrapping itself around him until he dropped the gun.

Clay hadn't yet processed the fact a blanket had disarmed him, and he reached down to the floor to pick up the gun, but Marie was quicker, and the gun flew from the floor before he could pick it up, landing in a light fixture, out of Clay's reach.

In shock, Heather stared at Clay Bowman, who glared angrily in her direction. Enraged, Clay walked toward Heather, prepared to kill her with his bare hands, and unaware they weren't alone. But before he took two steps, a ball of black fur and razor-sharp claws flew into his face. Clay wailed in pain, unable to push away the angry feline.

Stunned at Max's attack, Heather stood with the spirits and watched as Clay, in a panic, tried to get the cat off his face. He fell to the floor and rolled around in pain, his hands injured by the claws as he unsuccessfully attempted to pry the rabid animal from his face.

"That's enough, Max," Marie told the cat before lifting the still hissing ball of fur and claws from Clay.

Heather cringed at the damage Max had inflicted.

"I'm going to kill you and that cat!" Clay stumbled to his feet.

Marie's energy threw Clay to the floor, and when it did, the walkie-talkie fell out of his pocket. He tried to reach for it, but Marie released her energy from Clay momentarily, pushing the walkie-talkie out of his reach before pinning him to the floor again.

Betsy pointed to the walkie-talkie. "He was talking to someone named Rodney. Rodney is helping him!"

"Let's get him tied up, shall we, before we have to deal with whoever else is out there," Marie suggested. "I need some rope."

"I'll get something," Heather said before dashing off. She returned a few minutes later carrying two rolls of duct tape. "This is the only thing I could find."

Marie eyed the duct tape. "Well, we must make do. Heather dear, can you please start one roll for me? Pull off about two feet."

Clay, who continued to lie on the ground, confused why he couldn't stand up, watched as Heather pulled a long strip of duct tape from the roll, yet did not tear it off.

"What do you think you're going to do with that?" Clay barked at Heather.

Heather just smiled and let go of the duct tape.

Still on the floor, Clay stared at the roll of tape floating in his direction, the piece Heather had pulled from the roll waving like a strange tail. He didn't need Marie's energy to hold him in place at that moment. Mesmerized, his eyes widened in horror as he began rolling down the hallway while the tape wrapped around him, securely wrapping him in duct tape, holding down his arms and then his legs. When Marie depleted that roll of duct tape, she started on the second until Clay lay helpless on the floor, resembling a mummy with bandages pulled from its face to reveal bloody scars.

"How did he get in here?" Eva asked.

"He was in the basement. They talked about a tunnel," Betsy explained.

"I'll be right back." Eva disappeared.

Since Clay could not see or hear the spirits, he assumed he was alone in the room with Heather.

"What are you going to do?" Clay growled.

"I think we need to find Rodney," Heather said.

Clay glared at Heather. "What do you know about Rodney?"

Eva returned the next moment. "No one is in the tunnel, but that's clearly how Clay gained entrance. The doors on the Marlow end have been unlocked and are open. There are lit lanterns in the tunnel. Someone has been staying in there."

Heather looked at the walkie-talkie. "These things don't have a big range. This Rodney has to be close by."

"Let me go, or else you're going to be sorry. It'll be worse for you," Clay shouted.

Heather reached down and pulled off both of her socks. She tucked one sock into another and handed it to Marie. All three spirits looked at Heather. "I can't have him yelling in the background while I try to catch this Rodney dude. Can you please shove these in his mouth to shut him up?"

Clay started to shout something, only to have the socks fly into his mouth. He tried spitting them out, but Marie took the remaining strip of tape and wrapped it around his face and mouth, holding the socks in place.

Heather cringed. "I imagine those are stinky. I wore them jogging today."

"What's your idea?" Marie asked while Clay squirmed in frustration on the floor, trying to get loose.

"You go outside, and I'll try to flush out this Rodney by making static noises on the walkie-talkie. Listen for it. Check the backyard and around the alley first."

Marie vanished, and Heather gave her a few minutes before she turned on Clay's walkie-talkie and started making spitting sounds into the device.

"Clay?" the voice on the other end called out.

MARIE WENT FIRST to the garage to grab some rope. She didn't want to use duct tape again, plus she didn't have enough. Marie found some rope, and instead of taking it with her, she placed it on the garage roof. She didn't want Clay's partner to see a rope floating in his direction and scare him away before she could catch him.

She moved over the bushes along the alley, listening for any strange sounds.

"Clay? Is anything wrong?" a voice said.

Marie smiled when she saw the man hiding in the bushes, clutching a walkie-talkie matching Clay's. Focusing her energy on the man, she watched as he lifted into the air and began floating toward Marlow House.

The man screamed and kicked his feet. From his pocket, he pulled out a gun and started shooting. Marie immediately dropped the man to the ground, knocking the breath out of him. Her energy took his gun and placed it on the roof of Marlow House's garage and then retrieved the rope.

INSIDE MARLOW HOUSE, where the twins continued to sleep peacefully, Heather, Eva, and Betsy, who remained in the entry hall with Clay, heard Marie's voice call out, "Yeehaw!" And then, to their astonishment, a man wrapped tightly in a rope came floating down the hallway from the kitchen, with Marie straddling him, riding her bound prisoner as if he were a horse, while she waved a gun over her head.

"Playing cowgirl, Marie?" Heather asked.

THIRTY-FOUR

Duct tape covered every inch of Clay Bowman, from his ankles to his upper chest, winding tightly around his body, immobilizing his limbs. In his futile attempts to escape, he had exhausted himself and now lay on his side. Tears ran down his cheeks, the salty moisture irritating the bloody and stinging scars left by the demon cat. He could barely breathe with the foul socks shoved into his mouth.

He suspected the lack of air to his brain was responsible for his hallucinations. Moments earlier, Rodney had floated into the entry hall while tied up like a calf at the rodeo, with a gun circling over his head. Clay might be crazy, but he wasn't crazy enough to believe any of that was actually happening. He wondered if something other than a lack of oxygen was behind the hallucinations. He didn't believe anyone could have slipped him drugs, so the next logical conclusion was some toxic environmental poisoning. *Yes, that has to be it*, Clay thought. There must be toxic gas or mold in the tunnel behind the hallucinations.

Clay wondered when Heather would call the police, or did she plan to wait for the Marlows to come home? She kept talking to herself in a bizarre fashion. One moment she looked to the right, as if someone stood there; she would say something and then turn in the other direction and act as if she was speaking to another person.

He suspected whatever toxic chemical poisoned the tunnel's air had leaked into Marlow House, which would explain not only Heather's bizarre behavior, but why the cat had attacked him unprovoked.

RODNEY LAY ABOUT fifteen feet from Clay in the entry hall, staring blankly in Clay's direction. While he didn't have a sock shoved in his mouth, he seemed incapable of uttering a sound. He lay on his side with his eyes wide and all the color drained from his face.

"I won't call 911. I'm just calling Brian. He's working today, anyway." Heather looked at Marie. "I'm going to grab my phone and check on the babies. Keep an eye on these guys. And I'm not convinced there aren't more than these two, so please stay alert." Heather started to go to the living room but paused a moment and looked at Betsy. "And you. Please don't leave. We need to talk."

When Heather returned a few minutes later, she carried her phone and had already finished calling Brian. "The twins are getting a little restless. I think they're waking up. Marie, before the police get here, can you get me the gun?" Heather pointed to the overhead light fixture. "And I should probably take the other guy's gun."

Clay's gun floated down from the ceiling and landed in Heather's hand, followed by Rodney's gun.

Now, with a gun in each hand, Heather looked at Betsy. "By any chance are you Betsy Francas?"

Betsy stared at Heather. "How did you know?"

Heather shrugged. "Long story. But before the police get here, can you tell me everything you know about these two, including what you overheard them say? And please stick around after the police leave. Danielle will want to talk to you."

Before Betsy could answer, the babies started crying.

TEN MINUTES LATER, Brian and Joe arrived at Marlow House with backup. The front door was unlocked, and they walked in. Even Brian, who'd gotten the abbreviated version from Heather, was not prepared for what he found when entering the house. If Heather hadn't told him Clay Bowman was one of the would-be kidnappers, he would not have recognized him because of his bloodied face. It looked as if someone had taken a razor blade to Clay, with his blood-soaked beard and red stripes covering his forehead and nose.

Brian knew where to find Heather, because when rushing by the living room window on the way to the front door, he'd seen her sitting on a blanket spread out on the floor with the twins. It looked as if she were alone in the room, yet Brian knew Eva and Marie were somewhere in the house.

HEATHER SAT on the blanket with the twins, with Max curled up on her lap. Next to her sat Betsy, who had just watched her change diapers and now looked down lovingly, speaking sweetly to the babies. It was obvious to Heather the twins, like Connor, could see spirits, as they responded to Betsy's attention with cooing, kicking feet, and excitedly waving hands.

Minutes earlier, Brian and the other police officers had rushed by the front window. Voices and the sound of movement now came from the hallway, yet Heather remained with the twins.

After some time, Brian, Joe, and several other officers entered the living room, with Clay and Rodney by their side. While the rope and duct tape had been removed, both men were now handcuffed. When entering the living room, Brian pointed toward the fireplace, and then the two officers led Clay and Rodney there and made them sit on the hearth. Clay no longer had her socks shoved in his mouth. She told herself she needed to get a new pair of socks.

"Heather, are you alright?" Brian asked.

"I'm fine, thanks." Heather smiled at Brian.

"Are the twins okay?" Joe asked.

"They are troopers. Slept through everything." Heather grinned.

Joe glanced around. "Where are Walt and Danielle?"

"They're at brunch at Pearl Cove." Heather cringed. "I haven't even called them yet to tell them what happened."

"Why don't you first explain to us what happened," Joe said.

Heather glanced over at Clay, who remained sitting silently on the fireplace, glaring in her direction. The scratches were now bright red and slightly inflamed. "Our old friend Clay here somehow got into the tunnel and managed to unlock the doors leading to Marlow House's basement. I suspect he broke into the Crawford house, because the Crawfords haven't been home."

"Any idea what he was planning to do?" Joe asked.

"He was going to kill me, kidnap the twins, and hide out in the tunnel and wait for Walt and Danielle to pay the ransom."

"I was not!" Clay shouted. His partner, Rodney, remained eerily silent, his eyes dead while he stared ahead.

Heather pointed to Clay. "He has a ransom note with him. It might be in his jacket."

"We already found it," Brian said, holding up a piece of paper.

"Can you read it to me?" Heather asked.

Brian opened the note and read aloud, "We have kidnapped your babies. If you want to see them again, do not call the police. Do not tell anyone. You are to follow our instructions, or you will never see them again. Danielle Marlow is to go to the bank and remove all her gold coins and the Missing Thorndike. She is to return to Marlow House with the gold coins and necklace for further instructions. Walt Marlow is not to leave the house. You are being watched. If you do not follow our instructions, you will never see your son and daughter again." Brian refolded the note.

"Why do you think Clay was going to kill you?" Joe asked.

"For one thing, he said he was going to," Heather said.

"I never said that to you!" Clay shouted.

Heather looked at Clay. "No, your partner there, Rodney

Whoever-He-Is, told you on that rinky-dink walkie-talkie to kill me and leave the ransom note on my body."

"You couldn't have heard that," Clay snapped.

Heather shrugged. "This is an old house. Sound travels."

Brian interrupted and asked, "Heather, whose guns are these?" He pointed to the two guns sitting on the coffee table.

"Oh, those belong to Clay and Rodney. Rodney is the quiet one over there." Heather pointed toward the fireplace.

Joe could no longer hold back. He had to ask the question he had been wondering since he first stepped into Marlow House. "How did they get tied up?"

Heather took a deep breath and glanced down briefly at Max. "The babies were sleeping in here when I noticed voices. No one was supposed to be here. I stepped out into the hall, and then suddenly, there was Clay, pointing a gun at me. And then Max, well, he just appeared out of nowhere. He flew at Clay's face. As you can see, he did a number on him. Made him drop his gun." Most of that was true.

"How did you get him tied up?" Joe asked.

Heather shrugged. "It was a little awkward. But I had him at gunpoint."

Clay glared at Heather.

"How did you get the other one tied up?" Joe asked.

"By that time, I had Clay's gun. Rodney was outside and came in to find out what was taking so long. I got the drop on him, got some rope, and tied him up. Then I called Brian." Heather smiled sweetly.

Brian started to tell the officers to put Clay and Rodney in the police car when Heather stopped him. "Can I get a picture of his face first?"

Brian arched his brows at Heather. "That's rather ghoulish, isn't it?"

Heather shrugged. "I just want to show Danielle what her guard cat is capable of."

"Okay, but I think I'm going to have to take Clay to the ER

before we go on to the station. Those scratches already look inflamed."

Heather grinned at Clay. "Yes, they are, aren't they?"

Overhearing Heather's comments, Clay shouted, "You're sick!"

"And you intended to kill me," Heather countered.

After Heather took Clay's picture, the officers put Clay and Rodney in the police car, while Joe and the other officers went down to the Marlow House basement to investigate the entry to the tunnel, leaving Brian alone with Heather—if you didn't count any ghosts. When the officers were all out of earshot, he knelt down next to Heather and whispered, "I'm waiting for Joe to point out your plot hole."

Heather frowned. "What plot hole? I came up with a great story."

Brian let out a sigh. "First, you said something about over-hearing Clay's walkie-talkie conversation with Rodney, and how sound travels in this house."

"So? What's wrong with that?"

Brian chuckled. "Then you say you heard voices. No one was supposed to be here. You walked out to the hall, and there was Clay pointing a gun at you."

"Yeah, so?"

"If you heard Clay talking to Rodney on the walkie-talkie about killing you, why would you go out into the hallway? And when you did, you shouldn't be surprised to find Clay pointing a gun at you."

Heather groaned. "Drat, you're right. Although, I didn't say I was surprised he was standing there pointing a gun at me. Just that he was there."

Brian leaned closer, gave Heather a quick kiss, and said, "Fine-tune your cover story before you come down to the station. I'm glad you're okay." He then looked up and said, "Marie, if you're still here, thank you for watching over Heather and the twins."

"You are very welcome, Brian," Marie said.

Brian gave Heather another kiss and, before standing up, said, "You'd better give Walt and Danielle a call."

Heather nodded. "What are you going to do about the tunnel?"

"Isn't Adam listing the Crawford house?"

"Yes."

"We'll be calling Adam. Like you said, they had to gain access that way."

AFTER BRIAN LEFT, Betsy said, "I'm so confused."

"About what?" Heather asked.

"I'm a ghost, right?"

"Yep. Although I know some prefer to be called a spirit."

"And Marie and Eva are ghosts too, right?"

Heather nodded. "Correct."

"But you're not a ghost, and neither are these babies' parents. Right?"

"You don't seem confused to me."

"Why is it you and they can see us? I know others can't. But the one who kissed you, he knew about Marie, but he couldn't see her."

"I'm a medium, and a few of my friends are as well. Do you know what a medium is?"

"Yes. But I never thought they could really communicate with ghosts."

"Well, they do. And while my friend Brian knows about mediums and ghosts, he's not a medium. And some people, like Joe, who was here asking me questions, he doesn't believe in mediums or ghosts."

"Interesting."

"But now I have some questions."

"Yes?"

"Were you murdered?"

THIRTY-FIVE

On Monday morning, while Heather dealt with kidnappers and the police, Lily and Ian dropped Connor off at his grandmother's house while they ran errands and looked at light fixtures for Ian's new office. When they returned home, they noticed several police cars parked in front of Marlow House.

"Oh no, I hope everyone is okay!" Sitting in the passenger seat, Lily turned around while Ian pulled into their driveway, her eyes not leaving Marlow House and the police cars. "Heather and Marie are babysitting the twins while Walt and Danielle are at brunch!"

Ian and Lily got out of their car and rushed across the street to Marlow House. When they got to the front door, they found it open, and inside were police officers, with some standing in the entry hall talking, others taking photographs, and some coming and going from the basement.

The first person they recognized was Joe, who was talking to another officer. Joe looked up when Ian and Lily walked into the house.

"Are the babies okay?" Lily blurted.

Joe looked at Lily and Ian and nodded. "Yes, they're in the living room with Heather."

"What happened?" Ian asked.

"Kidnap attempt."

Lily's right hand flew to her mouth. "Oh, my gawd!"

"Heather's in the living room; she can explain everything. I need to finish up here." Joe turned back to the officer he had been talking with to resume their conversation.

Lily and Ian hurried to the living room. When they walked in, they found Heather sitting with the babies on a blanket spread on the floor, with Max sleeping on the edge of the blanket.

"Heather!" Lily cried out, rushing toward them.

"IS CONNOR WITH HIS GRANDMA?" Heather asked after moving to the sofa with Lily, where they both sat, each holding a baby. Ian had gone back out to the entry hall to talk to Joe and the other officers.

Lily cradled Addison in her arms. "Yes. So what did you tell Walt and Dani?"

"When I finally called them, they were just getting ready to leave the restaurant. I told them not to worry, everything is fine, but some things happened, and don't freak if they come home to police cars in front of the house."

Lily groaned. "Knowing Dani, that's going to drive her insane not knowing what happened."

"I didn't want to blurt out someone tried to kidnap the twins. Or that Clay Bowman somehow unlocked the doors at their end of the tunnel."

Lily glanced around the room. "Is Marie here?"

In answer to Lily's question, a throw pillow lifted from the sofa and then fell back down.

Lily looked at the throw pillow. "Hi, Marie. Thank God you were here!"

"Eva was here too. But she left with Betsy."

Lily frowned. "Betsy?"

"Yep. Betsy Francas, the woman who made the twin quilt. Well, she's a ghost now."

"So she is dead? Was that who they found in Jameson's root cellar?"

Heather nodded. "Yep. Someone murdered her."

"Is she responsible for what's been going on in the nursery?" Lily asked.

"You mean is she our poltergeist?"

Lily nodded.

"I don't think so. Walt and Danielle stopped over to the Jameson place yesterday, and Danielle got out of the car and looked around. They didn't see Betsy, but she saw them, and she followed them back here. So until yesterday, Betsy's ghost had been hanging out at the Jameson place."

"Who murdered her?"

"She didn't tell me. With everything that happened this morning, she was overwhelmed. Eva suggested the two of them go somewhere and talk."

Motion from the window caught Lily's attention. "Um, Danielle and Walt just ran by."

Heather glanced at the doorway from the hallway, waiting for the anxious parents to run into the room.

———

LILY AND HEATHER had moved to the recliners facing the sofa, where Danielle now sat, nursing the twins, with Marie by her side. After Heather explained all that had happened, Walt left for the entry hall to find Ian and talk to Joe and the other police officers.

Heather stood up. "Danielle, I want to show you something." As she approached Danielle, she took out her phone. "Remember how I told you Max attacked Clay?"

"Yes."

"I don't think you appreciate Max's fierce loyalty." Heather pulled out her phone, opened her photo app, and pulled up the photo she had taken of Clay. She showed it to Danielle.

Danielle's eyes widened. "Holy crap! Max did all that?"

Still sitting on a recliner, Lily cringed. "Heather already showed me. It's brutal."

"Yep, he did all that." Heather pulled the phone from Danielle, gave the picture another quick look, and closed the photo app. "Marie had to pull him off Clay."

Marie glanced briefly at Max, who napped under the coffee table. "I didn't do it for Clay. But the way he was flailing about, I was afraid he would knock Max to the floor and then try kicking him. I remember when he tried that with Hunny."

Danielle smiled down at Max. "Someone's getting chicken for dinner."

After Danielle finished nursing the twins, Marie helped her change their diapers. Once they were dry and content, Danielle returned with them to the sofa. "When Chris gets back, I want to talk to him again about finding a buyer for the gold coins. And I also think we need to find a home for the Missing Thorndike."

Lily looked at Danielle. "What are you saying?"

Danielle looked down at her babies. "This isn't the first time someone tried extorting us for the gold coins and necklace. But this time, it put Addison's and Jack's lives at risk. It's just not worth it. There's no guarantee Marie or Walt will be here to save the day when it happens again, and it will happen again."

"How will selling the gold help?" Heather asked.

"If someone tries to extort us for money, it's more difficult to take that much cash out of the bank. It draws too much attention to the kidnappers. But going down to the local bank and me taking something out of a safe-deposit box is a totally different thing."

"You also want to get rid of the necklace?" Lily asked.

"I'm going to talk to Walt and Eva about lending the necklace to a museum. Not our little museum here. I was thinking there has to be some sort of theater museum somewhere, something for silent screen stars. That would be a perfect place to have Eva's necklace on display."

Lily looked over at the babies. "I understand what you're saying.

It's too easy for someone to extort you when you keep a fortune in a local safe-deposit box."

"And if it weren't for Marie, it would be gone by now, anyway."

BRIAN and another officer sat with Clay in the emergency room as the nurse cleaned the inflamed wounds covering Clay's face. The prisoner sat on an exam table, his wrists handcuffed behind his back. Clay winced from pain as the nurse dabbed moist cotton balls over the scratches and applied ointment.

"How did this happen?" the nurse asked. "It looks like someone locked your head in a cage with a pissed-off cat."

"That cat was crazy," Clay grumbled. He looked at the nurse, who had just finished cleaning up his face. "I need to have a blood test, too."

"What are you talking about?" Brian asked.

"There's mold or something in that tunnel."

Brian frowned. "Mold?"

"Yeah. I spent the night in the tunnel last night, and this morning I've had all kinds of crazy hallucinations. It's got to be some sort of toxin. Probably why that cat flipped out."

"What kind of hallucinations?" the nurse asked.

"A baby quilt attacked me." Clay began.

The nurse frowned. "A baby quilt?"

"Then Rodney floated down the hallway. Literally a couple of feet off the floor. Guns twirling over his head. All sorts of crazy stuff."

The nurse looked at Brian. "Maybe we should take a blood test."

BRIAN HAD CALLED the chief before leaving Marlow House to ask him if he wanted to come down to the station and be there when they brought Clay and Rodney in. Since the chief couldn't drive yet, Joe had volunteered Kelly to give him a ride, and the chief accepted the offer.

Clay and Rodney were in lockup, and the chief was in his office on Monday afternoon, discussing the case with Joe and Brian, who stood by his desk, when Fred Lyons walked into his office.

"Fred," MacDonald greeted him while remaining seated behind his desk.

Fred glanced at Joe and then Brian, giving them both a nod before looking back at MacDonald and asking, "He's here?"

MacDonald nodded. "He's in lockup." The chief turned to his two officers and said, "I called Fred to tell him we have Clay."

"And he tried to kidnap the Marlow twins?" Fred asked. The chief had given him the abbreviated version of what had happened over the phone.

The chief nodded. "Yes."

"Oh crap," Fred groaned, taking a seat facing MacDonald. He rested his face in his palms and shook his head.

"Umm, we'll leave you two to talk," Joe said.

"But before we go, I think we found your coin collection," Brian said.

Fred looked up at Brian. "You did?"

"Yes. Clay wasn't working alone. He was working with some guy named Rodney Healy. We found his truck parked down by the pier. What we assume is your coin collection was found shoved under the seat of the truck. It looks like some of the coins are missing."

Fred nodded and put his face back in his palms.

Brian and Joe left Fred and the chief alone, and the chief filled Fred in on Clay's arrest.

"Clay somehow got his hands on the keys to the doors on the Marlow side of the tunnel, which is how he got in. We found the keys in the tunnel and showed them to Walt, and he said they're the duplicates that the museum made for their upcoming tunnel display. I called Millie Samson. She said the last time she saw the keys was last Saturday, and she didn't realize they were missing. She thought one of the docents moved them. We aren't sure how they ended up with Clay."

Fred groaned again. "I think I know."

ERIC AND ZACK sat next to each other in the interrogation room, with their mother on the other side of Zack, their uncle Fred on the other side of Eric, and Chief MacDonald sitting across the table from them.

"Boys, have you seen these before?" MacDonald dropped the keys on the table between Eric and Zack. The boys looked at the keys and then looked briefly to their uncle, who stared at them.

"What is this about? Why are we here?" Debbie demanded.

"Debbie, let the boys answer the chief's question," Fred snapped.

Debbie glared at her brother-in-law but said nothing.

"Umm, there were keys like those at the museum," Eric said.

"These are the keys from the museum." The chief reached across the table and picked them back up. "Who do you think took them from the museum?"

Eric shrugged in response, but Zack blurted, "Where's our dad?"

"You gave the keys to your dad, didn't you?"

Eric and Zack briefly looked at each other and then looked back at the chief.

"Did our dad tell you that?" Zack asked.

"What's going on? Where's Clay?" Debbie demanded.

"Did you know Clay was in Frederickport?" Fred asked Debbie.

Debbie bit her lower lip nervously and shook her head. "He's here?"

"Did you help him plan the kidnapping?" Fred shrieked.

Debbie furrowed her brows and looked confused. "Kidnapping? What are you talking about?"

THIRTY-SIX

E ver since Clay Bowman tried framing Heather for the murder of Brian's ex-wife, Kelly had been nicer to her. *Nice is probably the wrong word*, Heather thought. Less judgmental? Nah, Kelly was still judgmental, but now she occasionally defended Heather, which felt a little strange.

Heather didn't imagine they were going to suddenly become best buds. But Kelly was married to one of Brian's close friends, and if they could be around each other without the former friction, Heather took that as a win, especially during times like this morning.

Brian and Heather sat in a booth with Joe and Kelly, having breakfast at Pier Café on Tuesday morning. Over bacon, eggs, and pancakes, they discussed the previous day's drama and arrests.

"I wouldn't be surprised if they're both going for the insanity defense," Joe said. "Clay's partner in crime hasn't said two words since we arrested him. We ask him a question, and he just stares out in space with those blank eyes, like no one is home."

Instead of adding a comment, Brian took a sip of coffee and glanced over to Heather, keeping his thoughts to himself.

"And after toxins didn't show up in the blood test, Clay kept insisting there was something wrong with the tests, because there is no way a blanket attacked him and knocked the gun out of his hand." Joe shook his head at the idea, picked up his coffee cup, and took a drink.

Brian chuckled. "Which was helpful, because with that statement, Clay basically confessed."

"Wasn't the blanket that he claimed attacked him actually the baby quilt Lily and I found at the estate sale?" Kelly looked at Heather.

Heather stared down at her eggs and speared a bite with her fork. "Yep."

"Perhaps the quilt did attack him," Kelly suggested.

"Oh yeah, right," Joe scoffed.

Kelly shrugged. "It's possible, considering what we've seen over there." Kelly looked back at Heather. "Did the quilt attack him?"

Without looking up from the plate, Heather considered the question. Quietly, she laid her fork down on her napkin and looked up to find everyone at her table looking at her. "Going on the record and claiming a baby's quilt disarmed a kidnapper while I stood ten feet away would probably jeopardize the case against Clay. That's something I'm not willing to do. No. I would never go on the record and make that claim."

Kelly stared at Heather. "Off the record."

Heather looked at Kelly and nodded.

Exasperated, Joe threw back his head and scoffed.

With a shrug, Heather picked up her fork and continued eating. Kelly turned to Joe. "We both saw what happened in the nursery."

"Yeah, well, Clay could be right, and some hallucinogenic toxins have come up from the tunnel," Joe countered. "And that's what's making us imagine weird things when we're over there."

Brian chuckled. "Joe, I doubt you and Kelly would experience the same hallucination. While you can't wrap your head around the possibility something from the paranormal realm is responsible for what you saw at Marlow House, I'm actually comforted by the fact that whatever it is, it helped save Heather and prevent a kidnapping."

ON THE OTHER side of Beach Drive, at Marlow House, Danielle and Walt sat in the living room with Marie, with Max curled up on Danielle's lap, while the babies napped in the portable cribs nearby.

"I certainly hope they won't let Clay Bowman out on bail this time," Marie said.

Danielle absently stroked Max's head. "I seriously doubt it."

"What about his partner?" Marie asked.

Walt placed his arm around Danielle's shoulders, gently pulling her closer to him as they sat together on the sofa. He looked over at Marie. "I spoke to Edward this morning. The other man's name is Rodney Healy, and he's from the same area Clay was living in before moving back to Frederickport. He has an impressive rap sheet. Someone at Clay's old station told Edward that Rodney was one of Clay's informants."

"Sounds like he was more than an informant," Danielle scoffed.

"Is Edward working today?" Marie asked. "He really needs to rest, or he won't heal properly."

"He was at home when I spoke to him," Walt explained. "But he did mention he was going into the station this afternoon."

"When I spoke to the chief last night, he said Debbie Bowman confessed to knowing her husband was in town but swears she didn't know about the kidnapping. The chief believes her. One of her sons also confessed to taking the keys, but said when he took them, he didn't know their father was in town. The boys just wanted to see the tunnel, and when they broke into the Crawford house, Clay showed up. He had been following them," Danielle explained.

Marie let out a sigh. "Well, having been a mother to a son, and having two grandsons, I can understand how the boys would want to explore the tunnel. It just got a little more involved than they bargained for. Sad, those boys have a father like that. I wonder what's going to happen to them now. Will charges be filed against them and their mother?"

Danielle shrugged. "I imagine if Debbie and the boys cooperate with the police, they won't file charges against them."

They discussed the matter a few more minutes when Marie said, "Not to change the subject, but did you notice what happened last night? Or should I say, what didn't happen?"

Danielle smiled at Marie. "No knocking."

Marie nodded.

"Is this just a fluke? I haven't heard doors slamming lately, and the last time anyone saw a stuffed animal thrown across the room was Friday. And now we go an entire night without the knocking. I'd love to discuss this with Eva," Danielle said.

Marie glanced around, as if expecting her friend to turn up at any moment. "I'm surprised Eva isn't back yet."

"I hope when she returns, she has Betsy with her. I have a lot of questions I need answered," Danielle said.

They continued to discuss recent events for another fifteen minutes, when snowflakes fell from the ceiling. They all stopped talking and looked up for a moment, waiting for Eva's arrival.

A moment later Eva appeared, standing between the sofa and recliners, with Betsy by her side. As soon as they were both fully visible, all traces of snow disappeared.

"Danielle, I would like you to meet Betsy Francas," Eva introduced.

"Hello, Betsy," Danielle greeted her. "Thank you for your help yesterday."

"It wasn't much, really. I wanted to do more, but it seems like all I could do was warn them."

Eva motioned to Walt. "And this is Danielle's husband, Walt."

Betsy turned her attention from Danielle to Walt. "Eva told me about you. Fascinating."

Walt smiled at Betsy. "As my wife said, we are thankful for your help. And if there is anything we can do for you, please let us know."

Eva interrupted Walt and suggested they sit down before they continue. She motioned for Betsy to take the empty recliner next to Marie as she hovered nearby in an imaginary chair.

After the two spirits sat down, Betsy looked at Walt and Danielle and said, "Eva explained how much time has gone by since…since that day. My girls, they're adults now. The person who killed me didn't just steal my life, they stole my chance to raise my children. They let my daughters grow up believing I had abandoned them. What a horrible thing to do to a child. I only want one thing, and that is for my daughters to understand I didn't abandon them. I loved them and never deserted them."

"One way to do that is to identify your body," Danielle said. "They've tried using your DNA. Umm…not sure if they used DNA way back when you were alive. But basically, it's taking samples from your remains and matching it with a family member. Unfortunately, when they ran your DNA after they found you, there were no close matches. And while the police chief wants to try running it against a sample from your brother, he's trying to figure out what he can say to justify the request for your brother's DNA, because you were never reported as a missing person, and the only reason the police chief knows about your connection to where your body was found is information from Marie. A ghost."

"Oh, I see," Betsy murmured.

"Who killed you?" Danielle asked.

Betsy's apparition seemed to shrink. "I'm not quite ready to discuss that. Betrayed by someone I loved for so many years is difficult to talk about."

Danielle nodded. "Okay. But then, can I ask you, are you responsible for what has been happening in our nursery?"

"You are obviously talking about the poltergeist," Eva answered for Betsy.

Danielle looked at Eva. "Yes."

Eva glanced at Betsy and back at Danielle. "After much discussion, and considering everything, I'm convinced the answer to that question is yes—and no."

Danielle frowned. "I don't understand?"

"It might help if you could bring in the quilt. It's still in the entry hall," Eva suggested.

Walt started to stand up to retrieve the quilt, but Marie told him to sit down, she would get it. Marie vanished and a moment later returned with the quilt. She placed it on the coffee table, already neatly folded.

"What some people call poltergeists aren't actually ghosts—despite the fact geist is the German word for ghost or spirit. They believe the acts of the poltergeist—such as the slamming of doors or throwing objects—is from the energy that comes from people, living or dead. It's not a conscious act from the source generating the energy," Eva explained. "I believe the energy we experienced in the nursery initially came from Betsy's death trauma and the pain of her being separated from her daughters. That energy attached itself to the quilt, because the quilt was one thing that Betsy had poured her love into during her pregnancy, the love for her unborn babies."

Danielle looked down at the quilt. She started to ask Eva if it was possible for the energy to detach from the quilt and return to the original source—Betsy—but instead of asking, she froze when something about the quilt caught her attention. Staring at it for a moment, she gently lifted a sleeping Max from her lap and set him on the sofa next to her. She leaned over and picked the quilt up from the table. Danielle rubbed its edge between her fingers, studying it for a few more minutes before looking up at Betsy.

"What is it?" Marie asked.

"Betsy, when you were killed, were you wearing what you have on right now?" Danielle asked.

Betsy glanced down at her blouse and then looked up at Danielle. "Yes. Why?"

"And that's the same blouse you had on when you were put in the root cellar?"

"Yes."

"What is it?" Walt asked.

"Look at Betsy's blouse. That fabric." Danielle held the quilt up for Walt to see and pointed at one of its appliques. "That's the same fabric as her blouse."

DANIELLE FOUND the chief in his office on Tuesday afternoon. He sat behind his desk, talking on the phone when she walked in. He looked surprised to see her. When she saw he was talking on the phone, she started to leave, but he waved her in, pointed to an empty chair, and continued with his phone conversation.

Danielle quietly sat down in the chair facing his desk, setting the neatly folded quilt, which she had brought with her, on her lap, and waited for him to finish the phone conversation.

When the chief ended the call, he looked up at Danielle and was about to ask a question when Danielle blurted, "Do you have photos of the body you found in the root cellar? Her clothes."

The chief frowned. "Yes. Why?"

"We can identify the body, at least enough so you can ask Betsy's brother for a DNA test." Danielle jumped up from the chair and took the quilt to the chief, dropping it on his desk. She then explained how Betsy had made her blouse and had later used the leftover fabric in the twins quilt.

MacDonald picked up the quilt and studied it. "Interesting."

"I know what you're thinking now."

Still holding the quilt, he looked up at Danielle. "You do?"

THIRTY-SEVEN

"You're wondering how you're going to explain how someone looked at this quilt and recognized some of the fabric as the same fabric from the blouse worn by the remains found years ago, in the Jameson root cellar."

MacDonald leaned back in the desk chair and studied Danielle, who stood over his desk, looking down at him. He smiled at her. "And you're going to tell me?"

Danielle grinned. "Of course. You see, after Lily gave me this quilt, I was curious about its history. Who made it? Someone obviously made it with love for twins. But who?" Danielle began pacing the office. "So I did my Nancy Drew thing and eventually ended up talking to Gemma Francas, the second wife of Dan Francas. She told me Dan's first wife, Betsy, had made the quilt for their twins." Danielle stopped pacing and looked at the chief.

"Go on."

Danielle resumed her pacing and explanation. "Gemma told me Betsy abandoned her twins—simply walked off and left her husband and babies. Now, I might understand her actions if she'd had postpartum depression. Women can do horrible things under postpartum depression. Things they would normally never do." Danielle stopped pacing and looked back at the chief.

"Go on."

"I couldn't accept that someone who made this beautiful quilt, that was obviously made with love for her babies, would just walk away forever. Eventually, she would have come back. Yes, some women, some mothers, abandon their children. But I didn't feel it was the case with Betsy. So I started looking to see what had become of her. I couldn't find a divorce decree for her marriage. I found that odd, considering Gemma claimed they married two years after Betsy took off. Heather talked to her brother for me, and he never heard from her again. So I asked myself, did something else happen to Betsy? Something more sinister."

MacDonald smiled at Danielle. "And what did you tell yourself?"

"Well, while looking for information on Betsy, I discovered they stayed at Elenore Percy's house when they moved to town."

MacDonald arched his brows. "Didn't Marie tell you that? Or did she mention that before she died?"

Danielle smiled sweetly. "Marie? Umm no. It wasn't her. Someone mentioned that when I started asking people about Betsy, but I can't recall who it was. Anyway, this person also mentioned that Elenore Percy's house was next door to the Jameson house, where the police found a body in the root cellar years ago. So I started wondering, could it be Betsy?"

"Interesting. And convenient. And then what did you do?"

"I came to you, of course. Started nagging you to let me see the old files on the case, and from the photos, I recognized the fabric in your Jane Doe's blouse."

"That is some impressive Nancy Drewing and creative writing there."

"Well, are we going to identify the remains and inform those young women that their mother did not abandon them? She loved them."

MacDonald sat up straighter at his desk. "Did Betsy tell you who murdered her?"

"No, but I'm pretty sure who it was."

DANIELLE SAT in the evidence room, flipping through the photographs the chief had given her. They had been taken back when Betsy's body had been found in the root cellar. He hadn't shown her all the photographs taken that day, only the ones that included clear shots of her clothing. The chief had left her alone in the room so he could go take a phone call.

"The chief told me what you were doing."

Danielle looked up and saw Brian Henderson had just walked into the room.

"Do you think I'm crazy?"

"Yes. But what does that have to do with anything?" He glanced at the pile of photographs. "Gruesome pictures?"

"Nah. The chief left out the gruesome ones. He also showed me the actual blouse."

"I know. He told me."

"It's the same fabric. Of course, it's not in terrific shape, but clearly the same fabric as what's in the quilt."

"The chief wants me to interview Gemma Francas."

Danielle turned in her chair and faced Brian. "Really?"

"Yes. And he wants you to go with me."

Danielle arched her brows. "I'd love to, but that surprises me. Why would he want me to go with you?"

"Because you've already talked to her. That way, she'll be less inclined to walk back some of the things she told you that she may not want to tell me. Once I tell her Betsy was murdered and didn't leave that day, I imagine she'll want to change her story."

"You aren't bringing her into the station to question her?"

"Later. But the chief feels, and I agree, we might get more out of her if we approach this as a more friendly and casual chat. You up to it?"

"When do you want to do it?"

"Today?"

"Umm, can I go home first? It's almost time to feed the babies."

Brian nodded. "No problem. You go home; call me when you're ready. I have to take the chief home, anyway."

HAD Gemma Francas looked out her peephole and seen a police officer standing on her front porch with Danielle Marlow, she probably wouldn't have answered the door. But she had just walked out to her mailbox to pick up her mail when the police car pulled up in front of her house and parked.

She acted surprised to see Danielle get out of the car with the policeman. Gemma removed her mail from the box while she watched Danielle and the officer walk toward her. She recognized the officer but couldn't remember his name.

"Danielle Marlow? What's going on?" Gemma asked when Danielle reached her, the officer by her side.

"Hello, Mrs. Francas. This is a friend of mine, Brian Henderson, with the Frederickport Police Department."

Brian handed Gemma his business card. "Hello, Mrs. Francas. I need to ask you a few questions, and when I heard Danielle knew you, I asked her to come with me so you could have someone familiar with you, to make you more comfortable, considering what I have to tell you."

Gemma frowned. "I don't understand."

"Can we go inside and talk?" Brian asked gently.

Gemma reluctantly turned around and led the pair to her house. A few minutes later, the three sat at Gemma's kitchen table.

"So, what do you need to tell me?" Gemma asked.

"I hate to have to tell you this," Brian began, "but someone you knew, who I understand was a close friend of yours, was murdered. Your husband's first wife, Betsy Francas."

Gemma shook her head in denial. "No. That can't be true."

"Her body has tentatively been identified. While taking additional steps to confirm her identity, we need to question people who were close to Betsy. I understand you were childhood friends."

"Umm…yes. When did she die?"

"It looks like you may be one of the last people to have seen her alive. Other than the murderer, of course."

"Are you suggesting Betsy has been dead all these years?"

"Unfortunately, yes. I understand you and your husband married about two years after his wife disappeared?"

Gemma stared at Brian for a moment. Finally, she said, "She left willingly. It wasn't as if she was missing."

"I understand. And you were married two years later?" Brian asked.

Gemma didn't answer immediately, but looked anxiously from Brian to Danielle, back to Brian. Finally, she said, "You'll find out anyway. Dan and Betsy never divorced. He wanted to divorce her and legally marry me, but we didn't know where to find her. We obviously didn't know she was dead. And since we couldn't find her, Dan couldn't get a divorce."

"It is possible to get a divorce if one spouse goes missing," Brian said.

Gemma shrugged. "Well, Dan didn't want to go through all that. I suppose if we lived in a state with common law marriage, which Oregon doesn't have, we would be legally married anyway if what you say is true about Betsy."

"What color hair did Betsy have?" Brian asked.

Gemma frowned at Brian. "She was a strawberry blonde. Just like her daughters. They look just like her."

"Where are they now?" Brian asked.

Gemma shrugged. "I have no idea. I haven't seen them for years. They didn't even bother coming to their father's funeral."

"I understand Betsy came to you and told you she was leaving her husband and babies."

"Yes."

"Tell me about that day."

Gemma glanced again at Danielle and back to Brian. "I stopped over at her house."

"Now this was when they were staying at Elenore Percy's house, correct?" Brian asked.

"Yes." Gemma froze for a moment, glanced at Danielle, and then continued, "Betsy, Dan, and I had been friends since childhood. We were all very close. And then Betsy married Dan. She had the twins, and he got a job here. My parents died a few months before Betsy and Dan announced they were moving. When they left Vancouver, I felt so alone, so I decided to move here too. I didn't tell them. I wanted to surprise them. But when I showed up at the house, umm…Betsy was not acting like herself. The quilt she had made during her pregnancy was sitting on her kitchen table, all folded up neatly. She told me she couldn't do this anymore. I didn't know what to say. She just took her ring off, set it on the quilt, and left. At the time, I assumed it was postpartum depression, and that she'd come back."

"And you told her husband what happened when he came home."

Gemma nodded.

"How did he react?"

"He was devastated, of course."

"Did you stay with him that night?" Brian asked.

Gemma looked taken aback at the question. "What are you suggesting?"

"I think Brian meant to take care of the babies. You told me you stayed to take care of them," Danielle reminded her.

Gemma shook her head. "No, I didn't spend the night at the house. I just came over when he was at work."

"Do you have any idea where Betsy went after she left the house?"

"No."

"Did she leave in her car?" Brian asked.

"No. They only had one car, and Dan had taken it to work. Someone picked her up."

"Who?"

Gemma shrugged. "I don't know. I think it was a man, but I'm not sure."

"Can you describe the car?"

"That was such a long time ago. I don't remember."

"I'm wondering." Brian sat back in the chair. "That night, after you returned home, perhaps Betsy came back. Perhaps to pick up something she left, or she had a change of heart. But when Dan saw her, he was too angry to talk and lashed out. Things got out of hand. And then he carried her body next door and buried it in the root cellar. I've checked, and no one was living on the Jameson property during that time, and that's where we found the remains that we believe are Betsy Francas, and we'll verify it once the DNA test is complete."

Gemma stood up and glared at Brian. "Are you going to accuse an innocent man who is not here to defend himself?"

"You don't believe it's possible Dan murdered Betsy?" Brian asked.

"Absolutely not! He was the most loving and gentle man. He would never hurt a soul."

"Then do you have any idea who might have killed Betsy?"

Gemma sat back down in the chair. "How would I know? I had just arrived in Frederickport."

"They found her body a short distance from where you last saw her."

Gemma shook her head. "Dan didn't kill her."

"I'm sure he didn't mean to kill her," Danielle said.

"He didn't kill her." Gemma began to cry. "You won't sully Dan's name. He was the best man I ever met." Tears streamed down her face, and she turned to Brian. "He was my friend, too. But it wasn't enough for Betsy to just marry him. She convinced him to find a job here and move away from Vancouver. She didn't care that I had just lost my parents and would be all alone. And when I came to surprise her, she was angry with me. Accused me of trying to come between her and her husband. I couldn't believe what she was saying, and I became angry too. I slapped her. She stumbled. Fell. Hit her head. I didn't mean to hurt her." Gemma folded her arms on the table and buried her face in her arms as she sobbed hysterically.

Danielle and Brian looked at each other in silence, both surprised at Gemma's confession.

THIRTY-EIGHT

Danielle, Lily, and Heather sat at the kitchen table at Marlow House on Tuesday evening, sharing two cinnamon rolls between them, while Walt and Ian visited in the parlor with Connor.

"I can't believe we're eating these before dinner," Heather said before popping a bite of the sweet sticky roll in her mouth. She glanced over at the Crock-Pot sitting on the kitchen counter. Walt had started a large pot of chili for dinner while Danielle joined Brian at Gemma's house. They were waiting for Brian and Joe to get off work before eating, because Walt hadn't just invited her and Brian to dinner; along with the Bartleys, he had also invited Joe, Kelly, Adam, and Mel.

Lily pulled off a piece of one roll they shared. "We need to eat them before Connor walks in here and demands some. He doesn't need the sugar."

"What about the calories? All that running for a cinnamon roll." Heather let out a sigh and took another bite.

"Well, I read on the internet that breastfeeding can burn up to 700 calories a day. So I figure that means I could burn 1,400 calories a day. And I also read an average cinnamon roll has 250 calories, so that means I can have almost six cinnamon rolls a day."

Lily gave a snort yet didn't comment.

Heather looked at Danielle. "To begin with, Old Salts are not the average cinnamon roll. Second, not even you would eat six cinnamon rolls while you're nursing. Otherwise, the only thing you'd be feeding Addison and Jack is sugar water."

Lily gave another snort, and Danielle giggled.

Now finished with her portion of cinnamon rolls, Lily licked off her fingers and asked, "What happens if Gemma decides to lawyer up and gets the confession tossed out? After all, she hadn't been read her rights."

Danielle grabbed a nearby napkin and wiped off the corners of her mouth before saying, "I asked Brian about that. He said a spontaneous confession is typically admissible even if a person hasn't been read their rights. Brian doubts that even with a lawyer, her confession will be thrown out. No one asked her if she killed Betsy. And while she gave her confession in defense of her husband, her husband has been dead for years."

"So what now?" Lily asked.

"Brian said they're calling Betsy's brother to get the contact information for Betsy's daughters," Danielle explained. "And they still plan to do the DNA, but they don't doubt the remains belong to Betsy."

Heather stood up and began removing any evidence from the table that they had been eating cinnamon rolls.

"I can't imagine how those girls are going to deal with this," Lily said as she handed Heather her wadded-up napkin. "How would you feel learning the only mother you grew up with murdered your real mother?"

Heather dumped the trash in the kitchen garbage can and glanced over to Lily. "It doesn't sound like Gemma had a terrific relationship with them, anyway. Not like they are about to learn something horrible about a person they loved. They haven't seen her for years."

Lily nodded. "True."

Heather returned to the table. "I wonder why Dan never tried to divorce Betsy. It's a no-fault divorce. Weren't they a thing back then?"

"I have a theory," Danielle said.

Lily grinned at Danielle. "One thing I love about you, Dani, you always have a theory."

Danielle rolled her eyes at Lily and continued, "Gemma could have discouraged him from getting a divorce and suggested they just tell people they were married. I don't know what reasons she would have given him, but I can see not wanting to open that can of worms. If he started looking for Betsy to initiate a divorce, even if he didn't need her cooperation, he might start wondering why he can't find her. Why she never contacted her brother or other friends. He might suddenly realize his wife was a missing person."

"Or Dan secretly hoped Betsy would someday come back to him, and he didn't want to be legally bound to Gemma when she did," Lily suggested.

"Yes, that's another possibility," Danielle agreed.

"You both could be right," Heather said. "It's possible Dan didn't want to start a divorce for the reason Lily suggested, and Gemma didn't press the matter, because like Danielle said, she didn't want to open up that can of worms."

THE FIVE COUPLES sat around Marlow House's dining room table, enjoying Walt's chili and the cornbread Adam and Melony had brought over. Connor sat in his highchair between his parents, eating a peanut butter sandwich with a sippy cup of milk and slices of pear.

Adam had just told everyone about Bill bolting the door shut to the tunnel from the Crawford side yesterday morning, while Clay was obviously already in the tunnel.

"At least we know some troublesome spirit hadn't been moving the books around." Melony snickered and then told them about how Adam was freaking over the rearranged books, but now they knew Clay had been the responsible party.

"Like I keep saying, there is a logical explanation for everything," Joe insisted.

"Sometimes there is also an illogical explanation," Kelly countered.

"We've found our explanation for what was responsible in the nursery," Danielle announced. "And we believe it is no longer an issue, which is why the twins are again napping upstairs."

Melony looked at Danielle. "You think whatever was happening has stopped for good?"

Danielle looked at Ian. "Maybe you can explain."

"We've been researching this type of phenomenon and believe it wasn't a ghost—" Ian began, only to be cut off by Joe.

"Exactly what I have been saying," Joe said.

Ian smiled at Joe but continued, "It wasn't a ghost, but it was possibly the energy created from the trauma of Betsy Francas's murder, transferred to her quilt."

"Oh brother," Joe groaned. "You aren't serious?"

Melony gave Joe a dismissive wave before looking back at Ian. "Oh, hush, this is interesting."

"And now that Betsy's murder has been exposed, her murderer confessed, she can be at peace." Ian didn't mention that his research included information from Eva passed on to him.

Joe let out a sigh and grabbed another piece of cornbread.

"And this means we're moving into Marlow House in a couple of weeks so they can come in and finish up the construction," Lily announced. "And I will not worry about something throwing stuffed animals at me."

"Are you sure it will be safe here?" Kelly asked.

"If things start flying around Marlow House in the next couple of weeks, we'll reconsider, but I think we're good."

"Have you contacted the family of Betsy Francas yet?" Melony asked Joe and Brian.

"Joe called the brother," Brian said. "He really fell apart."

"That doesn't surprise me," Lily said. "The guy just found out someone murdered his sister."

Joe shook his head. "It wasn't just that. He reacted like someone who had just learned that the person he helped send to the electric chair was innocent."

"It's not like he was responsible for her murder," Kelly said.

"I can understand his reaction," Heather said. "We told you how Chris and I met him when we were trying to help Danielle learn more about the quilt. He really had issues about his mother, who abandoned the family. And then he's told the sister he loved did the same thing to her kids. I suspect that's why the guy is still single. He's got some genuine anger issues. And then he learns the sister he's hated for years—the same sister he once loved—didn't deserve the hate."

"What about the daughters?" Melony asked. "How did they take it?"

"They said little," Brian said. "I think they were in shock. One asked about her mother's remains. We explained she had been buried at the local cemetery."

"I wonder if they're going to want to move the body," Ian asked.

Brian shrugged. "They didn't say."

"I talked to Chris tonight," Heather said.

"When's he going to be back?" Adam asked.

"He'll be back in the morning. And I'll have to go back to work."

"At least you had a few extra days off to relax," Adam snarked.

Heather chuckled. "Yeah. Work would have been more fun. Anyway, Chris said to let the daughters know the foundation will pay for a new headstone for their mother's grave. They just need to pick it out. And if they want to move their mother's remains, the foundation will cover it."

Adam shook his head. "It has certainly been a crazy couple of weeks."

"And now the local jail is full," Ian said.

"Not really. They transferred Clay and Rodney to a more secure facility. And Gemma is under observation at a hospital," Joe explained.

"Why would they need to put Gemma under observation?" Adam asked.

"Not sure what Brian and Danielle did to her, but when she got to the station, she started hysterically sobbing and wouldn't stop," Joe said.

"To be fair, she started sobbing the moment she confessed," Danielle corrected.

AFTER EVERYONE WENT HOME on Tuesday night, Danielle took her shower and then sat in a rocking chair, nursing her babies, while Walt sat in the rocking chair next to her. Also in the room were Eva, Marie, and Betsy, who had been in the nursery with the twins all evening, while Danielle and Walt had been downstairs with their guests.

"We were really close as children," Betsy told them when discussing Gemma's confession. "When Dan and I started dating, I thought Gemma was jealous of Dan because he was taking more of my time. But I eventually realized it was the other way around. She was in love with him. That's why I wanted to move."

"Did Dan know how she felt?" Danielle asked.

Betsy nodded. "Yes. We discussed it. It made him uncomfortable. When Dan and I started dating, Gemma became more clingy around him. She was always finding a reason to touch him, like take hold of his hand or lean against him. It was as if she thought she was dating him, too. In fact, after we got married, he told me Gemma was acting bizarre, as if she thought we were both his wife, and he said he didn't want two wives. So when I suggested we move after the babies were born, he was all for it."

"What happened that day?" Danielle asked. "The last day you saw her."

"Dan was at work, and I had just finished feeding the babies when I heard the doorbell. When I answered it, there was Gemma, all smiles. Of course, I let her in the house. I assumed it was a surprise visit. I didn't even entertain the possibility that she had upped and moved to Frederickport. But as soon as she was inside, she said something like, *surprise, I'm your new neighbor*, and then announced she had bought a house right up the street from the one we were buying."

Danielle cringed. "I can't even imagine how you felt when you realized she was going to be your neighbor."

"I snapped like I had never snapped before. I yelled at her, told her to leave us alone, that Dan was my husband, not hers. And that we had moved to Frederickport to get away from her. Obviously, it was a stupid thing to say, considering what happened next."

"I wonder if she often regretted slapping you. If she hadn't, you wouldn't have fallen and hit your head, and she wouldn't be where she is now."

Betsy frowned at Danielle. "She never slapped me. I turned around to get the phone to call Dan when she hit me over the head with one of Elenore's iron statues. I remember falling to the floor, my head throbbing, and I looked up and saw her holding that statue over me. I tried to get up, and she hit me again, and I fell back down and couldn't move. She picked up my left hand, and I could feel her pulling off my wedding rings. Everything went black, and then I woke up as she was pushing me into the root cellar."

"She knew you were still alive when she put you in the root cellar?" Danielle sounded horrified at the thought.

Betsy nodded. "She knew."

THIRTY-NINE

E dward MacDonald's sister urged him to stay home, telling
him he had been doing far too much since his knee replacement surgery. She pointed out the woman had died years before he
ever moved to Frederickport.

He disagreed with his sister. After all, Betsy's body had been
found when he first started working at the Frederickport Police
Department, and he felt it was his duty to attend her funeral, as a
sign of respect.

The chief no longer used a walker and had advanced to a cane.
His doctor also gave him the green light to drive again, so he didn't
need to ask his sister to drive him to the funeral or ask one of his
friends to bring him.

Chris had amended his offer to move Betsy's body and had
suggested moving both Betsy's and Dan's body to adjacent plots in
the Frederickport Cemetery. The daughters accepted this offer.
They also announced they wanted to have a funeral for their
mother, but instead of a church service or one in the cemetery
chapel, they opted for a gravesite service.

The weather proved ideal, with a clear blue sky, sunshine, and
barely a breeze. When MacDonald arrived at the cemetery, familiar

faces greeted him, including the Marlows, the Bartleys, the Nicholses, the Morellis, along with Heather, Brian, and Chris. Danielle and Walt had brought the twins along in their double stroller, while Lily had left Connor with her in-laws. They had all arrived early, and the service was not supposed to start for another twenty minutes.

"IT'S A LOVELY HEADSTONE," Betsy said as she ran her fingers over the granite. Unlike the marker placed by the Jameson estate, this one included her name, birth and death date, along with an inscription written by her daughters. Her fingers briefly disappeared within the stone. "That was nice of your friend."

Eva smiled at Betsy. "I'm glad you like it."

Betsy looked over at the crowd gathering. "I wonder if anyone from my family is going to come. Who are all those people?"

"Some of them went to church with your husband," Marie explained. "And some are friends of your daughters."

Along the nearby walkway Danielle, Heather, Lily, and Kelly stood around the stroller, looking down at the babies and talking, while Joe and Brian had stepped away to talk privately with the chief. Ian, Walt, and Chris stood about six feet from them, discussing Ian and Lily's plan to move temporarily into Marlow House while they wrapped up the home addition.

Heather was just about to say something when a man walked up and interrupted her. It was Betsy's brother, Hector Burr Jr. She immediately recognized him and introduced him to her friends. As Heather made introductions, Betsy suddenly appeared at her brother's side.

Hector looked immediately at Danielle and reached out and took her hand, looking into her face. "You're the one who figured this all out. Thank you."

"You're more than welcome. I just couldn't imagine someone who put such love into a quilt would abandon her babies."

He released Danielle's hand and glanced briefly toward the

gravesites. "You had more faith in my sister than I did. I will always regret my lack of faith. I should have been the one to search for her."

"Oh, Hector, I know how much Mama hurt us both. You especially, because you remembered her. I forgive your lack of faith. I love you."

Danielle reached out and took back his hand. He looked into her face, and she smiled. "I sincerely believe, with my whole heart, that your sister is looking over you right now. And she not only forgives you, but she understands and loves you."

Hector flashed Danielle a sad smile while he gave her hand a gentle pat before pulling away. A tear ran down his cheek. "I hope you're right."

WALT AND DANIELLE opted to stand at the back of the small group of mourners attending the gravesite service because they had the twins with them, and if either baby started crying, they wanted to move them away from the group so as not to disturb the service.

Betsy's family had arranged for a friend from Vancouver, who had known Betsy most of her life and who was now a pastor, to preside at the service. After he spoke, Hector stepped up and said a few words about his sister, including how her absence had left a painful void in his life. After Hector, each of Betsy's daughters spoke. They told their mother that they loved her and prayed she was now at peace.

The fact both daughters were about twenty years older than their mother at the time of her death struck Danielle, making her wonder how Betsy felt, seeing her daughters looking older than she had ever been. According to Hector, growing up, the daughters looked just like their mother, which now afforded Betsy a glimpse into what she would have looked like had she lived longer.

When the service ended, Walt and Danielle stayed back with their twins and didn't leave because Danielle had brought something to give to Betsy's daughters. But right now, they were standing some distance from the dispersing crowd, watching as different people introduced themselves to Hector and his nieces.

As the crowd melted away, Hector looked in Danielle's direction. Earlier, when talking to him, Danielle had asked him if, after the service, he could introduce her to his nieces, as she had something to give them.

Several minutes later, Hector and his nieces approached Walt and Danielle. Danielle introduced Walt to Hector, and Hector introduced Betsy's daughters to Walt and Danielle. Also by Hector and his nieces' side was Betsy, who couldn't keep her eyes off her daughters.

Karen reached out briefly and touched Danielle's hand. "Our uncle has told us how if it weren't for you, we would probably never know the truth about our mother. Thank you."

"I'm just glad the truth finally came out."

"Things make a lot more sense now. Especially since we've learned Dad was never married to Gemma," Jillian said.

"How so?" Danielle asked.

"Karen and I never understood why Dad stayed with Gemma," Jillian said. "Gemma was always fussing over Dad; she was almost suffocating in her adoration of him. Yet he always, well, seemed to push her away."

"How was your relationship with your father?" Danielle asked.

"I think, considering everything, we had a good relationship. As good as possible with someone like Gemma always trying to insert herself. When Dad died, Karen and I decided not to attend his funeral because we didn't want to see her. Instead, we had our own private service at Cannon Beach, where Dad used to take us when we were little," Jillian explained.

Danielle smiled. "I believe your dad would have liked that."

"Even though Dad was often distant, we knew he loved us," Karen said. "As we got older, sometimes he would look at us and get this sad, faraway look in his eyes and then say how we looked so much like our mother. Unfortunately, if Gemma overheard, it would send her off."

"You never had a good relationship with Gemma?" Danielle asked.

"Like I said a few minutes ago, it all makes sense now. I spent a lot of time in therapy after I left Frederickport. When Karen and I were younger, I'm talking fifth grade and younger, we assumed Gemma was our real mother. She was a good mom back then, even loving. We were her little girls. We loved her. But then, as we got older, something changed. It was like a switch flipped, and she went from loving us to hating us. We were in eighth grade when we learned about our real mother. Or should I say, we learned Gemma's lie."

"I don't understand. Why do you think she started hating you?" Danielle asked.

"I'm now convinced she started hating us because we started looking so much like our real mother. Not long after we left Frederickport, Uncle Hector gave us a box of photos of our mother growing up, including her school pictures, the ones they take every year. Up until our preadolescence, we looked a little like both of our parents. But around third grade, we started looking more and more like our mother. Her sixth-grade school pictures looked just like us at that age."

"She hated that you looked like your mother?" Danielle asked.

Jillian nodded. "I'm sure of that now, especially knowing that she killed our mother because she was in love with our father. But I don't believe Dad ever really loved her."

"I remember after we were told our mother abandoned us, Gemma would tell us—when Dad wasn't around—that we were impossible to love, and that's why our birth mother left," Karen added.

"Did your father notice the change in your relationship with Gemma?" Danielle asked.

"He noticed the tension, but never witnessed the things she said to us. In fact, she was sickeningly sweet to us when he was around. If we tried to talk to him about her, he would tell us it was natural for us to get annoyed with her because we were getting that age. In fact, I think that's why dad told us about our real mother. Since he assumed the only problem was our changing hormones, he thought if we learned Gemma loved us despite not being our biological mom and had stepped up to be our mother, that we would appreciate her more and we'd be more tolerant. But all it did was give Gemma more ammunition for abuse."

"I'm so sorry," Danielle muttered.

Jillian gave a shrug and then reached out and hooked her sister's arm with hers, pulling her closer to her side. "Thank you. We're okay and much better now that we know the truth about our mother. Both Karen and I are married to wonderful men. I have two beautiful children, and Karen has three."

"I'm a grandma!" Betsy gasped.

"We considered bringing our husbands and children," Karen began. "But we both decided they're too young. Oh, they're not babies. I have two in high school. But this is so much to take in right now. We decided to come here with just Uncle Hector. And later, when all the kids are older, we'll come back and visit Mom's and Dad's graves."

"There is something I want to give you." Danielle reached into the storage basket under her stroller and pulled out the twin quilt. She handed it to Karen and Jillian.

"Is this the quilt Mom made for us?" Jillian asked as she took hold of the quilt's top left corner, while her sister took hold of the quilt's right top corner.

Danielle smiled. "Yes. Your mother would want you to have it."

Betsy's daughters held up the quilt, studying their mother's handiwork.

Tears filled Karen's eyes. "It's amazing."

"Show them!" Betsy said excitedly.

Danielle flashed a quick glance at Betsy and smiled. She looked back at Betsy's daughters.

"I just figured this out last night," Danielle lied. Betsy had showed her after Gemma's arrest.

"Your mom obviously intended to use this at the bottom of a shared playpen, or on the floor for you both to play on. But I'm pretty sure that she wanted to someday give you both the quilt. Your children are probably too old for it now, but maybe you can pass it on to a grandchild."

"How could she have given it to both of us?" Karen asked. "You think she wanted us to share it or have it cut in half?"

Danielle grinned. "Sort of. This is what I found." Danielle reached over and took the quilt from the sisters. She showed them a hidden zipper tucked away along its center. When unzipped, the halves of the quilt separated, making two crib-sized quilts.

"If you look closer," Danielle said, "Just a little work with a seam ripper will remove the zipper completely, which will leave you with two beautiful and complete baby quilts, and no zipper to scratch a baby or distract from the quilt's appearance."

Karen took back the quilt and looked closer. "Wow, that's ingenious. But we probably shouldn't remove it."

Danielle shook her head. "Don't even consider leaving it intact. Your mother obviously wanted you both to someday have half of the original quilt. Considering all that she was denied, give her this. She lovingly made this quilt during her pregnancy, even planning for the day you were older and she would hand this down to you as adults. She wants you each to take her love with you. Give her that."

FORTY

Danielle stood on the first-floor landing at Marlow House, holding Addison in her arms as she watched Kelly pick up a box of toys from the stack of random containers Ian had left by the staircase before he took off with Walt to the hardware store.

"You really don't have to take those upstairs. The guys are planning to do that when they get back." Danielle glanced up the stairs and saw Marie standing at the top of the staircase, watching.

"I want to help," Kelly insisted. "And I told Lily I'd fix Connor's room up so she doesn't have to do it."

Danielle stood quietly and watched as Kelly awkwardly moved up the stairs with the large box. "Please be careful! Don't fall!"

Danielle returned to the living room, where she found Lily sprawled out on the sofa, leaning against an armrest, with her knees bent and the soles of her bare feet on a sofa cushion, while Jack lay across the top of Lily's thighs, his feet resting on her large belly as he looked into her face. Holding onto his tiny hands, Lily wiggled them gently while whispering nonsensical baby talk. Lily's own son was spending the afternoon with his grandmother, to keep him out of the way while they set up his temporary room at Marlow House.

"You really need to tell Kelly not to take all that stuff upstairs.

Walt can do it in about two seconds when he gets back. Heck, Marie's here. She can do it."

Lily glanced up at Danielle and smiled. "Kelly wants to. And Marie can't very well move the boxes while Kelly's here. Neither can Walt." She looked back at Jack and resumed the baby talk.

"She's going to wear herself out, and I don't want her to fall."

Lily looked up again. "She won't fall. Marie's keeping an eye on her."

"It's still silly. She's going to be exhausted when she's done." Danielle started for the recliner, but Lily stopped her.

"Can you shut the door first?" Lily whispered.

Danielle turned around and shut the door from the living room to the hallway.

"I wanted to talk to you without Kelly hearing."

Danielle walked to the recliner and sat down. "What about?"

"Has Betsy moved on? I know she hadn't as of yesterday."

"Yes and no." Danielle leaned back in the chair and repositioned Addison to make them both more comfortable.

"What does that mean?"

"She's not in Frederickport anymore, but she's not ready to move on. She plans to stay with her daughters, get to know them and her grandchildren. And who knows, one of her younger grandchildren might be able to see her."

Lily cringed. "That would be wild. Not sure if that's a good thing or not."

"I'm just glad Betsy can finally be with her daughters. Even though it will be a one-sided relationship."

By the time Walt and Ian returned from the hardware store, Kelly had already hauled all the boxes for Connor's room upstairs and had started to fix up his room.

"I wish Kelly hadn't moved all those boxes herself," Ian said when he and Walt walked into the living room. The only reason he knew his sister had moved the boxes was because Max had told Walt when they walked into the house, and Walt told Ian.

Lily looked up at Ian and smiled sweetly. "I tried to tell her to wait for you."

Ian eyed Lily suspiciously. "Why don't I believe you? I'm going to check on my sister." He dropped a quick kiss on Lily's brow and whispered, "You're evil."

"I'm not evil," Lily told Danielle and Walt after Ian left the living room. "But sometimes Kelly is a little like Connor."

"How so?" Walt asked.

"Sometimes we just need to wear Connor out so he'll fall asleep and give us a break."

Danielle chuckled. "Has Kelly been driving you crazy?"

Walt walked over to Lily and picked up Jack, who had just started to squirm. He put the baby over his shoulder, gently patting his back, as he began pacing between the recliners and sofa while listening to Lily and Danielle.

"Not crazy exactly. She can just be a little exhausting sometimes, but I must admit, she has her moments. She convinced her mom we weren't pranking them. And that whatever happened upstairs has moved on, like all spirits are supposed to do. Of course, Joe is not thrilled and thinks we've all lost our minds, not just his wife, yet he is sort of the odd man out in this whole thing."

"She seems happier," Danielle said.

Lily nodded. "I think she loved helping Ian research paranormal phenomena. It made her feel more a part of his life again. Unfortunately, it also energized her in that she is determined to now be the best sister and sister-in-law, which means when Joe is working and she has some free time, she wants to hang out."

"She just wants to help," Danielle reminded her.

Lily let out a sigh. "I understand. But sometimes it's exhausting."

"And now you want to exhaust her?" Walt teased.

Lily grinned at Walt. "Something like that."

KELLY WAS JUST COMING DOWNSTAIRS when she heard the doorbell ring. By the time she reached the first-floor landing, Walt had already answered the front door and led Chief MacDonald into the house. She followed them both into the living room.

"Chief, look at you getting around town!" Danielle greeted when he walked into the room, with Walt and Kelly trailing behind them.

"I went into the station this morning, and I was on my way home. I was going to call you and tell you what happened, but I thought I should probably tell you in person."

Danielle frowned. "That sounds serious."

Five minutes later, they all sat around the living room, Walt, Danielle, Lily, Ian, Kelly, with the chief sitting in a recliner, his leg with the new knee elevated. Marie hovered nearby in an imaginary chair while Kelly and Danielle each held one twin.

"There won't be a trial for Clay," the chief began.

"Did he make a plea deal?" Danielle asked.

MacDonald shook his head. "No."

Kelly frowned. "They didn't grant him bail again, did they?"

"No. Nothing like that. He ran into some people he knew, and the authorities are trying to say it was a suicide, but—"

"He's dead?" Danielle blurted.

"Yes. They found him in his cell. While they claim it's a suicide, I also heard from someone I spoke to at the jail that there was quite a commotion the first night he showed up. There were some inmates who recognized Clay from when he was on this side of the law, and it didn't sound as if he treated them much better than he treated Heather."

"When did this happen?" Walt asked.

"Last night. They called me this morning, and then I made a few calls myself."

"Have they told his wife yet?" Walt asked.

"Yes. But that's another story altogether." MacDonald shook his head.

"What do you mean?" Danielle asked.

"Apparently, Fred and Robyn are getting a divorce. From what I gather, he did not want Debbie and the boys to keep living with them."

Danielle cringed. "I wondered about that."

"Supposedly, Debbie was already making plans to divorce Clay. I guess she had convinced herself Clay hadn't murdered Camilla, but I suspect she might have forgiven him for that. But kidnapping babies, no. That was a bridge too far for her."

"I can't say I blame her. But why are the Lyonses splitting up now?" Lily asked.

"Because Robyn wanted her sister and nephews to keep living with them, and Fred said absolutely not. They had to leave. From what I understand, Robyn and Debbie intend to move from Frederickport with Debbie's boys. I'm not sure what Fred plans to do or where he will live, because, supposedly, Robyn wants him to sell the house."

"Wow. Poor Fred," Danielle said. "He really blew up his life, pulling that stupid nepotism crap."

"That's for certain." MacDonald shrugged. "To top it off, he turned in his resignation."

"Who's going to be city manager?" Ian asked.

MacDonald shrugged again.

"I agree with Dani. Wow," Lily said.

They all sat in silence for a few minutes, considering what the chief had just told them. Finally, Ian said, "There's still the trial for Clay's accomplice."

"I'm not sure when that's going to be. He's been moved to a mental ward. He still hasn't spoken a word since his arrest. From what I've been told, he sits all day with his arms wrapped around himself, rocks back and forth, and stares off into space," the chief explained.

"What did Heather do to him?" Kelly asked.

Danielle and Lily exchanged glances, as did Walt and Ian, while Marie, who sat nearby on an imaginary chair, said, "It serves him right. Coming in here trying to destroy people's lives. I'd like to think of it as karma."

"I mentioned the other day that Gemma's no longer under observation. And her attorney did initially try walking back her confession, but it ended up in a plea deal," the chief said.

BY MONDAY EVENING, Lily and Ian had moved into a bedroom on the second floor of Marlow House, while one of the other bedrooms on that floor had been set up for Connor. They had turned over the parlor to Ian, where he set up his computer to use as his makeshift office. With the Bartleys temporarily moved out of their house, Ian's father could now bring in the construction crew to finish up the addition without working around the family.

Connor was upstairs in bed, and the twins had been fed and laid in the nursery cribs, while the adults sat downstairs in the living room. They weren't too concerned about Connor being in a strange room while his parents were downstairs visiting, as they had left Marie upstairs with Connor, reading him a bedtime story.

"Thanks so much for letting us stay," Lily told Walt and Danielle for the tenth time.

"Hey, you're always welcome," Danielle insisted. "And thanks for sharing your nanny."

They all laughed.

"I'd feel guilty, but Marie does seem to enjoy spending time with the little ones," Lily said.

"I'm just glad this poltergeist thing is over, and we don't have to worry about mystery ghosts anymore," Danielle said.

Unfortunately, Danielle spoke too soon.

RETURN TO MARLOW HOUSE IN
The Ghost Who Sought Redemption
HAUNTING DANIELLE, BOOK 35

Two newborns and a toddler under one roof, with another on the way, can be challenging for any parent, but add an unwelcome spirit with the sketchiest of reputations, and you'll have the local mediums scrambling for a resolution before the toddler spills the tea.

BOOKS BY ANNA J. MCINTYRE

COULSON FAMILY SAGA

Coulson's Wife

Coulson's Crucible

Coulson's Lessons

Coulson's Secret

Coulson's Reckoning

Now available in Audiobook Format

UNLOCKED 🔒 HEARTS

Sundered Hearts

After Sundown

While Snowbound

Sugar Rush

NON-FICTION BY
BOBBI ANN JOHNSON HOLMES

HAVASU PALMS, A HOSTILE TAKEOVER
WHERE THE ROAD ENDS, RECIPES & REMEMBRANCES
MOTHERHOOD, A BOOK OF POETRY
THE STORY OF THE CHRISTMAS VILLAGE

Printed in Great Britain
by Amazon

42767705R00162